G&B Detective Agency
Case of the Lonelyfarmer.com

By R. L. Link

A Max Mosbey and Skip Murray G&B Detective Novel

G&B Detective Agency
Case of the Lonelyfarmer.com
All rights reserved.
Copyright © 2018 by Rollie Link

ISBN-13: 978-1981214808
10:1981214801

G&B Detective Agency
Case of the Lonelyfarmer.com

Prologue

It appeared that the Downtown Merchants' Association was not a presence on this end of Main Street. It was dirty and littered. There was dried vomit on the curb in front of one of the bars, left there by a patron at bar closing the night before. Drunks and near drunks stood outside the doors of the bars smoking cigarettes and grumbling about the new city ordinance that didn't allow them to smoke inside. As the two officers made their way from one bar to another, the smokers greeted them like old friends. Some of them the two officers knew, some they didn't. Some of them used to play in the same Parks and Rec softball leagues and tournaments that the two officers had played in at one time, sponsored by the various bars and restaurants, and a few of them, past their prime, still did. Some they had arrested.

Air conditioning assaulted the two police officers as they opened the front door to the Star Lounge. The seedy Main Street bar was dark, but cool. It was a hot and humid evening, and Max and Skip had been patrolling the two blocks of bars that congregated at the end of the street, a couple of pizza joints huddled amongst them that catered to the evening drinkers and drunks. The two were sweating under their bulletproof vests, loaded down with thirty pounds of gear. On top of that, Max had a Smith and Wesson snub nose thirty-eight backup gun in a holster attached to his left ankle and a lead-weighted sap riding in a pocket on his right pant leg. Skip traveled light, compared to Max, but he was still carrying a load. The air conditioning in the bars was a welcome relief from the July heat and humidity outside.

Max and Skip shook hands with some of the regulars as they made their way through the bar. Max separated from Skip, who was talking to the bartender, and ambled toward the stage in the back where a local band was playing. They weren't really very good, but they were popular on Main Street nonetheless. The people who frequented the Main Street bars weren't particular. The musicians on stage smiled and nodded to Max as he walked by. Max passed the stage to enter a hallway that ran to a door farther back. On one side of the hallway was the men's room, on the other the women's. Max checked that the door in the back was unlocked, according to the fire code. Max opened the door and looked into the dimly lit storeroom behind it. Some old tables with chairs stacked on them lined one wall. It was quiet in the room, but he could hear voices through the door on the other end of the room that led out to the alley. Occasionally patrons used the back doors and the alley to make their way from one bar to the next. Max waited in the storeroom, trying to make out what the voices outside were saying. He walked closer to the door and stood for a moment, then opened it and walked out into the hot, humid air.

The two men in the alley jumped as soon as the door opened and Max appeared. One of them threw something into the storm drain where they stood. Max could smell the fragrance of marijuana hanging in the still evening air.

"Hey Max," one of the men nervously said.

Max knew the one who spoke by sight. He didn't know his name, though. The other was a stranger. Max reached down to the portable radio on his belt and clicked the transmit button three times in succession, then stepped into the alley and away from the wall, where he could maneuver if necessary. The two men fidgeted.

"Sucking some butts out here tonight?" Max asked.

"Yep," the man that Max knew spoke up. "Just smoking a cigarette."

"What kind of cigarettes you smoking?" Max asked.

"Marlboros," the stranger sneered.

Max turned his attention to the stranger. He could see that the stranger was building up to something. Max started to sense trouble. He shifted his left foot forward and brought his left hand up, palm open, subtly taking up a fighting stance.

"Smells like Mexican Marlboros to me," Max drawled. "Doesn't it to you guys?"

The stranger fidgeted some more, looking like he wanted to do something, but he wasn't quite sure what. Max was trying to keep an eye on the stranger and keep the other man in the corner of his vision at the same time, but the men were starting to move apart.

"Why don't you girls just stay where you are," Max instructed them.

The stranger started to say something but was interrupted when the back door slammed open and Max heard Skip's voice.

"You harassing these two, Max?"

"Yep," Max responded, "Got me a couple of pot smokers hiding out here."

Skip moved to the right of the stranger, where he had a clear view of both men. The stranger was caught in a position where he had to turn his head away from one officer to look at the other. The other man stood still.

"Man," the fellow that Max knew said to the stranger, "just be cool. These guys are good guys."

Max did not look at him. "No, we're not really," he said dryly.

"Why don't you two get up against that wall," Skip instructed, "and spread 'em out."

The one man did as instructed, but the stranger hesitated a moment.

"Hard way or the easy way," Skip said.

The stranger reluctantly took up a position facing the wall next to his friend, hands up. While Skip kept an eye on the two, Max patted down the men for weapons, running his hands up and down their legs, around their waists and up under their arms. Max pulled a folding hunter out of the back pocket of the stranger and stuck it in his own pocket. He found a small metal pipe in the stranger's front pocket. Max went from the stranger to the other man and searched him the same way. When he was satisfied, Max stepped back, leaving both men facing the wall.

"So where's the pot?" Max asked.

"We don't have no pot," the stranger said.

Max addressed the other man. "Where's the pot?"

The other man was resigned but silent.

"Okay," Max said. "Here is the deal. I'm calling for a dog. The dog sniffs dope. And when he gets a scent, he starts ripping things apart until he gets ahold of it." Max waited a moment to let it sink in.

"I'm not out here all night to play games with a couple of shitheads, so we're gonna get this done here and now. You can give it up, or the dog will find it."

As Max was finishing, he heard Skip talking into the radio. "We need a K-9 in the alley, one hundred block of Main, north side."

The radio crackled in response. "Seventy-six, be there in a few."

Several seconds passed in silence, then the stranger took his right hand from the wall and started reaching toward his waist.

"Do it nice and slow," Max instructed him.

The stranger reached into the front of his pants and ran his hand down into his crotch, then he pulled it out and dropped a sandwich bag containing a half ounce of marijuana on the ground. Max walked up behind him, put a hand against the man's back, pressing him against the wall, and pulled the baggie out with the toe of his boot. Keeping his hand on the stranger's back, Max bent down and retrieved it.

Max opened the bag, held it under his nose and let the odor waft from the bag. "Well, I don't know enough to tell if this is good shit or not, but I do know it isn't horse shit." Max waited for a response. "Horse shit smells like marijuana when you burn it." Max waited for another response. "No kidding, I learned that in the academy."

The two men neither moved nor said anything.

"Disregard on the K-9," Max heard Skip say over the radio.

"Ten-four."

A patrol car was coming up the alley. Max couldn't make it out very well in the poor lighting, only well enough to determine that it wasn't the K-9 car. The car pulled up and an officer got out.

"What do you guys have?" the officer asked.

"Hey Milton," Max greeted him. "Got us a couple of dope smokers here."

"Yeah, and Max is giving them a lecture on horse shit."

Milton looked a little confused at Skip's comment, but let it go. Max and Skip were always off in their own Max and Skip world, and it took too much effort for Milton to keep up with them, so he didn't try.

Max was holding the bag of marijuana in his hand. Skip and Milton handcuffed the two men and turned them around. Max took the pipe out of his pocket and handed it to Skip. Then he walked to the storm drain, opened the baggie and poured the contents between the grates, letting it fall into the water running below the street. Skip took the pipe, and with the arm of a well practiced pitcher, expertly threw it up on the roof of a three story building on the other side of the alley. Max took one man by the arm, turned him around and took off the cuffs. Then he did the same to the stranger, taking the folding hunter out of his own pocket and slipping it into pocket of the stranger, where he had found it during the search.

"The night's done for you two." Max said. "I see you out here again tonight and you are both going to jail." The two said nothing. They turned away from the officers and started walking down the alley. Max watched them for moment, then turned to Milton.

"*Que pasa, amigo*?" Max asked Milton.

"Nothing," Milton answered. "Just wanted to see what you guys were getting into."

"Same old, same old," Max said. "Hey, will you give us a ride to the station to pick up our car? I'm tired of walking."

Milton walked over to his patrol car and opened the back door. "Gotta ride in the back, because I have all my stuff in the front."

"Beggars can't be choosers," Skip answered.

Chapter 1

Monday

Max drove his Mustang into the parking lot in front of Filo's Coffee Shop and parked. He glanced over at the offices for G&B Detective Agency across the street. Monica's car was parked in her reserved space directly in front of the entrance. Skip's Mercedes was parked next to it. Max wasn't surprised to see Skip's car there, but he was curious why Monica was in the office so early. She usually didn't show up until after nine, and later if she had an early class.

Max went into the coffee shop and walked to the counter. The barista looked up. He was making a cappuccino. Max looked around the coffee shop. He was the only one there, besides the barista.

"I got you Max," the barista said as he was finishing up his art work on the surface of the drink.

"Okay, thanks," Max replied, eyeing the cappuccino. "Medium dark brew," he added, turning and walking to a table near the window.

Max took his seat and looked across at the offices again. He saw Skip crossing the street, walking toward Filo's. "What the heck?" Max said to himself. He watched Skip step over the curb and walk across the grass to the parking lot. Skip looked up and Max waved. Skip raised his hand in a half hearted attempt to return the wave and crossed the asphalt parking lot, making a line for the door. The barista caught Max's attention as he placed a cup of dark brewed coffee in front of Max and the cappuccino on the table across from him.

Skip came through the door and across the open room to the table where Max was sitting. He sat down across from Max and took a sip from his cappuccino.

"Man, they make good cappuccinos here," Skip commented.

"So what's up?" asked Max.

"Just came over to have coffee with you," Skip replied. "Didn't want you sitting over here alone."

"That's nice of you," Max said.

"Hey, just taking care of my partner," Skip smiled.

"Anyone ever tell you that you're full of shit?" Max said.

"I think you have before." Skip took another sip of his cappuccino. Max was looking out the window at the street.

"What's Monica doing in the office so early?" Max asked.

"Essie's preschool is having a field trip somewhere. She had to drop her off early, so she stopped by to study a little bit before class." Skip paused for a moment, looking out the window in the same direction as Max. "I think that she has a test today."

Max and Skip sat in silence for a while, each thinking his own thoughts. Max could tell that Skip was working up to something, but he was willing to wait. He was sure that Skip didn't come over to Filo's just to make small talk.

"How were the overnights?" Max asked.

"Down, everything is down," Skip said, unconcerned. "I think we're gonna start out slow this week. We haven't been making much money lately. We were down last week."

"Down how much?" asked Max.

"I don't know," said Skip. "More than you and I both made in a year before we won the lottery."

"Well, that isn't all that much," Max replied. "It's Monday, and it's always down on Monday. It will come back up. We've got all week."

"I'm not worried about it," said Skip. "Just something to do."

The two private detectives sat in silence again. Max went to the counter for a refill. Skip finished his cappuccino. When Max returned and sat down he looked across the table at Skip, getting his attention.

"What?" Skip asked.

"What?" Max replied, smiling.

Skip looked at Max askance. He laughed.

"What do you think about taking on another case?"

"I don't know," responded Max. "That last one was kind of fun for a change."

"That's what I was thinking," Skip continued. "It gave us something to do." He shrugged his shoulders.

"Better than watching the stock market go up and down all day," Max said.

"Better than sitting here, looking out the window all day," Skip added.

"Got something in particular you want to investigate?" asked Max. "Or are we going to advertise?"

Skip collected his thoughts for a moment before he responded.

"So there is this guy, he used to work with Marjorie at the clinic when she worked there. Name's Travis Bentley. He is a psychiatrist-slash-psychologist. But he doesn't work at the clinic anymore. Now he has a private practice. He specializes in substance abuse. He contracts out and does those OWI classes, works a lot of weekends and evenings doing them. He's registered with the courts and all, so he has all these people who get probation and deferred judgements and such. He also does drug classes. Same thing, he gets a lot of clients from the courts. Small time druggies is all."

Skip paused for a moment. Max sat, waiting.

"Okay, so like I said, this Travis works nights, weekends, all the time. He has this private practice, and he is trying to make a go of it. And he is. He's doing pretty well. He keeps busy. And he's good, so I hear."

Skip paused again, took a breath, then resumed. "So he was working at home the other day, and he got on his wife's computer to check his email or Facebook or whatever, and he brings up a new tab, because he doesn't want to mess up his wife's stuff, and you know how that page comes up blank, or sometimes it has icons for recently and frequently visited sites on it?"

Skip waited for Max to answer.

"Yeah," Max replied. "I know what you are talking about. A little gear up in the corner turns it on and off."

"Exactly," said Skip. "So our man Travis gets the blank page, but he hits the little gear, for whatever reason, and up come some interesting sites."

Skip paused again.

"Go on," said Max. "Like maybe porn sites?"

"No, not porn," replied Skip, "but online dating sites, Craigslist personals and pages like that."

"Oh, man," Max exclaimed. "That's interesting."

"Yep," Skip resumed. "So Travis thinks that his wife is up to something, and he thinks that he knows what it is, but before starts jumping to conclusions, he calls up Marjorie and asks her if she thought that we might follow his wife around to see what she is up to. Sort of corroborate his fears."

"Is this something that you really want to do?" Max asked. "Kind of sleazy. I mean, follow some guy's wife around taking pictures…" Max considered a full-on rant, about graduating to doing workman's comp cases and chasing juvenile delinquents around for juvenile probation, but decided not to poke at his friend so early in the morning. Instead he sat, waiting.

"You know how Bev was Gloria's friend and she asked us to look for Bev's missing dog? You remember that one, don't you? Remember how you said that we would do it, just for her?" Skip spoke matter-of-factly, emphasizing the "we." "You remember all that, right?"

"Yep," Max replied. "I do remember that."

Skip sat staring at Max across the table. He didn't respond. The two sat there for a moment looking at each other.

"Okay," Max finally broke the silence. "When do we start following her around?"

"I got Travis coming into the office at ten," Skip replied. "We'll go from there."

The two sat for a few minutes more.

Skip stood and picked up his empty cup. Max did the same, taking his mug of coffee.

"Let me get this topped off and I'll walk back over with you," Max told Skip as he started toward the counter where the barista was waiting for him.

"Fill 'er up," Max said. "I'll bring the cup back later."

"Ten-four," replied the barista, smiling as he took the mug from Max to refill it.

Skip was waiting at the door as Max got his fresh mug of coffee and came his way. He held the door for Max and the two walked toward the offices of G&B Detective Agency across the street.

"Got anything else going?" Max asked Skip as they waited for traffic.

"Thinking about closing the pool up for the summer," Skip replied.

"Need help?" Max asked.

"I think I can get it," Skip remarked.

"Why don't you just hire someone to do it?" Max asked.

"I like to do it," Skip said.

"Bullshit," Max laughed.

Chapter 2

Monday

Max and Skip sat in the waiting area of the detective agency chatting. There were two leather chairs across from Monica's desk, with a round end table between them. Max and Skip spent a lot of time in those chairs talking and looking out the window. When they returned from Filo's, they had taken up residence in the chairs, and now, nearly an hour later, they were still there. Monica had chatted with them when they had first sat down, but she left for class. Skip had filled her in on the case that they were getting ready to investigate, and she said that she would come back after class, just in case they needed her. She was surprised that the two millionaire detectives were going to take on another case. After the Tucker case they had both sworn not to take another one. But she had to admit to herself that she had fun looking for the tiny dog and all the other aspects of working the case. It was better than sitting at her desk, answering the phone and telling people that G&B Detective Agency wasn't taking any cases. She found that she enjoyed investigative work. The two detectives watched her get into her car and leave.

After she left, a silver Prius pulled into the parking lot and started to park in Monica's reserved space directly in front of the door. The two detectives watched through the window from their easy chairs. Seeing the sign, the driver backed out of the space and moved to the empty one next to Max's yellow Mustang.

"Travis?" Max asked.

"Yep," Skip replied.

The two watched the driver get out of his car. Max would have described him as an average guy. Average height, average weight, average looking. Skip would have described him as a white male adult, five-eleven, medium build, mid-forties, well dressed, full head of black hair thinning on top. Travis walked up on the sidewalk and entered into the reception area where Skip and Max were sitting.

Skip stood up and held out his hand.

"How are you, Travis?" he asked. "My partner, Max," he motioned toward Max, who was getting up from the chair.

Max shook hands with Travis.

"Let's go to the conference room and talk," Skip said, leading the way to the first room down the hall on the right, which also served as the play room for Monica's daughter Essie when she wasn't at preschool.

As Max and Travis went into the conference room, Skip turned the other way into the room across the hall. Travis glanced toward Skip. The room he was going into looked like a bar. Not just a room with a bar, but a real bar.

"Need something to drink?" Skip asked.

"No," Travis replied. "Well, maybe some water."

"Bring me a Coke," Max called out.

In the conference room was a formal conference table surrounded by leather chairs, each one occupied by a stuffed animal. Max walked around the table, tossing each animal into the corner as he motioned to Travis to take a seat recently vacated by a large pink rabbit.

Travis looked around. There were children's toys laying everywhere. There were crayons and coloring books laying on the table where Travis took a seat. Max swept them to the other end of the table, knocking some of them on the floor and going around to pick them up.

"Our receptionist, Monica, has a little kid. She brings her here once in a while, when she isn't at daycare," Max explained. "She plays in here."

"That's nice," Travis said. "I mean, nice that you let her do that."

"There's a big room in the back that has a bunch of playground equipment in it," Max added. "Gotta keep the help happy, you know." Then in a quiet voice Max said, "Actually, she kind of runs the place."

Travis didn't reply.

Skip came into the conference room and put a bottle of water in front of Travis. He tossed Max a Coke across the table and slid a small spiral-bound notepad and pen in front of him. Skip took a seat at the end of the table and opened up his own leather-bound notebook.

"Sorry about the mess," Skip said nonchalantly. "Okay, let's just start from the beginning. What's your wife's name?"

Travis took a deep breath and collected his thoughts.

"Well," he began, "I work a lot of evenings and weekends leading substance abuse classes. Most of my clients are court ordered, but some are there voluntarily. Sometimes I'm home during the day while my wife is at work. So I was home on Friday, getting ready to do a weekend OWI class. You know: people get probation for OWI, and instead of doing two days in jail, they do two days in a hotel, where I give them their court-ordered alcohol awareness class. I set them up for the weekends. I'm court certified. That's what I do."

Travis paused for a moment. "So on Friday I had all my stuff packed up, my laptop and everything, and I wanted to check my email to make sure that nobody was trying to skip out. They do that. They sign up for the weekend, then they make up an excuse not to be there. So I got on my wife's computer. And when I pulled up the browser, she had a bunch of open tabs. I didn't want to mess them up, so I opened a new tab. When the new tab came up, it was a blank page. I don't know if I meant snoop or what, but I hit the icon that opens the page to recently viewed sites. That is when I saw that she had been getting on a dating site: lonelyfarmers.com." Travis stopped for a moment, gathering his thoughts. "And then I saw that she had been on Craigslist. So I clicked on that, and I followed it as far as I could, you know, and she had been in the personals. I didn't know what to think. It has been bothering me all weekend. And then I remembered that Marjorie told me that after you guys won the lottery and quit the police department, that you started up a detective agency. So I called her up last night and asked her how to hire you guys to check it out."

Travis looked from Skip to Max and back. Skip was taking notes. Max hadn't written anything on his notepad.

"So, question," Max spoke up when Travis was finished. "Why not just ask your wife what the deal is? Why not just follow her yourself?"

Travis looked down at the table, then back up at Max. "I don't know. I guess I'm afraid of the answer. I guess that I'm afraid she will think that I'm spying on her."

"So you don't want her to think that you are spying on her, but you want to hire a couple of private detectives to spy on her?"

"I don't know," Travis continued, "I keep telling myself that it's nothing. That she is just curious. Maybe it's just harmless. I don't want to make it more than it is, if that is the case."

Max and Skip sat pondering what Travis had said. Skip was unusually quiet. He was the one who normally had all the questions.

"So what would you tell one of your clients to do?" Max asked.

Travis gave Max a sad look, and shrugged his shoulders.

"What's your wife's name?" asked Skip again.

"Peggy," Travis answered.

Skip wrote the name at the top of his notes.

"You got a picture of her?" Max asked him.

Travis took out his phone and brought up a picture of him and Peggy. It was a selfie taken on vacation the summer before. There were mountains in the background. He showed it to Max and Skip without comment.

"Can you send that to me?" Max asked, handing Travis a G&B Detective Agency business card and pointing to his email address printed on it.

When Travis looked back up from his phone, Skip asked him, "Where does Peggy work? What does she do?"

"She works at an ethanol manufacturing plant, BioForce Ethanol Manufacturing. She is in charge of a department there. She reviews and approves contracts with subcontractors, oversees their work, coordinates with inspectors."

"What kind of subcontractors?" Max asked.

"Cleaning—I mean janitorial and equipment cleaning. Those are two separate things. Security—they subcontract out security. Facilities maintenance. She doesn't have anything to do with expansion, though. That is another department."

"So she's pretty high up that ladder?" Max asked.

"Yes," Travis said, a bit of pride showing in his voice. "She is up there. She has seven people under her. She answers to one of the VPs."

"She makes good money, I expect?" Max commented.

"Yeah, she makes real good money," Travis responded. "I couldn't have started my private practice without her having this job. I mean, I'm doing quite well now, but in the beginning she floated the whole thing."

"So what kind of schedule does she have?" Skip asked. "What time does she go to work? What time does she come home? What time does she go to lunch? Does she just go to the office every day, or does she travel around?"

"She goes to work early," Travis responded. "She is supposed to be there by eight, but she always gets there early. She likes to be the first one in. She gets off at five, but she works late sometimes. Not often. She gets an hour for lunch. I think that she takes it over the noon hour. She's pretty conventional. She likes routine. It doesn't vary much."

"Monday through Friday?" Max asked.

"Monday through Friday," Travis affirmed.

"What does she do in the evenings?" Skip asked. "What does she do on the weekends, when you are working? Does she have hobbies?"

Travis thought for a moment. "I don't know," he answered. "I mean, I used to think that she just watched TV, worked in her garden, visited with her friends. We talk. When I get home, I ask her what she did, and she always says that she didn't so anything special. Sometimes she goes shopping and she shows me what she got."

"How long you been married?" Max asked.

"Fourteen years," Travis answered.

"Any kids?" Max asked.

"No kids," Travis answered. He didn't elaborate.

The three sat in silence for a moment. Skip was going over his notes, running down through them with the point of his pen. Max was staring out the door into the hall. He heard the door open and recognized the sounds of Monica coming in and sitting at her desk.

"Okay," Skip broke the silence. "We'll take the case. We'll see what we can find out. We'll give it a week. We will follow her around and see where she goes and what she does. If all she does is just innocent stuff, then we will tell you that you have nothing to worry about, or at least we didn't see anything that you need to worry about. If she isn't doing anything, we aren't going to give you an accounting of her every move. And you still pay the fee. If we see that there is something going on, well, then we will report it to you. We will report it in detail. We won't keep anything from you. How's that sound?"

Travis gave the two detectives a serious look. "That is all I ask," he agreed.

"One more thing," Skip added, "What does she drive?"

"Brand-new silver Lexus convertible," Travis answered.

"That shouldn't be too hard to spot," Max remarked.

Skip stood up. Travis and Max followed. They shook hands and Max led the way from the conference room. As they passed into the reception area, Monica looked up from her desk. The first thing that Travis noticed was how strikingly pretty she was.

"Monica," Skip announced, "Travis. Travis, this is Monica, our receptionist. You can call in and talk to her any time. Monica is our go-between. You can tell her anything that you want to tell us. She will pass it on. She is privy to everything we do here, so…" Skip trailed off.

"Nice to meet you, Travis," Monica said, flashing her smile. She stood up and shook hands with him, then sat back down. "If you call and I'm not in, leave a message."

Travis smiled back. "Well, I guess that is it," he announced. "I'll wait for you to call me, I guess, unless something else comes up."

Travis walked out the door. The three watched him cross over to his car, get in and back out of the parking space.

"He thinks you're cute," Max said.

"I used to make a living being cute," Monica shrugged as she went back to her school work.

Skip noticed that Monica's car wasn't in her reserved space.

"Where's your car?" he asked her.

"Milton took it to Express Lube to get the oil changed," Monica replied, not looking up from her studies. "He's off today."

"So now you've got Milton taking your car for oil changes?" Max said in an accusatory voice. "What's the deal with that?"

"He thinks I'm cute, too," she replied, looking up.

"That is sexist," Max responded.

"No, you're sexist," Monica responded back.

"Whatever," Max said. "OK, we are going to get to work on this case. You gonna be around this week?"

"I'll try to be here as much as I can," Monica said in a more serious voice. "I got a lot of things to do, but I'll try to be here. I can study here as well as anywhere, and I'll bring Essie over when she gets out of preschool."

"Do your best," Max said.

"Well," Skip spoke up, "I'm saying that we go over to the ethanol plant and see if we can find a place to wait for Peggy to go to lunch, and then start following her around."

"Sounds good to me," Max agreed. "What are we going to drive?"

Both Max and Skip were looking out at the two cars parked in front of the agency: Max's yellow Mustang and Skip's silver Mercedes. A maroon Nissan Sentra was pulling in off the street and parking in the reserved parking space in front of the agency. Skip looked at Max. "I think every other Sentra I have ever seen is maroon or silver, don't you think?"

"What am I supposed to drive?" Monica piped up.

"Take your pick," Max responded. "'Oh lord, won't you buy me a Mercedes Benz.' Isn't that the way the song goes?"

"I'm thinking more on the lines of a yellow 'Stang for Milton and me to drive around on his day off."

Max narrowed his eyes at Monica, but she had seen the look before and wasn't at all intimidated by it.

"Okay, done deal," she declared as Milton was coming through the door.

"What's a done deal?" Milton asked her.

"We're taking Max's Mustang this afternoon and driving it down to Saylorville Lake for some sightseeing, top down."

Milton looked at Max, who shrugged his shoulders, dug his keys out of his pocket and tossed them to Milton. Monica reached over and took them out of his hand.

"I'm driving," she declared.

"So much for sticking around the office," Skip mumbled.

"Don't worry," Monica teased. "We'll go fast."

Chapter 3

Monday

The two detectives were in no hurry, so they hung around the office for a while, waiting for lunch time. Monica and Milton drove off in Max's yellow Mustang, heading to Polk City and Saylorville Lake. Max was in his office surfing the net, and Skip was on the Morningstar site reading the financial news. Just before eleven-thirty Skip called across the hall to Max's office.

"You ready to roll?"

"About," Max replied. "You packin'?"

"No, I'm not packing," Skip said.

"Are you bringing a camera?" Max asked.

"I'm bringing my phone. It has a camera," Skip replied.

"Okay, I'm not gonna bring my pistola, but I will bring my binoculars and my camera with the telephoto lens, because that's why I bought it, to take pictures," Max called back.

"Okay, let's go then," Skip said.

He met Max in the hallway. Max had his Cannon camera case hung over his shoulder and a pair of Burris binoculars in his hand.

The two detectives walked out the door and Max locked it.

"Who's driving?" Skip enquired. "You look like a bird watcher, by the way."

"Your case, you're driving," Max said.

The two got into Monica's Sentra and Max put his camera and binoculars on the back seat. Skip started the engine and backed out of Monica's reserved parking space. Skip drove from the parking lot to the street, then pointed the car toward the east. He navigated to the on ramp to US Highway 30, known by most of the old-timers as New 30. New 30 wasn't actually that new; it had been there as long as Max and Skip could remember. Highway 30 split into New and Old just west of the Ames city limit, with Old 30, formally known as Lincolnway, traversing the town and New 30 running a mile south and parallel, east and west. Old 30 ran east out of Ames for thirty miles or so, through the towns of Nevada, Colo, State Center, then toward Marshalltown where it merged again with New 30 to continue to the east. Old 30 was the original route of the Lincoln Highway, the first US highway to connect the east coast with the west coast. Three ethanol plants were located between Ames and Nevada, the county seat: two were on Old 30, five miles east of Ames and two miles west of Nevada. The other, BioForce Ethanol Manufacturing, was a mile directly south of them on New 30.

Both detectives were familiar with the area. Max had grown up on a farm south of there a few miles. Skip had grown up in a small town situated in the southwest corner of the county. However, the two had not known each other growing up. Max was a few years older than Skip, and had enlisted in the navy after high school. Skip had gone to Iowa State University after high school on a baseball scholarship, and Max had gone to college at the same time on the GI bill after he was discharged from the navy. But still the two did not meet until they were both testing for the police department.

Max and Skip had taken notice of each other during the physical agility part of the testing. There were a dozen young men in the group, gathered on the first floor of State Gym at Iowa State University. To pass, each had to run a mile in less than eight minutes. Neither of the two were concerned about the time: Skip was an athlete, and Max was just plain determined.

The track was an indoor track, twelve laps to the mile. As the group began the run, Skip took the lead, with Max right behind him. After two laps, Max realized that he was not going to outrun Skip, but he was determined to stay with him as long as he could. Lap after lap, Skip would pull away just a little bit, Max doggedly keeping the lead as narrow as he could. By the time Skip came around on his tenth lap, he had started to pass the slower runners, with Max less than half a lap behind him. By his eleventh lap, Skip had passed all the other runners except Max, who was himself gaining on the pack. After his twelfth lap, Skip crossed the line to finish the run. As he pulled to the side to let the group pass, they pulled up behind him, leaving Max to bring up the rear. Max crossed the line at six minutes and fourteen seconds.

As Max crossed the line, Skip remarked to one of the timers monitoring the run that Max had finished, but that the rest of the runners still owed a lap. The monitor looked at Skip in confusion. Skip pressed it: it wasn't fair, he said. He and Max had finished the run, the rest still needed to run another lap; they had quit early. Still the monitors were confused. Max walked up to Skip as he became more agitated and put his hand on Skip's arm. He told Skip to forget it. That it didn't make any difference. That he had passed the run with time to spare, and that was all that counted. The two were hired less than two months apart. Twenty years they worked together, friends from the very first day.

Skip drove into a huge farm implement dealership across from the BioForce ethanol plant and parked the car where they had a good view of the parking lot across the four lanes of Highway 30. Skip positioned the Sentra between two monstrous John Deere combines. It was just before noon, and the implement dealership was quiet. The two waited a moment to see if anyone would come out to investigate what they were up to, but no one seemed to notice them there. Max retrieved the binoculars from the back seat and trained them on the parking lot, systematically scanning the cars for a silver Lexus convertible. It took him several minutes to locate it, but he finally did.

"Got it," Max said.

"What's going on?" asked Skip.

"Nothing," said Max. "All's quiet on the western front. It's early."

Max settled back in the seat.

"Company," Skip said, looking in the rearview mirror, where he was watching a sheriff deputy's car pull up behind them. Skip could see the deputy on the radio calling in the plate number. The two waited. The deputy finally walked up to the passenger's side door. Skip rolled down Max's window. The deputy peered into the car.

"What's up guys?" the deputy casually asked.

"Hey, Carlisle," Max said.

"What you guys doing here in Monica's car?"

"Watching that parking lot over there," Max replied.

Carlisle leaned down and looked into the car. "You guys on a case?"

"Yep," Max said.

Carlisle glanced over across the highway at the parking lot in front of the ethanol plant. "Not much going on."

Max didn't say anything.

"The guys over there in the dealership saw you two pull in here and they called. They thought that you were waiting to do a drug deal or something," Carlisle laughed. "I don't know why they thought that, but they did." Carlisle paused while he watched the parking lot again. "Then when I ran the plate, I thought what the fuck."

"Yeah," Max said, "We needed a car that didn't stand out and draw attention, you know?"

"So you borrow Monica's car and drive over here, park between two million dollars worth of machinery in broad daylight?"

"Gotta take what you can get," Max said.

"Monica and Milton are out sporting around in Max's Mustang," Skip added to the conversation.

"Them two are seeing a lot of each other since the missing dog case," Carlisle said.

"I guess," said Skip. "Wasn't a missing dog case, it was a stolen dog case."

Carlisle laughed. "Okay, whatever. I'm going to tell those guys that you two are just looking at these combines, but you don't need anyone to come out and talk to you yet."

"That's a good idea," said Max as he brought the binoculars back up to his eyes. "There's people moving over there and you're going to blow our cover."

Carlisle laughed again and tapped his knuckle on the door. "Okay stealth, good luck with your case."

The deputy went back to his car and backed out. Max trained his binoculars on the BioForce parking lot. A few minutes later he saw a woman that he recognized from Travis's picture, dressed in a business suit, come out and get into the car.

"She's getting ready to pull out," Max told Skip, who was already putting the car into reverse and backing from between the two combines. Max waved to Carlisle as they passed by him getting out of his car to go into the dealership. Deputy Carlisle casually waved back. The silver Lexus turned north toward Old 30. Skip waited for two more cars to turn, then followed all three cars north on the gravel road.

"Well, that was pretty sneaky," Max observed.

"She isn't looking back here. Besides, there's too much dust to make out what's going on behind her, anyway."

Skip pulled up behind the line of cars at the stop sign waiting to turn onto Old 30 toward Nevada. It looked like they all were turning the same way. Skip followed them to the edge of town where they all pulled into the parking lot at the West Café. Skip parked Monica's car and the two detectives entered the café just in time to see the woman from the Lexus sit down in a booth opposite a man who appeared to be waiting for her. There were already two menus on the table, and two glasses of water. The man smiled as the woman sat down.

"You two can sit wherever there's room," a waitress told the two detectives as she passed by. Max and Skip slid into an empty booth with a clear view of Peggy and the man.

The waitress came up and blocked it. "What can I get you to drink?" she asked as she set two menus on the table.

"Coke," said Max.

The waitress looked at Skip.

"Diet Coke, and we're ready to order."

Max was frantically looking at the menu.

"Burger and fries," Skip said. "And we need the bill so that we can pay up. We don't have a lot of time. We might need to leave quickly."

"I'll take the hot beef sandwich," Max said.

"I'll get it right out," the waitress replied as she wrote their order on a pad. "One bill, or two?"

"He'll get it," Max piped up.

The waitress looked over at Skip. He nodded his head.

Max glanced over at the other table out of the corner of his eye. Another waitress had just taken their order and left. Peggy was talking seriously to the man. He reached across the table and took her hand in his, smiling and nodding his head. After a moment, the woman pulled her hand away and looked around as if she was afraid that someone would see them holding hands. Max quickly averted his eyes. He saw Skip do the same. Max started talking to Skip. It wouldn't do for the two of them to sit in silence.

"What do you think?" he asked.

"They're chummy," Skip observed. "Wonder who he is?"

"Well, that is the next question," Max remarked. "Pretty fast moving case. I mean, we got her doing holdy-hands in the West Café already."

Max recognized the blank expression that Skip always gave him when Max stated the obvious.

"Just saying," Max responded to the look.

Skip did not say anything in response.

"Not liking this case already, are ya?" Max continued.

"Not really," Skip replied. "I don't like spying on people."

"Me neither," Max said. "But you know, we're private eyes. That's what private eyes do. Private eyes are seedy." Max waited for a response, but he didn't get one. Skip was watching Peggy and the man with her.

"You know," Max continued. "I don't like it, either. But this guy is Marjorie's friend, and that's what we do, right? Don't be so moody."

Skip looked up at Max and smirked. "You're too much," he said with a bit of a chuckle.

The waitress arrived with their orders. She set the plates in front of them, and placed the bill on Skip's side of the table.

"I told the cook you guys were in a hurry."

Skip dug his billfold out of his pocket and found his G&B credit card. "Thanks, appreciate it," Skip said to the waitress as he gathered up the bill and handed it to her along with the card. Peggy and the man were getting their orders as well.

Skip and Max wolfed down their food in silence, both of them glancing toward Peggy's table between bites. Several times the man reached over and touched her hand, as if to emphasize something that he was saying to her. He was doing most of the talking, she was doing most of the listening. She had a troubled look on her face.

"I wish that I could hear what they are saying," Skip remarked after he had stuffed another French fry in his mouth.

"Maybe we see if they have lunch together again tomorrow, and try to get a place next to them," Max replied.

Skip shrugged his shoulders. Max had finished his sandwich. He slouched down in the booth and stretched his legs. They watched Peggy and the man she was with out of the corners of their eyes. The man reached out, took Peggy's hand in his own again, gave it a squeeze and said something to her that made her smile. He let go of her hand and the two started to slide out of the booth. The man left cash on the table with the bill. Max and Skip followed them to the parking lot.

As the two detectives walked out into the sunlight, Skip turned toward the car, but Max stopped and waited. The man that was with Peggy had walked her to her car, spoken a few words through the open door as she got in, then closed the door for her. He turned and was walking past Max, who had casually moved to intercept him.

"Roger, Roger Leland," Max called out. It was clear that Max was addressing him. He stopped and gave Max a confused look. Peggy was already pulling out of the parking lot and turning toward the ethanol plant.

"Roger Leland," Max called out again, walking toward the man with his hand out. "Holy cow, I have not seen you for ages."

The man cautiously shook Max's hand. "Man, I can't believe it." Max heartily shook the man's hand and wouldn't let go. "Ben Ralston. You were in 4H with my older brother. Man, you guys were my heroes."

"I'm sorry," the man said as Max let him have his hand back. "I'm not Roger Leland. You got me mixed up with someone else."

Max feigned confusion. "You're not Roger Leland, from over by Shipley?"

"No," the man said.

"Dang," Max exclaimed after another moment of confusion. "I'm really sorry, man; I could have sworn you were Roger Leland. He was my brother's best friend when we were growing up. I'm really sorry." Max held out his hand again and the man took it. Max shook it, but this time he did not hold it.

"Man, I'm sorry. Ben Ralston, glad to meet you, anyway." Max gave the man his best "who the hell are you then?" look.

"Allan Proctor," the man replied, grinning at Max's embarrassment.

Max had taken out his wallet and was digging through it. He brought out a business card and handed it to Proctor. "I'm really sorry. Here, here's my card."

Proctor took the card and looked at it. "Independent insurance agent?" He gave Max a suspicious look.

Max laughed. "No, no man, I'm not drumming up business here." Max laughed again. "We're over here checking out corn yields. Bunch of farmers down around here got wind and hail damage back in July. We got us a team of adjusters in here all week. We're checking the yields on fields that wasn't hit, and we're comparing them to those that was. Figure out how much they lost because of the storm. That's how we determine it."

Max could see that Proctor was buying his story. Proctor was letting his guard back down. Max could read Proctor. The man's body language and expressions gave him away to someone like Max, who was trained to recognize and interpret them.

"What do you do, Allan?" Max asked casually.

"I own an industrial cleaning company," Proctor answered.

"Hey, that's cool," Max said enthusiastically. "You do any residential cleaning? I mean, sometimes I got a flooded basement or something and I need to get it cleaned up. Got a card? I could give you a referral."

Proctor pulled out a small leather wallet filled with business cards and peeled one off the top, handing it to Max. "I don't do any residential cleaning, just industrial, and I'm pretty busy right now, but I'm always looking for opportunities." He ended the sentence there, emphasizing "opportunities."

Max was looking at the card. "If I see any opportunities, I'll send them your way." Max smiled and put the card in his shirt pocket. "Hey, sorry again about the mix-up. I could have sworn you were Roger Leland." Max held out his hand again.

Proctor took Max's hand, shook it, then went toward his truck at the far end of the parking lot. Max walked over and climbed into the passenger side of Monica's car where Skip was waiting for him. The window was rolled down so that he could hear the conversation between Proctor and Max.

The two detectives watched Proctor get into a white Chevy Silverado that was covered with road dust, start the engine and pull out of the parking lot.

"You are something else, Max," Skip remarked.

"Just checking him out," Max said.

"Ben Ralston?" Skip lifted an eyebrow.

"Well, he was over the other day and I got some cards from him. I promised I would get him some referrals." Max smiled over at Skip.

"You could talk a drug dealer into selling you a dime bag in uniform, I'm telling you."

Max chuckled. "Done that once."

"I know," said Skip. "I was there. It cost me twenty bucks, remember?"

"Teach you not to bet against a sure thing," Max quipped. "Gonna follow him?"

"Got something else to do?" Skip asked as he pulled onto the highway.

"I don't think so," Max replied.

Chapter 4

Monday

Skip pulled out of the parking lot toward the east, the same direction that the white Silverado had gone. He could see it at a stop sign a couple of blocks ahead of him, with the left turn signal on. The two watched it turn into the parking lot of the True Value Hardware store. Skip pulled into the convenience store across the street and parked next to one of the gas pumps that faced the hardware store. Skip climbed out and started to pump gas into Monica's car. Max was on the phone calling the office. The phone rang twice before Monica picked up. Max was surprised that she was there.

"Hey," Max responded to Monica's voice announcing that G&B Detective Agency was not taking cases.

"What's up?" Monica asked, recognizing Max's voice.

"I thought that you and Milton were going down to Saylorville for lunch."

"Well, I thought that you wanted me to stick around and answer the phone," Monica countered.

"Okay," Max said. "I guess we did, I just thought that you were going to go down there, anyway."

"I work for you guys, you know," Monica said. "I was just giving you a tough time."

Skip leaned into the driver's side window and got Max's attention. "You want something from inside?"

"Yeah," Max pulled the phone away from his face. "Grab me a doughnut."

Max spoke into the phone. "Get on the computer and see what you can find on a guy named Allan Proctor. He owns an industrial cleaning business called Cleanguard, one word. I've got his card here."

"Will do," Monica said.

"Chocolate frosting," Max shouted out the window at Skip, but he was already going through the door.

"Call me back when you get something," Max turned back to the phone.

Max ended the call. Skip was coming out of the store with Max's doughnut balanced on a napkin in his hand. He handed it through the window to Max, then went to remove the nozzle from the tank. Max looked at the doughnut. It was chocolate covered. When Skip was done, he got into the car and sat while Max munched.

"Dessert," Max said. "Glad you got me a chocolate one."

Skip didn't respond. The white Silverado was still parked in front of the hardware store. There were two other cars in the lot.

"Got Monica checking out our man Allan there," Max broke the silence. Skip was watching the front of the store. The two waited a little longer. Finally, Proctor came out, got into his truck and drove out of the parking lot, again turning east. After he had gone a couple of blocks, Skip pulled into the street and followed. The two watched up ahead as the Silverado turned right. Skip hurried to the intersection where he turned as well, but the white Silverado was nowhere in sight. As they cruised south, both Max and Skip scanned parking lots, driveways and side streets for any sign of Proctor or his truck.

"Got 'im," Max suddenly announced. "Parked in front of the post office."

Skip drove around the block and parked the car where he had a clear view of the truck. They waited.

"He's just running errands," Max remarked.

"I know," Skip said absently.

Max's phone rang and he picked it up out of the cup holder where he had deposited it after he had called Monica. It was her on the other end.

"That was fast," Max said into the phone, not bothering to say hello.

"Nothing much on him," Monica said. "I don't see anything about an industrial cleaning company called Cleanguard at all. LinkedIn says that he's a member of the Iowa Pork Producers and that he has something to do with a Delvan Real Estate Development, but I followed up on that and it didn't go anywhere. There isn't a Delvan Real Estate Development that I can find. I checked him out in Iowa Courts Online, and there's nothing. Tried to find him on Facebook, but nothing there. Actually, there's just a bunch of nothing on him."

Monica took a breath and waited for a moment in case Max had something to say. When he didn't, she continued.

"So then I checked the county assessor's page, and he has two places listed in Story County. He has a 160-acre farm on 645th north of Maxwell, and 17 acres with a house on 650th south of Nevada."

Max rolled the information around for a moment, "What is it with Maxwell?"

"What's with Maxwell?" Skip asked Max.

"Just a second," Max said to Monica. He pulled the phone away from his mouth and turned to Skip. "Just this Proctor guy lives down by Maxwell. I'm wondering what it is with Maxwell all the time."

"Aren't you from there?" Skip asked.

"No, I'm from Shipley," Max replied. "I have lots of relatives around Maxwell, but I don't know any of them. They are all related to my grandpa's brother and I don't go to the family reunions."

"I thought that was why your parents named you Maxwell," Skip said.

"No, that is not why my parents named me Max. And it's not 'Maxwell,' just Max."

Skip laughed out loud. He liked messing with Max.

Max looked at Skip, waiting for another comment. Skip was watching and waiting for Proctor to come out of the post office and get into the Silverado.

"I think that you were talking to Monica on the phone," Skip remarked.

Max put the phone back to his mouth. "Okay, sorry about that, Skip was yanking my chain. What else you got?"

"Well," Monica said, "the place on 650th is only two years old. Looks like a really nice place from the picture on the assessor's site. The house itself is assessed at four hundred grand. Three car garage, one out building. Wasn't much on the assessor's site on the other place, except it says that it has a house, some buildings and some grain bins, so I pulled it up on Google maps and looked at the satellite view. It looks like there is a house, two long buildings, a big shed of some kind, couple of smaller sheds and two rectangular ponds back behind the two long buildings."

"Hog confinement," Max said. "That would go along with the Pork Producers thing." Max pondered the information that Monica had given him. "Anything else?"

"Not at the moment," Monica replied. "I'll keep checking around. By the way," Monica continued, "You ever check out yourself on the assessor's office site?"

"No, I haven't," Max replied.

"You ought to," Monica said.

"Why, what is there besides my place?"

"Nothing," Monica answered, "just says you have a lap pool in the basement."

"It says that on the assessor's site?" Max asked.

"Yep, among other things," Monica teased.

"Okay, whatever," Max said.

"Hey," Monica said as Max was getting ready to end the call, "how long you guys want me to stay? Milton is off today and we did really want to take the 'Stang for a spin."

"Go ahead and take off. We're going nowhere fast right now," Max said. "We're watching a parked truck. Thanks for sticking around, though. We'll catch you tomorrow morning before class and regroup."

"See you guys tomorrow, then." Monica ended the call.

Max put his phone in the cup holder and slouched down in his seat. "What is he doing in there so long?"

"I don't know," Skip replied. "But I don't think following him around all afternoon is going to do anything for us. We aren't getting paid to follow him around, we're getting paid to follow her around. "

"Monica got some info on him," Max said. "Sounds like he is a pig farmer, and that he has his fingers in real estate and maybe this cleaning business, but nothing much more. Just a regular farmer."

Skip started the car, pulled onto the street and drove past the Silverado. Max tried to look through the glass doors in front of the post office but he couldn't make anything out. At the corner Skip turned left and wound his way to the county fairgrounds and then drove south on S-14 to New 30. They took the highway west out of town, past the implement dealership and the ethanol plant. As they passed, they saw Peggy's car parked in the lot.

"This isn't going to be that easy, is it?" Skip commented "How are we going to keep an eye on her twenty-four hours a day? We can't sit over there in the implement dealership all afternoon, waiting for her to leave, just to follow her home."

"Right you are," Max answered him. "You're always the man with a plan. What's the plan?"

Skip kept driving west on 30 toward Ames in silence.

"What about sticking a GPS tracker of some kind on her car?" Max suggested.

"Do you have a GPS tracker that you could stick on her car?" Skip asked.

"No," Max replied, "but we could get one somewhere. We're a detective agency, might be a good idea if we had a GPS tracker."

"Where would you get one?" Skip asked.

"No idea," Max said. "Maybe Best Buy? You can track people through their phones. Like if you don't trust a spouse, you can track them that way. My daughter's friend was doing that with her boyfriend. But he also knew she was doing it. I mean, he was good with it, or at least he was saying that he was good with it. But maybe Travis could do that?"

Skip didn't say anything for a moment. "You know something, Max? We are piss-poor detectives when it comes to this kind of stuff. I mean following people around and digging up dirt."

It was Max's turn to ponder. "Lucky we don't have to make a living at it." Skip laughed.

Skip drove into the G&B Detective Agency lot and parked. The two went inside. Monica and the yellow Mustang were gone. Skip went to his office to call Travis. Max leaned on the door jamb while Skip placed the call and put the phone on speaker.

"Travis," Skip said when he answered the phone. "I need some sort of itinerary."

"Did you come up with anything?" Travis asked.

"We really haven't had a lot of time to see anything happen yet," Skip said. "We need to know when you are going to be home and when you aren't. Like, are you going to be home tonight? Do you expect Peggy to come home right after work?"

"Yes, I expect her home after work," Travis answered. "We don't have any plans for tonight. Tomorrow night, either. I do a twelve-step substance abuse program at the Willowbrook Church every Wednesday from six to nine. I usually leave for those before Peggy gets home. This week I have a drunk driver class Thursday evening, Friday evening and all day Saturday. I do those once a month." Travis stopped for a moment. "That's my week."

"Okay," Skip replied, "If anything changes, you need to call me up right away. If Peggy calls and says she is working late, she has somewhere she has to be, you need to call me up. You good with that?"

"I can do that," Travis sighed.

"Okay." Skip ended the call. He turned to Max. "That's about all we can do at this point, don't you think?"

"We still going to go watch her eat lunch tomorrow?" Max asked.

"I think we should," Skip answered him. "See if Proctor shows up again. But let's plan to see if she goes home on Wednesday and Thursday, then go from there."

"Sounds good."

Max left the agency, but Skip stayed behind. Max took Monica's car and drove to his house, which was less than a mile from the agency. It was after three when he pulled into his driveway.

"What were you up to today?" Gloria asked as he came into the house and out onto the patio, where she was working on her computer.

"Skip got us a case," Max replied, mixing himself a rum and Coke from the mini bar on the patio. When he was done, he carried it over to an Adirondack chair and sat down.

"Possible unfaithful wife case," Max continued. "We're going to follow her around for a week and see who she sees. Fact is, we went to lunch at a greasy spoon over in Nevada and watched her hold hands with a guy who wasn't her husband. It was so exciting that I almost fainted."

"An unfaithful wife case?" Gloria remarked a bit sarcastically.

"Yep." Max gave Gloria a smug look.

Gloria shook her head in disbelief.

"Hey, Skip is doing it for Marjorie. The husband is a friend."

"So you know who this paramour is? Does he have a name, or are you still sorting that out?" Gloria asked.

"Well, yes, we do," Max answered her. "His name is Allan Proctor. He gave me his card when I introduced myself to him in the parking lot as Ben Ralston, independent insurance agent."

"Okay, Mr. Ralston," Gloria mocked him. "And so you're sure that he wasn't messing with you, too, when he told you his name was Allan Proctor?"

"Gave me his business card."

"And did you give him one of Ben's business cards?"

Max didn't answer. Gloria went back to her computer.

"Just a second," Gloria said. "Allan Proctor, you said? I think that he was at a wine tasting I did for someone a year or so ago. Carl Zepman, the county supervisor. He had a wine tasting for some of the other supervisors and county bigshots. Bankers, real estate people, lawyers and like that. This guy Proctor ordered three cases of expensive wine. He made a big deal out of it, but the next day when I entered the order, his card was declined. When I called him up to verify the number, he cancelled the order. He's a real loud type. Wants to make sure everyone notices him. Kind of sleazy, but then when you're hanging out with politicians, lawyers and real estate agents, he fits right in. At least the others actually bought wine with valid credit cards."

"No shit?" Max exclaimed. "That's interesting."

"He's a real piece of work," Gloria said. "I've seen him around since, too. Haven't talked to him, though. I think he is avoiding me. By the way, he also had a wife with him at the tasting."

Max thought about it for a moment. "Wives come and go, but then Peggy is married, too, so I guess…" Max let it go. "Doesn't mean anything either way, I guess is what I was going to say."

"I'm driving Monica's car and she has the Mustang," Max told Gloria while she turned back to her work. "I'm going over later to switch back. You want to come along?"

"I don't think so," Gloria replied. "I have my Monday evening conference call with home office."

Max shrugged his shoulders and took another sip of his rum and Coke.

"Let me get this done," Gloria said. "We can have supper before the call, then you can take her car back while I'm doing that."

Chapter 5

Monday

Allan parked on the street in front of the post office, got out and took his notice with him inside. The rural mail carrier had tried to leave a package at the farm the week before, and it wouldn't fit in the box. Allan had found the notice on Saturday when he had gone over to do chores. He had no idea what it was.

Allan was thinking about Ben Ralston. He took the card out of his pocket and looked at it. What a toon. Allan could see through that guy the minute he opened his mouth. Read him like a book. Allan wondered how ol' phony Ben Ralston thought he was going to pull a fast one like that on Allan Proctor? In fact, Allan did know Roger Leland. Roger Leland was a farmer over on the other side of the county, and Roger Leland was at least ten years older than Allan. And Ben Ralston looked to be all of that as well. Who did he think he was kidding? Well, Allan didn't need any insurance, and he sure as hell wasn't going to buy it from Ben Ralston. Allan threw the business card into the mailbox on the curb as he passed by it on the way into the post office. Leave it to insurance agents to come up with some BS to shake someone's hand and put a business card in it.

There was just one clerk at the counter, and two other people were standing in line in front of him. Allan waited. The clerk was slow. Allan wanted to leave, but his curiosity was too much for him, so he waited. He pulled his phone out of his pocket and started reading his emails. He had received two text messages while he was with Peggy at the café and at the hardware store picking up a couple of spark plugs for his riding mower. Both were from his wife, Brenda. The first one said that Gordon had called twice and needed to talk to him. The second said that the hardware store had called to say that his spark plugs were in. He already knew that. What he didn't know was why Gordon wanted to talk to him so bad. It might be something about the tanker truck, but Gordon was good about keeping the tanker truck running. He usually didn't bother Allan about the truck. Allan couldn't think of anything else that Gordon might want.

The first lady in line took her package and walked past him on the way out. Allan gave her a big smile and nodded. The lady smiled back. Allan liked the way he could make women smile. Women liked Allan. He waited impatiently while the lady in front of him tried to decide what kind of stamps to buy from the display on the counter. It appeared that she knew the clerk, and they chatted while she looked at them. Allan was getting impatient. Finally, the lady bought her stamps and left. As she turned to leave, Allan gave her his patented smile and nod. She smiled back.

Allan laid the notice on the counter and the clerk picked it up. He glanced at it, then took it around the stacks of shelves behind him that were filled with mail. Allan waited alone. He looked at the stamp display. He looked at his watch. He didn't know what time it had been when he came in, but he was sure that he had been waiting at least ten minutes for the clerk. Allan could hear him rummaging around behind the shelves. He was just about to call out and ask what the holdup was, when the clerk came to the desk with the notice in his hand. He passed it over the counter to Allan.

"Maxwell post office," he told Allan.

Allan just stood looking at him.

"It is at the Maxwell post office, not here."

Allan let out a sigh of frustration. He knew that the clerk was right; his new place had a Nevada address, the old place had a Maxwell address.

"Okay," Allan said. "Sorry about that; I guess that's my fault."

The clerk did not say anything. Allan turned around and left the post office. He got into his truck and sat for a moment. There was a ticket under the windshield wiper. Allan rolled down his window and tried to reach it, but couldn't. He opened the door, got out and retrieved the ticket. He sat back down in the driver's seat to read it. Ten dollars for parking on a yellow curb. In the notes section, the issuing officer had scribbled, "blocking the mailbox." Allan looked out his window at the curb side mailbox that was, in fact, blocked from drive up traffic by the front of his Silverado. "Bullshit," he said to himself as his anger rose. "Just fucking bullshit." Allan fired up the truck engine and pulled away from the curb. He drove to the corner, turned left and wound his way toward S-14. He drove past the fairgrounds and to New 30, then turned and drove west toward the ethanol plant.

Allan turned into the truck entrance at the plant. The guard at the gate waved him right through. There were actual streets with signs that led to the back of the plant. It was almost like a small city, the way it was laid out. Allan turned on one street toward the back of the plant where it bordered the railroad tracks. There he found his tanker truck, but Gordon was nowhere to be seen. Allan parked behind the tanker, where he was not blocking the drive, and got out. The back door of the plant was open, and Allan went inside. A couple of workers were cleaning two huge stainless-steel ethanol tanks. Allan saw the two Mexican men, sopping wet with sweat, wearing long sleeves, rubber gloves, and bandanas on their heads. Each one wore a respirator mask and goggles. Allan had seen them around, but he did not know their names. They were hired by a company that Allan subcontracted with to do the actual cleaning. Allan said hi to them as he passed, but if either of the men responded, Allan didn't notice. Allan tried to stay away from the help. He wanted to be isolated as far as possible from the company that was supplying the Mexicans. Allan knew quite well that their documentation was questionable. He also knew that if ICE did a sweep, that the company Allan was contracting with for labor would just melt away, and a new one would pop up to take its place as soon as things settled down.

Allan walked through the plant toward the front, looking for Gordon. He passed through a set of doors, then another set of doors, and arrived in a hall near the front entrance to the building. A sign with arrows directed people to the different offices, but Allan knew where he was going. He went down the hall, his heels clicking on the tile floor and echoing off the walls as he walked. He finally opened a door and stepped into a reception area. The woman at the desk looked up.

"Hey, Peggy in?" Allan asked.

"Yes she is," the receptionist answered. "I'll let her know you are here."

The receptionist picked up the phone and punched a button. "Mr. Proctor is here."

The receptionist looked up. "Go on back."

Allan smiled and nodded. She did not return the smile or the nod. Allan walked past two unoccupied offices and through the door into Peggy's office. He closed it behind him and fell into the chair facing Peggy's desk.

"What do you think?" he asked Peggy.

"What are you doing here?" Peggy responded.

"Looking for Gordon," Allan said.

"Did you think that he would be here in my office?" Peggy asked, smiling.

Allan laughed. "No, but I thought that you would be in your office." He returned the smile and added a wink.

"Did you come in the back way?" Peggy asked him, leaning forward and lowering her voice.

"Yes."

"Did you see those two guys back there cleaning the vats?"

"Yeah."

"Did you talk to them?"

"No," Allan responded.

"Do you speak Spanish?" Peggy pressed.

"I know where you are going with this, Peggy," Allan countered.

"There is a lot of talk down on the floor of the plant, Allan. The guys are saying that those two are illegals, and that the ones before them were illegals, too. They are saying that you just traded two illegal aliens for two more illegal aliens. They are saying that they can't even talk to them, because they don't speak English."

"Well, it's not any of their business," Allan said. "I contract with Evergreen. They send the workers over to do the cleaning. They don't even work for me, they work for Evergreen."

"But you have the cleaning contract, Allan."

Allan shrugged his shoulders. "I don't know what to tell you, Peggy. I need people to clean those tanks, and I contract with Evergreen for those people. We've been over this before."

Peggy did not answer. She looked expressionless across the desk at him.

"Look, I'm not going to pretend that their documentation isn't questionable. Neither you or me are stupid. But here is the thing: I don't ask. I do my business, and Evergreen does their business. That keeps us pretty far removed from any legal implications." Allan paused for a moment. "You are a mile away from it, Peggy. BioForce is a mile away from it. But I complained to Evergreen about the workers they sent over the last time, because your guys here in the plant were pitching a fit, and these two guys are the ones they sent over to take their place. I don't know what you want me to do."

Peggy sat for a moment, still looking Allan in the face. "Allan, it isn't about how far removed we are, it is about illegal aliens working for BioForce, and the fallout when the feds come in and sweep them up. I'm thinking about BioForce; it is my job to think about BioForce."

"Peggy," Allan pleaded. "I don't know what you want me to do. I don't know where else to get workers. I tried to get reliable workers on my own, and I couldn't get them. That's why I contracted with Evergreen. The thing is, ICE isn't going to descend on BioForce for two maybe—or maybe not—illegal aliens, when they've got hundreds of them just north of here working on chicken farms."

Peggy sat back, resigned, but still didn't comment.

"Why do we always have to argue about this?" Allan asked. "Honey, things are going fine. Life is good. You and me, we got something that very few people have. Why do we always have to argue about Evergreen and the workers that they send over? I don't want to argue."

Peggy let her shoulders fall in defeat. Allan could tell that he had won, at least until it came up again. And he knew it would. Allan knew that Evergreen was sending over illegals to do the cleaning for him. Gordon had been shepherding illegals for a decade, maybe more. In fact, it was Gordon who had put Allan on to Evergreen in the first place. It was Gordon who had convinced Allan that if the feds ever picked up on it, Evergreen would be implicated, and then Evergreen would cease to exist. Cleanguard would never be held accountable. BioForce would be in the clear. All they had to do was plead ignorance. Another company would appear from Evergreen's ashes, pick up the reins — and the contract — with little more than a ripple of inconvenience for Cleanguard. Gordon had gone through that scenario several times over the years. He called it FMR: federally mandated reorganization.

"Hey," Allan continued, changing the subject away from illegal aliens. "Why don't we have a little picnic Wednesday evening? It's still warm enough. We can go to the lake, maybe build a fire in the fireplace at the shelter house, drink some wine and have a bite to eat. Maybe bring a blanket, snuggle up and keep each other warm after the sun goes down. What do you think?"

Peggy softened. "I think that sounds good. We need to talk about Travis and Brenda, and figure out what we are going to do. Maybe while we are snuggled up, we can come up with a good exit strategy."

"Good idea," Allan replied. "We've got to do this right. We need to take our time and do it right. We owe it to them."

Peggy felt relieved that Allan finally seemed ready to talk about Travis and Brenda. Every time she had brought it up before, Allan had skillfully changed the subject. Peggy didn't want to hurt Travis, but they were growing apart.

She and Allan were starting something special. He reminded her of that every day. He was right: they owed it to Travis and Brenda to think carefully about how they were going to go about the breakups. It wouldn't be easy, but in the end, it would be better for everyone.

Allan got up, leaned over Peggy's desk and gave her a kiss on the lips. She smiled. "Are we having lunch tomorrow?"

"You want to have lunch again tomorrow?" Allan asked. "Sure, we can do that. I don't think I have anything going. I'll have to check, though. If for some reason I can't make it, I'll let you know."

Allan walked to the door and turned. "But Wednesday evening is on for sure. We need it. We need some time, just you and me." He gave her his most sincere look and smiled lovingly at her.

"Get out of here," she said smiling back. "I have work to do."

Allan laughed and walked out, leaving the office door open. He walked past the reception desk and the receptionist looked up at him. Allan smiled at her, but didn't say anything when she wished him a nice day. Allan was already crafting his excuse to beg out of lunch with Peggy the next day. That wouldn't be a problem. He always had an excuse. He was a busy man, he could think of something.

Allan made his way back to the rear of the plant. As he approached the back door, he could hear Gordon speaking in Spanish to the two workers. Allan walked out into the sunlight and saw the three of them smoking cigarettes outside the door.

Gordon was Allan's number-one man. He was half Mexican on his father's side, born and raised up in Stanhope. His father had worked on one of the poultry farms outside of town and married a local woman. While Gordon's mother had never been anywhere close to Mexico, she spoke Spanish like a Mexican. She had lived with one after another for years before meeting Gordon's dad, and while many around Stanhope thought that Gordon's dad was going to be just one more Mexican through her bedroom door, the two eventually got married and had stayed together for three decades. Gordon was the only product of that marriage. He was born of hard-working Norwegian stock and even harder-working Mexican stock. He had the best and the worst of both coursing through his blood. Gordon's father never learned to speak more than enough English to buy gas and order a hamburger. He had died a few years earlier, leaving Gordon's mom with nothing. Gordon missed him.

"Hey," Allan said as he walked out the door, "what's with all the texts and phone calls?"

Gordon was leaning against the wall with his feet crossed, one over the other. He stood up when Allan came out the door and addressed him.

"We got a problem. I think that the pits are leaking into Indian Creek. All the grass is going dead on that low side, and it keeps creeping toward the creek. I think that you need to look at it."

"It's fall," Allan waved a hand dismissively. "Grass starts turning brown in the fall."

"No, I don't think that's it," responded Gordon. "The grass isn't turning brown because it is fall. You can see how it's creeping down toward the creek. There's green all around it. You gotta see it. If you look at the pits, you will see what I'm talking about. I'm kind of worried about it."

Allan sighed. "Okay, I'll go down there and look at it, see what's going on. You got a load?"

"Yeah," Gordon answered, "just emptied the tanks into the truck. I'm going to dump it. These guys finished up both those tanks. You want them to start on another one, or you want them to go home?"

Allan thought about it for a minute. "Tell them to go on home for now. I don't have any tanks right now that absolutely need cleaning. Maybe next week. Right now the guys down here are bitching about them being illegals, anyway, so it might be good for them to make themselves scarce for the rest of the week."

Gordon turned and spoke to the two in Spanish, giving them instructions. They both shrugged their shoulders and walked back into the building to get their things.

"They took it pretty good," Allan exclaimed.

"They're Mexicans," Gordon replied. "They just take it as it comes. They got a promise of work next week, they're happy."

Allan watched the two men come out the door and walk toward an old dilapidated Dodge pickup parked close by.

"Allan," Gordon interrupted his thoughts. "Will you please look at that pond and see what you think? You get this stuff in the creek, we're gonna have some problems."

"I'll look at it," Allan promised.

"Catch you later, then," Gordon said as he started toward the tanker truck.

"How are the hogs doing?" Allan stopped Gordon with the question.

"Fine," Gordon responded. "Going to grind feed tomorrow. We got plenty of bedding for now, but we might think about laying in some more before it gets too cold."

"I'll do that," Allan replied. Gordon was a good man, Allan thought. He would feel bad if he ever had to get rid of him.

Chapter 6

Monday.

After supper Max went out to return Monica's car. On the way he stopped at the Kum & Go to top up her car with gas, even though Skip had filled it up earlier, and then ran it through the car wash. When he was done, he drove across town to the townhouse Monica shared with her mother.

When he got there, he noticed Monica's mother's car parked in the space next to the garage, but no sign of his yellow Mustang. Max considered driving back home with the Sentra and picking his Mustang up the next day at the office, but he got the notion that Monica might have put it in the garage, so Max pulled in and parked next to Shawna's old Ford Taurus. He got out of the car, went up to the door and rang the bell. Max waited a minute or two, then rang it again. He heard footsteps coming to the door and Shawna opened it up. Essie, with wet hair and wrapped in a towel, was trying to get past her and out the door.

"Hey, you little outlaw," Max said to Essie. "Trying to make a break for it?"

Shawna was holding Essie back with one hand while she held the door open with the other. "Come on in, Max, and shut the door, before she takes off and runs naked through the streets."

Shawna was a strikingly pretty woman. She had gone through some rough patches in her life. It had not been easy for her to raise three kids from three different fathers with no help from any of them, but she had done as good a job as could be expected, under the circumstances, and even though she did not look any younger than Max, he had her by close to a decade. Still, one could see where Monica got her ebony beauty.

Max followed Shawna through the entryway and into the living room. Essie was tagging along beside Max, holding her towel up with one hand, and hitting him in the butt with her stuffed rabbit Oscar, which Gloria had given her for her third birthday.

"If that rabbit doesn't quit kicking me in the butt," Max growled, reaching half heartedly for the toy, "I'm going to take him home and make him sit in the corner 'til tomorrow."

Essie squealed and hit Max again with the bunny.

"Looking for a yellow Mustang, driven by a good looking Black girl and some big-ass dumb shit with a burr cut," Max said to Shawna, as he sat down in an easy chair.

"They left an hour ago," Shawna replied while she dried Essie's hair with the towel. "I think they were going to drive down to Saylorville and back before dark."

"No telling when those two will get back," Max observed. "They are a pair, those two, don't you think?"

Shawna didn't reply for a moment, absorbed with Essie's hair, working the tangles out of the wet locks.

"I don't know what to think about them," Shawna broke the moment of silence. "What do you think?"

"Cute couple," Max said. "I don't think it is anything serious yet. They're working it out. I think that they both want to take their time."

"I don't like it so much," Shawna frowned.

"What don't you like?" Max gently pressed her.

"Well, first thing, he's a lot older than her." Shawna looked up at Max.

"Okay," Max said. "What else?"

"No offense to you, or to Skip, or to anyone else, but I don't like her seeing a cop."

Max was taken aback a little. "What's wrong with cops?"

"Don't take it wrong, Max," Shawna continued. "Most cops are same as anyone, but there's some rotten ones." She paused for a moment, but continued before Max could comment. "I'm not saying Milton is a rotten cop, I'm just saying that I don't think it is good for her to get involved with cops. They work bad hours, they got a dangerous job and most people just don't like cops."

"You talking about yourself?" Max asked her.

Shawna paused for a moment pondering how to answer. "Honestly, Max, you're right. I don't particularly like cops."

"Thanks," Max responded.

"Come on Max," Shawna continued, "You know that you and Skip aren't like most cops. I got nothing but admiration for both of you. You guys have done more for Monica than I would ever have been able to do for her myself, and I thank God in my prayers that you two lifted her up when she was down, but you guys are not like most cops."

"Okay," Max said. "We've known where you stand on cops for a long time. It's no surprise revelation. We feel it, and we just walk around it, but Milton is a good guy. He has a lot going for him. He's going to go up the ladder." Max paused for a moment, then spoke again before Shawna could comment. "Besides, they're just out for a ride in the 'Stang. I don't see a ride down to Saylorville as a long term commitment."

"They got eyes for each other," Shawna answered him.

"Is there anything else you don't like about him?" Max asked. "Anything else we're tip-toeing around and don't want to say out loud?"

"Nothing at the moment," Shawna answered defensively.

"Nothing you want to talk about," Max countered.

"Max, I've always respected you, and you know that. I'm just voicing my concerns. You are like a daddy to that girl, and what you say, she listens to. So I'm just saying what I think about those two."

"Point taken," Max said tersely. "I'll keep that in mind for the future."

Max stood up and stretched his back. "When they get back, just tell Monica to drive the Mustang in tomorrow, and I'll trade with her then." Max started toward the door.

"Max, I didn't want to get something started," Shawna said, following him to the door. "I just wanted to talk it over with you, that's all."

Max turned and smiled at Shawna. "And that's what we did." Shawna looked tired. "It's all good, Shawna. Don't worry about it. Those two are going to do what they want, and neither you nor me are going to change the course. If we try, it just makes it harder on them, but it isn't going to change anything."

"You're right," Shawna sighed. "But I feel better talking to you about it, getting it out."

Max gave Shawna a wink and went down the steps to Monica's car. As he backed out of the parking space, Shawna was taking Essie back into the house. Max laughed. "Almost got away," he said to himself. Shawna had put Max a little on edge, but he let it go. Shawna probably hadn't been the best mother growing up, but there was no doubt that she cared about her kids. Max was good with that.

Max turned the Sentra toward home, lost in thought. He and Skip had spent the whole day working on the case, but all in all, they hadn't done much more than watch Peggy have lunch with a man who wasn't her husband. Where to now? He couldn't think of anything. He wondered if they would just go watch her eat lunch again tomorrow, or if there was something else they could do to further the case. What if she had lunch with the same guy? Would that even mean anything? They had promised Travis a week, and the first day had not turned up much. Allan Proctor: just a guy, as Monica had put it. Nothing more, nothing less. When you got right down to it, the two could have been nothing more than two longtime friends sharing a moment.

Max took a turn to pass by the agency on his way home. It was a few blocks out of the way, and he didn't know why, but he often just did things like that. Max still liked routine patrol. Max didn't like to be predictable. One last pass to make sure everything was secure. As he drove by the building that housed G&B Detective Agency, Max saw his yellow Mustang convertible parked in Monica's reserved space. Max slowed and pulled into the lot, parking next to the Mustang. He got out and walked to the door. He could see Monica at her desk and he knocked on the window to get her attention. Monica got up and came around to the door, unlocked it, then returned to the desk. Max opened the door, went in and took a seat in one of the leather easy chairs in the waiting area opposite her.

"Burning the midnight oil?" Max observed.

"It's only seven," Monica answered.

"I was over at your place looking for my car. I didn't expect you to be sitting here all by yourself," Max said, thinking as soon as he said it that Milton might be in the bathroom, or the bar. "You are alone, right? I can leave if you want." Max back-pedaled.

"No, I dropped him off," Monica replied. "We drove down to Polk City, had a bite to eat, drove around the lake. Milton likes driving the Mustang."

"I thought that you were doing the driving." Max said.

"Ha, like Milton isn't going to push me out of the way and hop right in the driver's seat, so he can put it to the floor, just to see how fast it will go."

"So you took him home?" Max asked. "What's with that?"

"I don't know," Monica said. "I just don't know where we are going with this. We've been going out since June, but it seems like there is something standing between us. I'm not sure he wants to carry all my baggage."

Max gave Monica a stern look. "Listen, don't put yourself down. Milton is lucky that you give him the time of day."

It was Monica's turn to give Max a serious look. "I have to be honest to myself: I was a stripper, I have a kid who has a no-good for a daddy. I came from trailer trash." She stopped for a moment. "I don't mean that I'm calling Momma trailer trash, but I did grow up in a house with wheels. And he is a lot older than I am, and then there's…" Monica trailed off.

Max let it go for a moment. "This have anything to do with Momma not liking Milton?"

"She talk to you about that?" Monica asked.

"Yes, she did, and you know, she isn't you. You need to decide what is best for you. Momma will come along. Besides, it isn't that she thinks Milton is a bad person, it is that she doesn't like who Milton is. There's a difference there, and she can get past it."

Monica shrugged her shoulders. "Doesn't change my history, though."

"There's nothing wrong with your history," Max said. "You made it through some tough times. That's good. It means that you have a better appreciation of the good times, and those good times should be right now."

Monica smiled at Max. "You're the best, Max."

"Hey," Max changed the subject. "You ever get on one of those dating sites?"

Monica wasn't surprised by Max's sudden topic change. "I used one called Africanroots.com for a while."

"You meet anyone on it?" Max inquired.

"Yeah, last winter," Monica replied. "I met this guy down in Des Moines. Nice guy. He worked for Wells Fargo. A loan officer. We went out a couple of times."

"Didn't last?" Max assumed, considering that he had never met the guy.

"Not really," Monica went on. "I didn't feel like he could deal with my baggage, either," she said in a tight voice, emphasizing the word baggage.

"No kidding?" Max said. "Is this baggage thing someone else's problem, or is it yours?"

"I don't know," Monica sighed. "You meet someone, you get to know them, they get to know you, then there comes a point where you have to tell them about it all." Monica went silent.

"You know something?" Max responded. "Milton knows all that already. And he is still hanging around like a pup wanting you to give him a pat on the head. I think that says something about Milton. I'm not pushing you at Milton, either; I'm just saying."

Monica smiled again.

"So this dating site, I'm guessing that it is for Black people to meet Black people?" Max resumed the conversation. "So if you want to meet someone Black, you go there. Lonelyfarmer.com, people looking for country folk?"

"Okay," Monica answered.

"So Proctor is a farmer, and he's looking around for a woman who likes farmers, and he finds Peggy. But Peggy isn't a farmer. She's a townie. Plus, she's married. So why would Proctor hook up with Peggy on lonelyfarmers.com?"

"Are you sure that he hooked up with her on lonelyfarmers.com?" Monica asked.

"Good point," Max countered. "Because I was wondering that a little while ago myself. In fact, maybe they aren't even seeing each other in that sort of way. Maybe they are just old friends. Maybe there is someone else out there that we haven't seen."

"Maybe," Monica agreed.

Max continued. "Could you get on lonelyfarmer.com? Can you get on there and see if they are both there? If they both are, can you see if they are doing anything through the site?"

"I don't know what I can see," Monica replied. "But I can sure get on there, create a profile and then look around for a middle-aged pig farmer that lives south of Nevada. I should be able to do that."

"Can you do it now?" Max asked. "I mean, is it hard to do?"

Monica was already typing. Max waited quietly.

"Okay, I just went ahead and used Moni for my name," Monica told Max. "What next? I need to describe myself."

"Tall, slender Black woman. Well proportioned. Long for the country life, looking for a pig farmer." Max laughed. "I don't know."

"Okay," Monica continued. "I don't have to say that I'm Black, because I'm going to post a picture. I'll say that I'm tall and slender, but I'm going to leave out the part about being well proportioned." Monica continued typing. "Love the country life, love listening to country music, line dancing and sitting in the quiet countryside listening to the calves bawling for their mothers. Looking for a cowboy to take me riding into the sunset." Monica looked over her work. "How's that sound?"

"It sounds like you are trying to hook up with a cowboy, not a pig farmer," Max commented. He thought for a moment. "That's fine, you aren't going to get on there and say that you like the smell of hogs. But add a little something. Say that you are a professional woman working for a large corn-based industry."

"Good one," Monica said as she typed. After surveying her work for a minute she glanced up. "Take a look."

Max went around the desk while Monica wheeled her chair out of the way. Max stood reading her entries.

"Dang woman," Max said his hick voice, which wasn't too far from his own. "You're just what I been a-lookin' for."

Monica's reached over the keyboard and let her hand hover over the "enter" key. "Should I do it?" she asked.

Max said nothing for a moment. "If you want to. But I'm looking at it and I'm telling you that you're going to get some responses. It is totally up to you. I don't want to push you into doing anything that you are not comfortable with, and I'm not sure how comfortable I am with this. Maybe we need to think this through a little more."

Monica brought her finger down on the key. "Done," she said. "I think that they have to approve it before I can do anything, so I can't go looking around for anyone yet. So we will have to wait until tomorrow and see what I can find."

Max sighed. "This is way beyond the call of duty, Monica."

"It's fine," Monica reassured Max. "I kind of want to see what kind of responses I get, anyway. It will be interesting. I might even use it for a psychology paper in one of my classes. It's research."

"I hope so," Max said. "Trade me keys, I want my car back."

Monica dug the keys to the Mustang out of her purse and exchanged them for her own keys.

Max headed toward the door. Monica was gathering up her things and shoving them into her backpack, getting ready to leave as well. Max stood holding the door for her. She looked up.

"I love you guys," she said. "I mean, you guys are my family."

Max smiled. "It's all going to work out. There's someone out there." Max stopped for a moment and chuckled. "I was going to say that I hoped it was Milton, but I didn't want to put any pressure on you, so I didn't say it."

Monica smacked Max playfully with her scarf as she walked past him. "Maybe it will be."

Chapter 7

Tuesday

Max drove into the parking lot of G&B early. Usually, Max would either stop at Filo's Coffee Shop and get a cup of coffee first thing or park his car at the office and walk over, but his curiosity was piqued. He could see that Skip's and Monica's cars were parked in front of the agency. Nothing unusual about that: Skip was nearly always in the office early, and Monica sometimes stopped in before her nine o'clock class. But what did strike Max as unusual was the beat-up old brown four wheel drive Ford F150 parked next to Monica's car. That one raised Max's pulse a little, and it was hard to raise Max's pulse.

Max walked through the door and saw Monica sitting silently, her backpack, loaded with books, sitting strategically on the desk, shielding her from the man sitting on one of the leather easy chairs across from her. Max addressed the man.

"Armand Higgins, long time no see. What can we do for you?" Before Higgins could say anything, Max turned to Monica and asked, "Where's Skip?"

"He went back to get something," Moncia responded just as Max heard Skip coming up the hall from his office.

Max turned his attention to Higgins.

"Well, I want to hire you guys," Higgins said to no one in particular.

Max and Skip stood looking at Higgins. Monica gathered her things to leave for class. "Well, I'll be looking forward to hearing about this one," she said as she squeezed past Max, keeping him between her and Higgins, and headed through the door. "Lock up when you leave."

Max took a seat at Monica's desk. Skip remained standing.

"What do you mean you want to hire us?" Max asked.

"Fish dying all over the place down there in the creek," Higgins said. "It stinks to high heaven. So I walked down there and looked around. Those townies own the creek and I ain't supposed to be trespassing. But I went down there to see what was stinking so bad, and the place is full of dead fish. They're all floating belly up behind a beaver dam down there. So I'm wondering: what is killing all them fish? I lived down there all my life. I was raised on that place, and I ain't never seen nothing like it."

"Why don't you just call the Department of Natural Resources?" Skip asked.

"A couple of things," Higgins replied. "One, I don't want no government people tromping around out there. Government people are what's wrong with everything, not what's right. Who knows what the fuck they would come up with? I can promise you something, whatever it was, it wouldn't solve the problem, it would just make more problems."

Max and Skip waited for Higgins to continue, but he sat looking at the two blankly.

"What's number two?" Skip prompted.

Higgins looked confused for a moment. "Oh, number two: I don't want anyone to know I was trespassing over there on the townie's property. I'm on probation, and I'm not supposed to be causing any grief for the townies."

"So you come to us?" Max remarked.

"Yep, you was the first people I thought of," Higgins replied proudly, "on account of you're detectives. Bev told me you only charged her two hundred dollars to find that dog of hers. I got two hundred dollars, and I'll give it to you guys if you can find out who is killing all them fish and then report it to the authorities. 'Cause it has to be something upstream, and I ain't in no position to go snooping around and getting myself into trouble. I turned over a new leaf."

"When were you talking to Bev?" Max asked suspiciously.

"During the trial," Higgins answered. "I made a deal with the state to give testimony on those two dog rustlers that shot me, in exchange for probation instead of jail time. So Bev and me were sitting around a lot, waiting to testify. I told her that I was sorry, and that I like Tucker a lot and that I wasn't ever going to hurt him. I think that she appreciated that. So we talked about Tucker a lot while we was waiting around."

Skip shook his head in wonderment. "Listen, we don't take a lot of cases. We only did that case with Tucker because Bev is a friend of Max's wife. No offense toward you, but we just don't need another case right now."

Higgins gathered his thoughts. "I know you guys ain't regular detectives. I know that you are choosy about who you work for. But here's the thing: you guys owe me. You guys almost got me killed. It still hurts me to breathe. I've been trying to change my life around, to think about things and to do the right thing, instead of just doing whatever the fuck I want. I'm also trying to get along with people better." Higgins stopped while he caught his breath. "I'm just asking you to figure out what is happening with these fish. One thing, I don't like the smell, but more important, I don't like to see someone destroying that creek. I grew up on that creek. I'm not just asking you to do it, I'm offering to pay you two hundred bucks to do it. That's a lot of money," Higgins said matter-of-factly.

It was a long speech for Higgins. Max could tell that Higgins had expected them to turn him down, and he had rehearsed what he was going to say. It was a strong and impassioned argument.

Max sighed. "We'll check it out."

Skip gave Max a look.

"If you don't want to do it, I'll do it myself," Max said to Skip.

Skip shook his head and turned toward Higgins. "Are you going home now?"

"I can," Higgins replied.

"Okay, we'll be down there directly. You be waiting for us, and we'll take a look-see. Then we'll go from there."

The three sat looking at each other, no one saying anything more. Finally, Higgins stood up. "Thanks, guys," he said as he made his way to the door. "I really appreciate it. I know that we didn't get off on a good foot during the Tucker thing, but I want you to know that ain't me anymore. I'm different now."

"Tie up your dogs," Max said as Higgins was opening the door to go out.

"Dogs have changed, too," Higgins said. "They ain't the same dogs, either."

"Tie them up or we don't get out of the car," Skip replied. He didn't have much faith in the reformation potential of farm dogs.

Higgins went out the door, climbed into his truck and pulled out of the parking lot.

Max shrugged his shoulders at Skip. "What the heck?"

Skip shrugged back. "I was almost gonna take it, anyway, you just beat me to the punch."

"We going right down?" Max asked. "If we are, I'm getting my pistol. I still don't trust him."

"Already got mine," Skip said.

"You're kidding."

"Nope," Skip replied. "I went back and got it from my office the minute Higgins came through the door."

Max laughed. "Will wonders never cease?"

The two gathered up their stuff and went outside to the parking lot, locking the door of the agency. Skip had left a note on Monica's desk telling her that they were headed down to Higgins's place, and that if she didn't hear from them later on, to call Carlisle and send him looking for them. Skip was packing his Sig .40 cal stuck in an inside-the-pants holster. Max had gone back to his office and retrieved his short barrel .38 special and a couple of speed loaders filled with Federal +P hollow points. Max walked over to the passenger side of Skip's car, but Skip was headed toward the Mustang.

"Let's take your car," Max shouted.

"I don't want to drive mine if we end up driving on gravel," Skip shouted back.

"You live on gravel," Max responded.

"I just washed it this morning on the way in," Skip replied.

Max sighed and walked over to the Mustang. Skip was already sitting in the passenger seat. "There isn't any gravel going to Higgins's place, anyway," Max grumbled.

"I have that guy Proctor's address," Skip said. "I want to run by there as long as we're down in that neck of the woods. Just want to see it."

"So I can just wash my car when we get back, and that will be okay," Max grumbled again.

"Yep," Skip replied.

The two left the parking lot and drove toward New 30. They took 30 east past Nevada and on toward the county road that was now called 650th street, which would take them south to Maxwell and Higgins's acreage. On the way, they passed the ethanol plant. Skip could clearly see Peggy's Lexus convertible parked in the lot as they drove by.

Skip and Max had made the trip to Maxwell several times during the dognapping they had investigated in June. When Max pulled onto the street in front of Higgins's place, he was surprised. In June, the acreage had been little more than a junk yard. Since then he had cleaned the place up. The barn where the dognappers had stashed their stolen dogs had a fresh coat of paint. It looked like the double-wide trailer that Higgins lived in had been power washed. The old Case tractor with flat tires that had been the one and only ornament in the yard was gone. The weedy grass looked freshly mowed.

Max pulled through the gate and into the barnyard. An old Toyota pickup was parked in front of the double-wide, next to Higgins's F150. Higgins's two Dobermans met Max's car as he put it into park and killed the engine. Max and Skip eyed the dogs. The last time they had been there the two dogs had tried to get in and rip the two detectives apart. Max had had to get their claw marks buffed out of the paint on his car. The two dogs now sat quietly on their haunches waiting for Skip and Max to get out.

"What do you think?" Max asked.

"You go first," Skip said, laughing.

Max cracked the door and the two dogs hopped up, but neither looked particularly aggressive. Max opened his door and put one foot out. The dogs trotted up to him, looking like all they wanted was some attention. Max reached out and petted one of them on the head. The other one tried to push his way in for a pet as well. Max stepped out of the car. He looked back in at Skip and shrugged his shoulders. Skip opened his door and the two dogs raced around to his side. Skip pulled the door shut, leaving it cracked a little. He put his foot out on the ground and got the same reception as Max had.

"Unbelievable," Skip exclaimed.

While the two detectives stood outside the Mustang with the two dogs, looking around, Higgins came out of the double-wide with a woman that Max and Skip recognized immediately. She smiled toward Skip as she walked toward the Toyota pickup.

"Bonnie," Skip addressed the woman. "How are you? How's business at Casey's?"

Bonnie stopped for a moment when Skip spoke. She looked at him shyly.

"It's good," she said. "I'm heading in right now. I just stopped in to see Armand for a minute on the way to work."

"Good to see you again," Skip said sincerely.

Bonnie got into the truck, started it and backed around so that she could drive out of the yard.

"Higgins, what's up with you and Bonnie?" Max teased.

"Just friends," Higgins mumbled, looking down.

Max was giving Higgins the once over, looking for any indication that he had the Browning Highpower on him, but there was nothing. Max was still not convinced that Higgins had turned into a model citizen. The old Higgins had been too unhinged for Max to think that he wasn't going to do something stupid. But Higgins seemed happy to see them.

"Wanna take a walk down to the creek?" he asked them in a serious voice. "I want you to look at it and tell me what you think."

"Let's go," Skip suggested.

The three men walked across the barnyard and through a gate into a pasture. The two Dobermans, Pete and Repeat, trotted along with them. The three were chatting about the weather and the lack of rain all summer when Max observed an interesting plot of plants growing along a fence row in the corner of the pasture.

"Is that pot?" Max asked.

"Where?" Higgins answered.

"Over there in the corner," Max pointed.

Higgins looked in that direction, but didn't answer. "Gotta climb over the fence here, and then we'll be on the townie's property. The creek is about a couple hundred yards beyond."

"Higgins," Max persisted. "Is that pot growing over there?"

"Well, if it is, it ain't mine," Higgins answered.

"If it ain't yours," Max asked, "whose is it?"

"Might be my cousin's," Higgins answered defensively. "Ain't mine."

"Is that the reason you might not want the DNR around?"

"Could be," Higgins replied.

"Let it go," Skip said to Max.

Max gave Skip a crosswise glance. "We aren't here to worry about pot," Skip said. Max shrugged.

Higgins stepped on the second wire of the three-wire barbed wire fence and pulled up the top one, making room for the two detectives to duck through. When Max was on the other side, he did the same for Higgins. They continued walking. The trail looked well traveled. The two detectives could smell dead fish.

Max, Skip and Higgins found themselves on the bank overlooking Indian Creek, looking down at the beaver dam below. As Higgins had described, hundreds of dead fish bobbed in the water. Most were small fish. Max could identify some bass, some crappies and lots of bullheads.

Higgins pointed at the carcass of a beaver floating among the fish.

"Shit," he exclaimed. "Look at that. A dead beaver."

"That doesn't look good," Skip remarked.

"Them beavers are good people," Higgins said, forcing a snicker from Max. Luckily, Higgins was too absorbed with the carcass floating against the dam along with the dead fish to hear him.

"Shit, man," Higgins exclaimed again. "This really sucks."

Max looked upstream. A path followed the bank.

"How far does that go?" Max asked, nodding toward the path.

"A couple miles, at least," Higgins answered.

"Let's go up there a ways and see what we see," Max suggested.

The path ran close to the bank on one side, and was crowded with trees and brush on the other. The three had to walk single file to navigate it. Max took the lead, with Higgins in the middle and Skip following up. The mosquitoes attacked them mercilessly as they worked their way up the river.

"We need a freeze to kill these bastards off," Max said as he slapped at the mosquitos landing on his arms.

They had only gone a hundred yards or so when they came to a deadfall blocking the trail. The three looked down at the river. Max could make out a dead fish here and there floating belly up in the slow current. The stream was low.

"You think it's just a kill off because the water is so shallow?" Max asked neither man in particular.

"Naw," Higgins answered. When it gets low like that, the fish gather up in the holes or at the beaver dams. I never seen nothing like this."

"Are there many beaver dams upstream?" Skip asked.

Higgins shrugged his shoulders. "I suppose so," he answered.

"Let's go back," Max suggested as he slapped at more mosquitos.

The three men walked back down the trail. They stopped at the beaver dam and looked around again. None of them had a comment. They left through the woods toward the meadow; when they got to the barbed wire fence, Higgins helped them through it as he had before. While they waited for Higgins to come through, Max glanced over at the pot grow in the corner of the pasture.

"What's the deal?" Max asked. "You really cleaned up your act, it looks like to me, so why the pot? Why take the chance? You know that if you get caught with it you're going to jail. They don't even have to charge you, they can just revoke your probation."

Higgins sighed. "You know, when I was layin' on that barn floor after those guys shot me, I thought that every breath was going to be my last. I laid there all afternoon and all night, and then my cousin came in. He got down on his knees, he called the ambulance and all the time he held my hand and begged me to keep breathin', to stay alive. He cried like a baby over me. That son of a bitch has never been anything but trouble for me, but when I needed someone more than I ever needed someone in my life, he was there, holding my hand, begging me to stay alive.

Higgins paused. "He planted that while I was in the hospital. He came and got me when I got out, he brought me home and he got Bonnie to help him get me back on my feet. He didn't even know Bonnie, he didn't know anybody, but he went into Casey's every day asking her to help him until she finally gave in and helped.

Higgins paused again. "By the time I had enough strength to walk out here and find it, damned grow was four feet tall. What am I going to do? Chop it down? I pretend that it's not there, and pray to God that no one finds it and sends me to jail for it."

It was an emotional speech. The two detectives stood silently looking across the meadow at the plants.

Higgins went on. "I don't know if you guys remember this, 'cause it was a long time ago. You guys were cops. Me and my cousin were out smokin' dope one night in the alley on Main Street and you two guys came out the door and caught us. My cousin had a baggie of pot stuffed down his pants, and I was taking a toke off of the pipe. You guys put us up against the wall. You said that if we didn't hand over the grass that you was going to call K-9 to find it. My cousin gave it up. Skip, you threw my pipe up on the roof of a three story building. Max, you dumped the weed down a storm drain. Then you told us to leave town. You know something? I never went back to Ames after that unless I had to. You guys gave us a break. Do you remember that?"

Max looked at Skip. "Not really," he said. "I mean, we did that a lot."

"I know you did," Higgins went on. "You guys are stand-up guys. This fish thing is driving me crazy. I don't want to see that creek and them woods die because someone don't care. Someone has to get to the bottom of it. But they got to get to the bottom of it somewhere else. They can't do it here. I don't want to go to jail because of my asshole cousin, but I can't do anything about that. I want you guys to get to the bottom of this. I want you guys to call the DNR, or whatever you have to do, and catch whoever is killing my creek. But you gotta make it happen somewhere else."

Higgins gave them a pleading look, waiting for something from either one of them.

Finally Skip spoke up. "Understood, we will figure it out."

"Thank you," Higgins replied. "Just help me out here, please."

The three men walked through the open gate that separated the pasture from the barnyard. The two dogs had been with them throughout the whole trek, and their short hair was covered with burrs. When they got to the Mustang, Higgins spoke up.

"Do I pay you guys up front, or what?"

"You can pay us when we're done," Skip replied.

"You take cash?" Higgins asked.

"Cash is fine," Skip responded.

The two detectives got into the Mustang and Max started the engine. He backed around and drove to the street. He could see Higgins in his rearview mirror, waving goodbye as they left.

"Wow," Max remarked.

Skip laughed a little. "Turn left and then right, I want to check out Proctor's place."

Max turned right onto the street that Skip had indicated and out of town.

"Where we going?" Skip asked.

Max turned to Skip. "What? Oh, sorry, I guess my mind is somewhere else." Skip's phone was telling Max to make a safe U-turn. "Keep going straight," Skip instructed him.

Chapter 8

Tuesday

Allan came into the house after mowing the yard. He had a big yard, but then he had a big mower. Allan was a farmer; he had machinery. The house was quiet. Brenda was at her part-time job at the hospital in Ames. The kids were at school. Allan went into his office in the walk-out basement. He had a view of the woods that lay behind the house and the creek below. It was the same creek that wound its way through the countryside, past his other farm, with its hog confinements, and found its way into the river. From there it flowed into the Mississippi and ultimately all the way to the Gulf of Mexico. But here, behind Allan's house, he could almost jump across it.

Allan opened his computer and checked his email. He had three email accounts, and he checked all three. One was what he called his regular email account. It was a Yahoo! account, the one he gave out to anyone who wanted to contact him for almost any reason. It was where he conducted his farming business. The second was the gmail account that he had set up earlier in the year for his industrial cleaning business. The third was his secret account with a fake name. He seldom used the secret account, but it was handy to have when he needed it. Allan was always careful with his email accounts. He never left them open on his computer, and they were all password protected.

Allan went through all the unread messages. Nothing of importance in any of them, so Allan took to surfing the net. He typed in lonelyfarmer.com and brought up the site. He logged in. Two women had contacted him. He looked through their profiles: both looked like recent divorcees looking for a rebound hookup. Allan wasn't interested. Allan looked around at other women in the area. Many of them he had checked out before, some were new. One piqued his curiosity. A professional woman who worked in a corn-based industry. Allan clicked on her.

The profile came up with a picture. "Cute," thought Allan. It wasn't often that he found a Black woman on the lonelyfarmers site. It didn't say where she worked, just that she worked in a corn-based industry. He wondered what that meant. She looked young. He looked to see if she had posted her age. She said that she was twenty three. Allan wondered again where she worked. Corn-based industry in Iowa usually means ethanol. Moni, no last name. Moni probably wasn't her real name. Allan read through her profile again. "Interesting," he thought. He wondered if Peggy knew this Moni.

Allan hit the return arrow and looked some more. Nothing else looked at all interesting to him after the Black girl. Allan actually found the site to be a little depressing. So many people with so little to offer. Allan wondered why Moni was even on there. He thought about Peggy, and the first time he had seen her profile on lonelyfarmers. She had caught his attention because he could see that she wasn't really serious. She was bored. She was curious. She was not desperate. He contacted her and she had gotten back quickly, but guardedly. After a little chit-chat back and forth, Allan had gotten her name. He then Googled her. It turned out to be a perfect setup: she was the director of a department at the BioForce ethanol plant that at the moment was accepting bids for ethanol tank cleaning and wastewater disposal services. Allan was all about servicing. He had a good-sized hog confinement setup on his farm, which he had to clean, so he already had some cleaning equipment. He even had a tanker truck. He figured he could probably scrounge up everything he would need to start a cleaning company. Everything but the knowledge. Allan didn't know the first thing about cleaning ethanol tanks. That's where Gordon had come into the picture.

Allan asked around about industrial cleaning and ethanol waste. He started at the co-op. He had asked at the seed store if anyone knew what kind of cleaning they did at the ethanol plants, and if anyone knew who was doing it now. He stopped into the implement dealerships. He contacted his connections in the Pork Producers. He even asked at the lumber yard. He searched the internet for hours on the subject. Allan spent a week looking for someone who knew something about cleaning ethanol tanks, and someone finally came through with Gordon's name and number.

The first time they met, at the bar, Gordon had struck him as nothing more than a laborer. Allan could tell that Gordon wasn't a businessman, but he was a hard worker, and that was what Allan needed: someone without a lot of ambition who would do what he was told. But Gordon was also a wealth of information when it came to cleaning the tanks used in the production of ethanol, and he told Allan that there was a lot of money in it. The two talked about it the whole evening. Gordon was looking for work, and Allan was looking for someone to help him start his business.

The next day, Allan made his move on Peggy. He turned on the charm. Peggy was lonely and wanted someone to talk to. Allan was right there, ready to listen.

She responded to him, and the two met. Then they met again, and again. Peggy admitted to Allan that she was married, that her marriage was a lonely one, because her husband worked evenings and weekends, leaving her alone at home. She and her husband were growing apart. Allan had nodded and told Peggy that he was also married, that his wife was a nurse and that she worked nights and weekends, leaving him alone a lot of the time, too. He talked about how lonely he was, how good it was to talk to her, and their relationship grew. It grew quickly. Peggy wanted something more in her life, and Allan was making sure that she saw what she was looking for in him. When Peggy had started to realize that she had something Allan was interested in, a lucrative cleaning contract, Allan had given Peggy a promise: someday they would have a life together. Peggy had happily given Allan the contract.

As soon as Peggy started talking about giving him the cleaning contract, Allan hired Gordon to help him get started. Gordon told Allan that the most expensive thing about cleaning ethanol tanks was getting rid of the wastewater. The tanks and plumbing were cleaned with caustic chemicals that had to be properly disposed of. Gordon told Allan that there was a place in Princeton, Missouri that had a federal permit to properly handle the wastewater, and that they got a nice fee for it. Along with that, there were transportation costs. Allan and Gordon together took a look at Allan's old tanker truck and decided that probably sooner than later they would want to replace it with something newer, but for a time it would suffice.

Gordon also told Allan about the undocumented workers who made it their occupation to crawl into the tanks and clean them with the caustic chemicals, and Gordon was an expert on how that process worked. Gordon told Allan that if he hired some guy off the street to clean the tanks, that there were a lot of federal hoops to jump through. It wasn't just about paying wages, there were benefits, social security, workman's comp, a medical plan, unemployment—not to mention all the trouble that blabbermouth employees could get him into with the authorities in all the agencies that regulated the industry.

"This whole business is chuck full of federal oversight," Gordon told Allan. That was why Gordon recommended contracting with Evergreen for laborers. If Evergreen supplied the workers, Allan would pay Evergreen, and Evergreen would be responsible for all the other headaches that came with it. All he had to do is write one check, to Evergreen. Of course, if anyone looked close enough, they might conclude that the Evergreen workers were not US citizens. But that was okay, because in America, a person was a US citizen until proven not to be. As Gordon said, "That is due process, innocent until proven guilty, legal until proven illegal." And that went for undocumented workers. Gordon went on to explain that the ethanol industry was tightly regulated, so Allan needed to make sure that he had deniability to protect his interests.

"If the shit hits the fan," Gordon had told him, "Evergreen will just cease to exist. If the authorities come in and try to pin anything on you, you tell them that you contracted with Evergreen in good faith. Then they go looking for Evergreen to pin the tail on the donkey, but by then, the donkey is gone." And according to Gordon, the best part of the plan was that the workers don't know anything, and they don't even speak English.

"You know what that means?" Gordon had asked Allan. "That means that they ain't going to go down to the local bar, get drunk and blab to anyone who wants to listen about what you are doing. Even if they do go down to the bar, no one who counts understands what they are saying.

If the feds go looking for witnesses, all they get is 'no hablo Ingles.'" Gordon assured Allan that Evergreen was the foolproof way to go.

"What about ICE?" Allan had asked him.

Gordon laughed. "ICE is not going to come around to see if you got a couple of illegals cleaning tanks. They don't have the personnel, the resources or the time. They want big busts. ICE is all about politics. They are looking for busts that make headlines, they want busts that make them look like they are getting tough on illegal aliens, and two illegals cleaning out a tank is not going to get them headlines. And besides," Gordon went on, "It's all on Evergreen. Evergreen is providing illegal undocumented workers to you. It's all on them, not you."

Gordon also told Allan that he was half Mexican, that not only could he drive the truck, he could ram-rod the help. Allan asked him if he could ram-rod the whole damned thing. Gordon said that he could. Allan was sold. He moved Gordon into the house on the old home place and went into the ethanol plant cleaning business. He set up a company, named it Cleanguard, put Gordon in charge and started distancing himself immediately. Deniability. Allan was learning fast. With Gordon running the cleaning business, Allan didn't have anything to do with the daily operations. Allan could see it all coming together.

Allan looked at his watch. He thought for a moment, then dialed Peggy's work number and waited. Allan always tried to call her at work. He didn't want his number showing up on her private phone. Her receptionist answered after only a couple of rings.

"Allan Proctor here," Allan said. "Can I talk to Mrs. Bentley for a minute?"

"She has someone in her office right now," the receptionist told him. "Shall I put you through to her voicemail?"

Allan thought for a moment. "That's fine," he replied.

Peggy's voice came on the phone, saying that she was busy at the moment and prompting the caller to leave a message at the tone.

"Peggy," Allan said into the phone. "I've got some equipment that has broken down at one of my other sites. I need to see about getting it fixed. I don't know how long it is going to take, so I may not be able to keep our lunch meeting today. Hopefully you can carry on without me. I'm looking forward to our Wednesday meeting, though. I'll see you then." Allan hung up the phone.

Allan got up and walked outside. He decided to drive down to the old place and see what Gordon was pissing around about. He climbed into his Silverado and started down the driveway toward the blacktop road that would take him south toward Maxwell and the farm. As he drove down the road, he thought about what to do about the grass, which he realized was really a problem, regardless of what he had told Gordon. At first Gordon had driven the old tanker truck down to Princeton on a regular basis to dispose of the wastewater. Everything in that regard had been on the up-and-up. After maybe a half dozen trips, usually every ten days or so, the old truck had started acting up. One day it was full of wastewater and Gordon couldn't get it to start. They had to have it towed to a garage. The mechanic got it going, but told Gordon that it was just a matter of time. The truck needed a new engine and the transmission wasn't in much better condition. Gordon had driven it down to the farm and parked it. Then he had called Allan.

At first, Allan hadn't understood what Gordon was suggesting. He understood that the truck was in bad shape, but he did not understand Gordon's solution to the problem, because Gordon had been cryptic about it. It took Allan a while to figure out that Gordon was suggesting they dump the wastewater into the manure pit underneath the empty hog confinement building on the farm.

"So what then?" Allan had asked.

"We'll pump it out later and haul it down to Missouri, but I got to empty the truck and have it back at the plant tomorrow. They are still cleaning," Gordon explained.

Allan didn't have a better solution.

"Go for it," Allan had told Gordon. "We can haul it down when we're done cleaning. Just dump it all in there." And so they had. But they had never got around to pumping it back into the tanker truck and taking it to Princeton. Instead, they pumped it into a holding pond to make more room. And now there was some sort of filtration going on, and Gordon wanted Allan to look at it. Allan didn't want to look at it. He knew that he had to, and he knew what he was going to see, but there was that deniability thing. What Allan didn't know wouldn't hurt him. But Allan knew that Gordon was going to be up at the plant all day working on the cleaning equipment, and Allan wanted to know just how big of a problem it was, so he was going to make himself take a look, anyway.

It was less than a ten minute drive from Allan's house to the farm. When he pulled into the drive he was reminded, as he always was, that this was his home place. When he and Brenda had gotten married and moved into the house there, it was already a hundred years old. Allan got out of his truck and walked back to the field behind the hog confinement buildings where the holding ponds were. He could smell the chemicals. They were overpowering the smell of the pig shit. That wasn't good. As he stood above the two ponds, looking past them toward the creek, his heart jumped in his chest. He took a deep breath of pungent air. "Shit," he said as he let it out. "Shit, shit, shit."

Chapter 9

Tuesday

"Turn left up here," Skip directed. Max did as Skip told him. As they approached a bridge that crossed Indian Creek on their route out of town, Skip told Max to stop on the bridge so that he could get out and look around. Max stopped in the middle of the bridge and watched as Skip got out and went to the rail to look over it into the water slowly flowing below.

"See anything?" Max called through the open door.

"Yep, we got some small ones floating belly up. Lots of minnows, and some bigger ones. I'm not a fisherman; I don't know what they are."

Max started to get out, but when he looked in the rearview mirror he saw a car coming up behind him. Skip was getting back in the Mustang. As soon as Skip closed the door, Max started driving. As they drove out of the city limits, the road turned to gravel. They continued on across the river bottom.

"In four hundred yards, turn right onto County Road 350th Street," instructed a woman's voice with a British accent from Skip's phone.

"Turn right up here," Skip told Max.

"Okay," Max replied to both of them.

The detectives looked across the flood plain at the tree line beyond.

"In two hundred yards, turn right on County Road 350th Street," the woman's voice instructed.

"Turn right up here at the next corner," Skip told Max.

"Okay," Max replied to both of them again.

Max turned on his right turn signal as he approached the intersection and started to slow down. In the rearview mirror, the car behind him was turning as well.

"Turn right on County Road 350th Street," the voice on the GPS instructed.

"Right here," Skip repeated the instructions.

"Sure you don't want to just keep driving straight?" Max asked. Skip snorted, but did not reply. Max turned the corner. The car behind him followed.

The road followed the river, parallel to the hills that marked the border of the flood plain. There were no buildings or farmsteads on the right, between the river and the road, but on the left, they drove past farmsteads built up high enough on the hill to keep them above flood level. After a couple of miles, the road rose out of the flood plain, but still ran parallel to the river, which now flowed through a narrow valley. As they continued, they approached Proctor's farm.

"Slow down a little," Skip told Max.

"I got someone right on my ass," Max replied. "I'll find someplace to turn around and we'll come back."

Max drove past Proctor's place while Skip surveyed the farmstead. It dropped off to the creek in the back. The old house sat close to the road. He recognized Proctor's white Silverado parked next to a pair of hog confinement buildings that sat north of the house.

"I'll turn around up here at the next place and go back," Max told Skip.

"Don't worry about it," Skip replied. "I got a look at it. I don't think there's anything else to see."

At Max approached the next farm, he saw a woman riding a horse English-style around an outdoor riding arena surrounded by a white three-rail fence. A nice brick one-story ranch style home sat beyond the outdoor arena, and next to the arena was a large Butler building, large enough to enclose an indoor riding arena and a dozen stalls. Max was familiar with the layout. He had grown up on a farm north of Shipley that was laid out much the same.

Max's father had raised cattle, and along with cattle came horses. When Max was young, his father would travel to South Dakota to buy feeder calves for their lots. As soon as Max was old enough to ride a horse, he had taken the trip with his father to ride through herds of Herford cattle, marking the calves that they wanted to feed out with huge yellow crayons. Then the marked cattle were separated from the herd and driven to semi trucks that would haul them to Iowa and his father's feed lots.

In the early days, before combines, when farmers still picked corn and stored it in corn cribs to let the corn dry on the cob, corn fields were surrounded by fences. The cattle, fresh from the range, were set loose in the fields to feed on the ears of corn that escaped from the corn picker and fell on the ground.

Until the snow came and covered the corn, the gates to the feed lots were opened in the morning to let the cattle forage. In the hour before darkness, Max and his father would saddle up their quarterhorses and ride out to herd the cattle back to the lots where they were held for the night, feeding on ground corn, vitamins and minerals, mixed to maximize weight gain. Later, during the winter months, the cattle were confined to the lots, standing all day at the feed troughs, eating and chewing their cuds.

In order to move the cattle from one lot to another, Max and his father would mount horses and ride through the herd, checking each and every steer to see that they were healthy and gaining weight. If one showed any indication it might be getting sick, it would be separated from the rest of the cattle and quarantined until the veterinarian could come and check it out.

When a steer was separated from the herd, it would take any opportunity to slip past the rider and return to the herd. The horses that they rode were trained to prevent the calves from getting back. They were cutting horses, trained to cut a calf from the herd and force it wherever the rider wanted it to go. Max grew up riding cutting horses. Later, when Max was in high school, he bought a roping horse and competed in the high school rodeo circuit, calf roping, and for a while as a heeler, throwing a lasso under the hooves of a steer that had just been roped by the header, in team roping competitions. Max knew his way around horses.

So as they approached the farm with the riding arena, Max appreciated the layout. Max looked at the name on the mailbox as he passed the driveway. "Beckman." The name immediately registered in his brain. As he drove by the arena he fixed his attention on the woman riding the horse around the arena and recognized her as well, as soon as he got close enough.

"Elizabeth Beckman," he said out loud.

"What?" Skip asked.

"That's Elizabeth Beckman on that horse," Max said. "You know her. Used to be a big shot at the university. Used to be on some committees with us when we were on the PD. We used to set up security for some of her events."

Skip didn't respond.

"When they used to assign us temporary duty with Special Olympics and stuff like that, you remember?" Max was trying to get Skip to remember who Elizabeth Beckman was. "Iowa Games?"

Skip was trying to place her. Max pulled over to the side of the road, letting the car behind him pass. As soon as the car was clear, Max did a bootleg turn in the middle of the road and returned the way that they had come. He drove past the arena and waved at the woman riding the horse before he turned into the driveway and parked the Mustang. He got out and approached the fence. The woman rode her horse up to where he stood, one foot on the bottom rail, both arms resting on the top rail.

"Max!" the rider exclaimed as she got close enough to recognize him. "I haven't seen you forever."

"Elizabeth Beckman," Max addressed her. "I had no idea the you lived out here."

Elizabeth rode her horse close to the fence where Max could reach out and stroke its neck.

"How long you been out here?" Max asked.

"Six years," Elizabeth answered. "After my husband passed away and I retired from the university, I moved here. I've always loved riding horses, so I was looking for a place to board a horse. I found this place and bought it instead."

"Nice," Max took in the whole place. "How many acres you got?"

"Twenty acres," Elizabeth answered. "Five acres that you see here, five acres of pasture and the rest is woods."

"This is real sweet," Max said.

"Thanks," Elizabeth was noticeably proud that Max appreciated her place so much. "Hi, Skip," she addressed Skip as he walked up beside Max.

"Hi," Skip said. He was still trying to remember her.

"What are you guys doing out here?" Elizabeth asked.

"Well," Max answered. "We don't work at the police department anymore. We have a detective agency, and we're working a case."

"I thought that you two won the Powerball lottery." Elizabeth countered.

"Well," Max continued, "we did. But then we decided to start a detective agency. So now we are private detectives, and that's what we do. G&B Detective Agency," Max added.

"What are you investigating out here?" Elizabeth asked.

"We were in Maxwell on a case, and we came out here to check out your neighbor's place," Skip answered her. "Proctor, down the road."

"What's he up to now?" Elizabeth laughed as she asked the question.

"Probably nothing," Skip replied. "He just popped up in another case that we are working, and we thought that we would drive by while we were in the neighborhood. Then Max saw your name on the mailbox and thought that he recognized you riding your horse."

"So what case do you have in Maxwell?" Elizabeth pressed.

"A dead fish case," Max replied. Elizabeth raised her eyebrows. "Guy noticed a lot of dead fish in the creek that passes behind his place," Max explained. "He thought that it was unusual, asked us to come down and take a look, see what we thought about it."

Elizabeth continued to give him the questioning look. "Dead fish? Isn't that something the state would be working on?"

"It is a long story," Max explained. "We know the guy. He just wanted us to take a look, that's all. So we came down to take a look. Then we thought that we would just take a look at this Proctor guy's place as well. Really, there isn't that much to it."

Elizabeth chuckled. "Well," she said, "Proctor's a piece work." She paused for a second. "He's okay, I mean, but he has always got some deal going. He sold me some alfalfa hay earlier this year, and it was moldy." She paused. "But then he said that he felt real bad about it, and that he would get me some hay that wasn't moldy. He brought me some bales of brome, but I wanted alfalfa. He said he would find me some more alfalfa." Elizabeth paused for effect. "I'm still waiting." She laughed.

"Seriously," Elizabeth continued. "He's not a bad guy, just always looking for some deal. Always trying to turn a buck. He means well. He doesn't go out planning to screw people, I don't think, but everyone knows that any deal with Allan will end up falling through somehow. He's just always got something going on."

Max and Skip didn't respond to Elizabeth's observations of Proctor.

"So Proctor doesn't live over here anymore, he lives up on 650th, is that right?" Skip asked what he already knew. "Anybody living in the house on this place now?"

"Yeah," Elizabeth said, "man named Gordon. I don't know his last name. He lives there, takes care of the place, feeds the pigs. Always seems to stay busy."

"You talk to him?" Max asked.

"Not really," Elizabeth answered. "Allan stops by sometimes to reassure me that he is still looking for some alfalfa for me and seeing if there is anything else he can sell me. He talks about Gordon and what a hard worker he is. The guy lives there alone. I think Allan just wants me to know that he doesn't have some derelict living there that I need to worry about. Tell you the truth, I don't think that I would recognize Gordon if I saw him on the street."

"Anything else?" Max asked.

"Not really," Elizabeth answered. "That's about it. Nothing much happens there. Gordon runs back and forth with that old tanker truck of theirs, hauling manure out of the pits, but that's it. Pretty quiet over there. Grinds corn and mixes feed on Saturday mornings."

Max changed the subject. "How many horses you got?" he asked.

"I have three of my own," Elizabeth answered. "Then I have six more that I board."

"That's a good number of horses." Max observed. "That's a lot of work."

"The others belong to friends," Elizabeth went on. "You remember Yvonne, don't you?"

"Yeah," Max answered, remembering her as a friend and coworker of Elizabeth's.

"Well, she has one horse here. I just board friends' horses. I don't try to make a lot of money with them. Just what it costs me to keep the place running."

Max smiled. "That sounds like you."

"We just have a good time out here," Elizabeth reflected. "My friends keep their horses here. I have the woods out behind the house. It's nice. We get together sometimes in the afternoon or evening, grill steaks. We have fun. Sometimes we have a bonfire out here and we all get drunk and run around naked." She might have been joking.

Max didn't know how to respond. "Sounds like fun," he replied.

"How's Gloria?" Elizabeth asked.

"Doing well," Max answered. "She is a wine consultant for a Napa Valley winery. She organizes wine tastings for them. Gives her something to do, and she likes wine."

"I knew that," Elizabeth nodded. "I ran into her at a wine tasting fundraiser she was doing a couple of years ago. You two need to come out here and she can do a wine tasting for everyone."

"And run around the bonfire naked," Max laughed.

"If you feel like it, you can," Elizabeth smiled and winked at Max.

The conversation stalled out. Max looked around. "We probably need to get moving," Skip suggested.

"I suppose," Max said.

"Stop by anytime," Elizabeth said. There was a genuineness in her voice as she said it.

"We will," Max replied. "We'll get together. It will be fun."

The two detectives turned and walked toward the Mustang. Max waved to Elizabeth as he got into the car. He pulled out of the yard, drove down the driveway, then pulled onto the gravel road. Elizabeth was riding her horse around the arena.

"I remember her now," Skip remarked.

"Great lady," Max said.

"Seems to be," Skip agreed.

Max drove the Mustang up the road. The lady with the British accent instructed them to make a safe U-turn as soon as possible. Skip was trying to figure out how to turn off the GPS. At the next intersection Max turned right, toward 650th Street, or the Maxwell Blacktop, as it was known for eighty years before they decided to give every road in the county a street name. The gravel road went over Indian Creek one more time along the way to the blacktop. Max stopped on the bridge. Skip got out and looked over the railing at the water flowing under the bridge. He stood there for several minutes.

"Anything?" Max asked when Skip got back in the car.

"One big one. Looks like a bullhead or a catfish," Skip observed.

Max shrugged his shoulders. "Wanna keep looking? Probably a bridge every mile."

"Not now," Skip responded. "We've got to concentrate on Peggy."

They reached 650th, and Max turned north toward New 30. As they passed Proctor's new place, Skip gave it a close look.

"Just nothing," he muttered.

"What?" Max responded.

"Just nothing," Skip repeated himself. "Just nothing there. We got nothing. We got our client, his wife, who we are investigating, and Proctor, a pig farmer who had lunch with her. We've got nothing so far."

Max looked at the clock on the Mustang's dash. "Quarter to twelve," he observed.

"Let's go see if Peggy's having lunch at the West Café, and if so, who she's having it with."

"Sounds good," Skip agreed.

"We have Higgins's case, too," Max remarked. "I mean, we have two cases."

"I'm aware of that," Skip replied.

Chapter 10

Tuesday

Max and Skip kept driving north past Proctor's new house. When they reached New 30, Max crossed and kept going north another mile, to where the blacktop crossed Old 30. He turned left and drove toward the outskirts of the small town of Nevada, the county seat. The two men were lost in thought as they drove into town. When they had traversed one end of the town to the other on Lincolnway, which was the Old Lincoln Highway, they arrived at the West Café. They scanned the parking lot for Peggy's Lexus, but it was not to be seen. They waited.

"So what we going to do when she gets here?" Max asked. "Are we just going to sit there and watch her eat lunch?"

"I don't know," Skip answered. "You got any ideas?"

"Depends," Max replied. "Proctor was down at his farm, and he didn't pass by while we were talking to Elizabeth. His truck isn't here. I'm wondering if they are even having lunch together today."

"He could have gone south and through Maxwell. We wouldn't have seen him if he went that way," Skip observed.

"Still," said Max, "He isn't here, and I didn't see him coming through town, so what makes us think that he and Peggy have lunch here every day? How do we know that yesterday wasn't just a business lunch? We agreed that other than a little holdy-hands, there wasn't much to report.

So I'm thinking that maybe we need to take another approach."

"What kind of approach are you thinking about?" Skip asked.

"Remember those dancers from Milwaukee that were down at Chris's in Cambridge back when we were on the PD? Remember how they got that guy to come up to the Howard Johnson in Ames and give 'em money for sex, but then they pepper sprayed him instead, shoved him out of the room and locked the door? Remember how we went down there to Chris's and pretended that we were customers for two nights, just to try and catch them doing it again?" Max paused, waiting for acknowledgement from Skip.

"So you want to go undercover and get pepper sprayed?" Skip asked.

"No, I don't want to get pepper sprayed. I don't think that Peggy takes people's money and then pepper sprays them. But I'm thinking that we need to nudge things a little if we want to find out what she is up to, or not up to, whichever the case may be."

Peggy's car pulled into the lot and parked close to Max and Skip in the Mustang. She got out and walked to the café. She didn't even glance toward them.

"Let's wait to see if Proctor shows up." Max suggested. "Then if he doesn't, I'm thinking that ol' Ben Ralston needs to introduce himself to Peggy and invite himself for lunch. What do you think?"

Skip thought about it for a moment. Max was good at undercover stings, there was no doubt about that. Skip had watched Max pull off more than a few. "Might as well," Skip shrugged. "I'm just concerned what the blowback might be if she finds out that Travis hired us to watch her, and then that we've been pulling an undercover operation on her on top of that. There's liable to be a big trust issue to deal with when this is over, and if she isn't doing anything, I don't want us making it any worse than it is already going to be."

"Something to think about," Max agreed, "but we gotta do something here. We're not getting anywhere as it is."

There was no sign of Proctor. The two sat for a few minutes, waiting.

"I'll go in and get a table," Skip finally said. "I'll text you when I get seated and give you the go. You come in, do your thing and I'll keep an eye out."

"Eye out for what?" Max asked.

"An eye out for whatever is going on," Skip answered.

Skip got out of the Mustang, walked across the parking lot to the café and inside. Max waited. Within a few minutes he got a text.

"By herself, ordered, doesn't look like she's waiting for anyone."

Max got out of the Mustang, locked the door and went into the café. When he walked in, he didn't wait to be seated. He gave the whole place the onceover. Max could size up a place with just one look. All of the booths were occupied. There were a few vacant stools at the counter. "Perfect setup," Max thought.

Max sauntered over to the table where Peggy was looking at the specials on the menu. Peggy ate at the West Café every day. She knew what the special was for every day of the week, but she still read them out of habit.

"Mrs. Bentley," Max addressed her. Peggy looked up. "Ben Ralston, friend of Allan Proctor's. Mind if I share a booth with you?"

Peggy smiled up at Max and motioned to the seat across the table from her. "Thanks," he said as he slid in and sat down.

"How do you know Allan?" Peggy asked when Max had settled in.

"Independent insurance agent," Max replied. "Our paths have crossed a few times. I'm down here with some adjustors, checking on yields for some corn that got hail and wind damage in June. We gotta determine the loss so that they can get paid for it. We're here all week."

"Where are you out of?" Peggy asked.

"Marshalltown," Max answered without hesitation. Max pulled a business card out of his billfold, took a quick glance at it to make sure that it was one of Ralston's cards, then slid it across the table to Peggy. Peggy picked it up and looked at it.

"It says that your office is in Ames," Peggy remarked, absently flicking the card as she examined it.

"Yeah, Ames and Marshalltown," Max explained. "We have offices in both cities." He didn't try to explain the discrepancy any further, steering the conversation smoothly and as seamlessly as if there were no discrepancy at all.

"So, you are a friend of Proctor's?" Max asked. "I saw you two in here eating yesterday."

"Sort of," Peggy answered. "He does some contracting for the company that I work for."

"The ethanol plant," Max pressed. "He told me that you work at the ethanol plant on New 30."

"Yes," said Peggy, "BioForce. What else has Allan told you about me?"

"Oh, nothing much," Max replied. "I don't really know Allan all that well, we've just done some business, you know, insurance claims and such. I talked to him yesterday in the parking lot. Hadn't seen him for a long time. We chatted a little, caught up on what we both have been up to."

Peggy felt a little uneasy. Allan was pretty careful about their relationship. They both had a lot to lose if rumors came out at the wrong time, and it was the wrong time as far as Peggy was concerned. Allan and she were still working out the exit strategy from their marriages. It seemed odd that Allan would be talking about her out in the parking lot to some insurance man that he hardly knew.

Max could see Peggy's defenses coming up. He changed the subject away from Allan. "So, are you seeing a lot of corn coming in? I mean, does it seem like the yields are high around here?"

"I don't know," Peggy answered. "I don't have much to do with that end of the business. I manage all the subcontractors. Cleaning, maintenance, security, that kind of thing. But I haven't heard that there is any shortage. I know that corn prices are really low, so I would guess that either the yields are high or the demand is low, that's how it works."

Max had been looking around for the waitress to place his order. She finally came up to the table and put a menu in front of Max. "What can I get you to drink?" she asked.

Max picked up the menu and handed it back without looking at it. "How about a Coke to drink, and could I get a hot roast beef sandwich?"

"You got it," the waitress said as she took the menu back from Max. She looked at Peggy. "Your chef's salad will be just another minute."

"Well," Max continued as the server walked away, "the wind and hail damage last summer was really localized. I guess if the yields are good, those guys are going to come out ahead. No skin off me," he laughed. "I get paid either way."

The waitress returned with Peggy's salad. "Be a few minutes," she told Max.

Max just smiled and nodded to the waitress. When she left, Max turned his attention back to Peggy. "So Allan must have the cleaning contract with you?" Max asked.

"He cleans the fermentation tanks," Peggy offered. "He has a crew that cleans the tanks on site, then hauls the wastewater out and takes care of disposing it."

"That a big deal?" Max asked.

"Kind of," Peggy said, at ease now that the conversation had moved into professional territory. "Federal and state regulations are very specific about how to handle the wastewater. Allan hauls it to a plant in Missouri that disposes of it properly in a way that prevents any environmental harm."

"I'll bet that keeps him busy," Max remarked. "He told me at one time that he had a big hog confinement. He still doing that?"

"I think so," Peggy answered. "He doesn't have much to do with the day-to-day operations at the plant. He has a man, Gordon, who manages his cleaning company. Allan is like the CEO. He just comes around to check on Gordon and see if he needs anything," she explained.

"Yeah," Max said, "I think that Allan has a few things that he is into. He keeps busy."

Max's food arrived and he started eating.

"So, did you know Allan before he started cleaning the tanks?" Max asked between bites.

"I knew him," Peggy said. "He's local. I used to see him around." She took a bite. "How long have you known him?"

"I don't know," Max said. "I've known him quite a while. Not well, like I said, but I've done some business with him over the years. We used to run in some of the same circles before he got married. Nice guy. Lovely family."

Max watched carefully for a reaction. Peggy grew silent. Her shoulders fell a bit, and she looked down at her food.

"Those kids of his are real corkers," Max said.

Peggy pushed a piece of tomato around on her plate.

"You got kids?" Max asked. "I see you're married."

"No kids," Peggy replied quietly. "You?"

"No," Max answered. "No kids. Me and the wife are both busy with our careers. We thought that we would eventually have kids, but we just never did. We're getting old enough that we probably won't have any." He let his voice trail off wistfully as he said it. "That's okay, I guess," he piped up. "Nothing wrong with not having kids." He smiled at Peggy. She seemed to perk up a little and smiled back.

"What's your husband do?" Max inquired.

"He's a psychologist-slash-psychiatrist," she answered. "He teaches substance abuse classes." Peggy did not expound on it.

"That's interesting," Max said.

"Not really," Peggy responded.

Max could sense that talking about her husband made Peggy sad, or maybe nervous. Max decided to take the conversation back to Allan and see what reaction he got.

"Ol' Allan was quite the lady's man back before he got hitched," Max chuckled. "He ever give you that wink of his? Probably see right through that, having a husband who is a psychiatrist and all."

"Oh yeah," Peggy perked up. "I've gotten it a few times."

"Something about that guy," Max shook his head affectionately. "I think everybody likes Allan. He's just that kind of guy."

Peggy smiled and nodded. "He is."

"I think he has to be one of the most thoughtful guys I ever met," Max continued. "Always thinking about other people."

"He does," Peggy responded. "He's a sweet guy. I like him. He's good to work with."

"Yep," Max said.

Peggy had finished her salad and was looking for the waitress. Max still had a few bites left of his roast beef sandwich.

"What do you need?" Max asked.

"The bill," she answered him. "I need to get back."

"Don't worry about it," Max said. "I'll take care of it. I just appreciate having someone to talk to. I usually eat alone, or with a bunch of other insurance agents, which is the only thing worse than eating alone." Max laughed. "I got it. Thanks, it was nice to talk to you."

Peggy got up out of her seat and extended her hand toward Max. Max took it and held it for a moment. Peggy pulled her hand away and turned toward the door. Max nodded to himself, then finished his meal. Max loved potatoes and gravy. When he was done, the waitress placed the bill on the end of the table. "Whenever you're ready," she told him.

"Ready right now," Max said before she could turn and leave. He pulled his billfold out and handed her a twenty-dollar bill. He didn't want to use the G&B Detective Agency credit card. He didn't know how well Peggy and the waitress knew each other, but he wasn't going to take a chance that the waitress would ask Peggy why she had talked to a detective. Skip must have already paid, because he followed Peggy out the door. Timing was everything, and Skip was picking up the surveillance. He knew his business.

When the waitress returned with his change, Max left a tip and walked easily out of the café into the bright sunshine. Skip was sitting on the back fender of the Mustang, waiting.

"Anything?" Max asked.

"Got in her car and left toward the plant." Skip replied. "What did you learn?"

"She's definitely got a thing for Allan," Max said. "I don't know what the relationship is between her and him, but there's something going on between them. Doesn't want to talk about Travis at all."

"Good-time girl?" Skip asked.

"I don't think so. I think that she is lonely." Max answered. "I held her hand when she shook to leave, and she was uncomfortable with it. I don't think that she is that way."

"Maybe you're not her type," Skip smirked.

"Doesn't make any difference, a good-time girl would have at least teased a little. I mean, teasing is the fun part. She didn't respond in that kind of way. Just the opposite."

Skip stood up and shrugged his shoulders. "If you say so, Casanova."

Max hit the button on his key fob to unlock the doors. They both got into the Mustang.

"Where to?" Max asked. "Wanna see if she made it back to work?"

"Drive around town," Skip said. "Let's just drive around and see if Allan is in town."

"Your case," Max replied as he pulled out of the parking lot and onto the street. Max cruised down Lincolnway and turned onto Main Street at the one and only stoplight in the town. When he got to the county court house, Max went around the block and drove back to Lincolnway. He drove past the hardware store, the Farm and Fleet and a couple of other restaurants. Max took a run out by the Justice Center, the annex building that housed the county jail, the county attorney's offices and the courtrooms that were no longer at the courthouse downtown. As a teenager Max had driven all over Nevada after school, wasting as much time as he thought he could get away with before going home to do chores. He knew his way around. There was no sign of Allan's Silverado.

As Max drove south out of town, toward New 30, Skip spoke up. "Take the long way home."

"What's the long way?" Max asked.

"Let's drive back down to Maxwell and see if he's at his place. Then let's cut across E-29 and come back up 69." Skip knew his way around as well.

Max turned east toward the Maxwell blacktop. When they got there, Max turned south and put the accelerator to the floor. The Mustang literally jumped, as if Max had put the spurs to it.

After a few minutes, Skip casually asked Max, "How fast we going?"

"Hundred-twenty," Max casually answered.

"That all it's got?" Skip asked.

"There's more," Max said.

As they flew past Allan's place, Skip glanced over. Allan's Silverado was sitting by the house. "Looks like he's at home," Skip observed.

The Mustang thundered down the two-lane blacktop. Finally, Max let up on the accelerator as they approached the hills that marked the river bottom, where Max could not see far enough ahead to continue at that speed. The car slowed down to fifty-five. It felt like they were creeping, after the wild ride they had just taken.

"That was childish," Skip reflected.

"I know," Max smiled over at Skip.

"Pull over before you get to the bridge," Skip instructed.

Max did as Skip asked and pulled off the blacktop and onto the shoulder. Skip hopped out as soon as he stopped and ran up on the bridge to look over the railing. Out of habit, Max had stopped with the two driver's side wheels on the traveled portion of the road to force any traffic around him and Skip, thereby keeping Skip safe from getting picked off by passing cars.

Skip watched the creek for a while, then glanced both ways and crossed to the other side to look over that rail. Then he turned around and made sure it was clear before he made his way back to the Mustang and got in.

"Nothing," Skip told Max as he got in the car.

Max checked his mirror and pulled back onto the roadway, continuing south. They wound their way along the river bottom into Maxwell. Max asked Skip if he wanted to go around past Higgins's place, but Skip shook his head. Max drove through the burg, past the Casey's, then south out of town. He took the county blacktop to the west, finding his way to US Highway 69 and back north to Ames. It was a nice ride, and Max enjoyed it thoroughly. He liked just driving around with no destination in mind.

Chapter 11

Tuesday

Carlisle drove past Higgins's house, then took the road that went past the park, the rodeo arena and out of town to the west. He was surprised by how Higgins had cleaned up his place since the case of the stolen dogs. Higgins had changed in a lot of ways. He was no longer firing off his 9mm Browning all the time, prompting the neighbors to call the sheriff. He also seemed to be getting out more, and whenever Carlisle ran into him, Higgins was all smiles and friendly. But nonetheless, Carlisle did not trust that Higgins had given up all of his bad habits, and Carlisle wasn't about to let him just fly under the radar after his sordid past.

Carlisle saw a truck parked at the other end of the bridge over Indian Creek, and a man in a DNR uniform leaning over the rail with a string. Carlisle pulled up on the bridge. The DNR officer looked over his shoulder at Carlisle, but continued to wind the string up on some type of reel that did not look anything like any fishing reel he had ever seen, which has caused Carlisle to be curious. Carlisle recognized the officer, but couldn't remember his name.

"What's up?" Carlisle asked the man, who had turned away from him again.

"Taking water samples," the DNR officer called over his shoulder.

Carlisle waited for him to bring up a bottle suspended from the end of the string, filled with river water. The officer put a cap on it, dried the bottle with a cloth that he pulled out of his back pocket, then put a piece of red tape over it, sealing the cap from being opened without removing the tape. The DNR officer wrote something on the bottle with a sharpie, then turned his attention to the deputy.

"Been taking samples all day," the DNR officer offered. "Yesterday, too. Some kind of pollution in the water, but we don't know what it is. Last week we found traces of it all the way down where the creek goes into the Skunk River."

"Like hog manure?" asked Carlisle, thinking about the hog confinement just up the creek a couple of miles. "Clear down where it goes into the Skunk river? That's a long way downstream from here," Carlisle reflected.

"I've been taking samples all the way upstream from where we first found it, looking for the source. This isn't hog manure, though; I think it's some kind of chemical."

"No kidding?" Carlisle said. "There's a big hog confinement up the creek a little ways. If it was hog shit, it wouldn't surprise me if it came from there."

"I know hog shit," the DNR officer repeated. "This is something else."

Carlisle thought about where someone might be dumping chemicals into the creek. "Maybe a meth lab?" Carlisle offered.

"Could be," the DNR officer agreed. "Have to be one hell of a big meth lab, though, to put enough chemicals in the water for them to show up all the way down at the Skunk. Anyway, I'm taking samples and we'll see what the lab finds."

"Sounds like fun," Carlisle said sarcastically.

"Job security," the DNR officer laughed.

"So when do you expect to get something back on the sample?" Carlisle asked.

"I've just been dropping them off to get them tested. They got an investigation going, but I don't know where they are on that. I'm not in the loop, I'm just the grunt. I don't know much about it, really."

"So you think it's serious?" Carlisle asked.

"I don't know," the DNR officer replied. "They got me on it full time, taking samples, so it must be something. But one thing I do know: I've got dead fish floating in the creek here. This is the first place since I started this that I've seen dead fish like this. I'm going to let the lab know about it when I drop off the samples this afternoon. This is my last one for today. I'm going to see if they'll send a state biologist out with me to look at these fish."

"Why are you just seeing them now?" Carlisle was curious.

The DNR agent shrugged his shoulders. "Maybe piled up above a low head dam somewhere?"

"I don't think there is any low head dam around here," Carlisle frowned.

"Log jam?" the DNR officer said, "Maybe a beaver dam?"

Carlisle shrugged his shoulders.

"I'll get a biologist to come out here and kick around," the DNR officer said. "That's their job. Until bow season starts up, mine's taking water samples. And I'll be glad when bow season starts, because I'm tired of taking water samples."

"Hey," said Carlisle, "if you do go up the creek to check it out, maybe I could tag along. I wouldn't mind taking a look up there myself. Might be a good reason for me to go up there and snoop around as well."

"Sure, why not?" The DNR officer nodded. "We could do that."

Carlisle pulled a business card out of his breast pocket, wrote his cell number on the back, then handed it out the window to the other officer. "Keep up the good work."

"Thanks," said the DNR officer as he took the card. "Catch you later."

"Don't be handing that number out," Carlisle said with a smile. "That's my personal cell."

"No problem," the DNR officer said as Carlisle pulled away.

Carlisle continued over the bridge and turned up 340th Street to the north. He drove past Allan Proctor's place and looked it over as he drove by. There wasn't anything going on there. If the pollution had been hog manure, Carlisle would have pointed the DNR in Proctor's direction. Proctor was a shithead as far as Carlisle was concerned. Proctor was no better than Higgins, just smarter, richer and better dressed. Carlisle had filed more than a few theft reports so that Proctor could report them to his insurance, and more than a few times Carlisle had thought that Proctor was pretty good at coming up with theft reports.

Carlisle drove past Elizabeth Beckman's place. Nice lady, he thought. Too bad she had to live next to Proctor's hog farm.

Carlisle continued his patrol, working his way through the back roads toward Ames, making a point to drive into some of the places that he knew were not often visited by their owners. Like most of the deputies, Carlisle had grown up in Story County. When he was a kid, everyone lived on their farms. They lived in old houses on small farms that had been farmsteads and in the family for a century. But that wasn't the way it was anymore. Small farms had been bought by big farmers, and big farmers became corporate farmers, and now most everything was run by farm managers. Nobody lived on most of the farms anymore, unless it was a hired hand. But there were still a lot of old farmsteads where no one lived, and hog confinements out in the middle of nowhere. Sitting ducks for opportunists. When he was on patrol with nothing in particular to do, Carlisle would drive into as many of them as he could, looking for broken locks or broken doors. Whenever he found evidence of a burglary, he would have to find out who owned the property, who managed the property, then get someone out there to see what was missing. It was a never ending job. And the insurance companies could care less. They just paid off and then jacked up the premiums. It was a game, and Deputy Carlisle often wondered if he was protecting and serving, or if he was just a pawn in the game. It was a game that Proctor played, too, and Carlisle didn't appreciate Proctor using him in the process.

Carlisle continued to work his way toward Ames. It was a beautiful fall day, sunny and warm. He looked out into the fields at the combines taking advantage of the weather to get the corn in. Harvest seemed to get earlier every year. The farmers were always in a hurry. They wanted to get crops planted early, and then get them out early. Carlisle liked patrolling in the early fall.

Carlisle turned onto New 30 and proceeded to the city limits of Ames. He took the first exit and pulled into the truck stop, heading for the Dairy Queen at one end of the building. It was getting close to lunch time, and Carlisle was a creature of habit. He stopped at the drive-up speaker to order his usual hamburger, fries and a Coke. He pulled up to the window and paid the young woman there. She was familiar with Carlisle's routine. He stopped in every Tuesday and Thursday. You could mark it on a calendar and set your watch to it. She smiled at him.

"How's it going today?" she asked.

"Same old stuff, just a different day," he answered.

While Carlisle waited for his order, he saw Milton pull in and park in the corner of the parking lot, away from the idling diesel trucks parked in rows behind the truck stop. When he got his food, Carlisle drove his patrol car alongside Milton's so that they could talk through their windows. They called that "twenty-fiving," for the ten code ten-twenty-five, which meant to meet somewhere. "Twenty-five me at the truck stop." Except the two officers didn't need to communicate the request, because Milton knew that Carlisle would be at the Dairy Queen getting lunch. Barring, of course, a call that would send one or both off to who knows where to check on who knows what. But the two monitored each other's radio traffic and had been doing their jobs for years, so they went with the flow, wherever that flow took them. Sometimes it seemed they could never make plans, on duty or off, because they were always on call.

"What's up?" Milton asked as Carlisle pulled up alongside his open window.

"Nothing much," Carlisle replied. "Just talked to some DNR officer who was taking water samples down on Indian Creek. Evidently someone is dumping chemicals in the water."

"Meth lab?" Milton asked.

"That's what I asked him," Carlisle replied. "He didn't know. All he knew was that it isn't manure and they found it clear down where the creek goes into the Skunk River."

Milton thought for a moment. "Man, that's a long ways, isn't it?"

Carlisle was biting into his hamburger and didn't answer.

"What else?" Milton asked. "What's Higgins up to?" Ever since the missing dog case a few months ago, Higgins had been a topic of their conversation.

"Nothin' I can prove," the deputy replied. "I think he has something going on back behind his place, but I don't know what. I think his shithead cousin and him are up to something."

"A meth lab?" Milton asked.

"Maybe, or maybe a grow," Carlisle answered. "The thing is, that DNR guy found some dead fish, so he's going to take a biologist up the creek to see what they can find. I'm going to see if I can tag along with them. It'll be a good excuse to get back there and take a look."

"Good idea," Milton said.

"So how's it going with Monica?" Carlisle asked.

"It's going," Milton responded.

"Serious?" Carlisle pressed.

"Not really," Milton replied. "It would be okay with me if it got serious, but she doesn't seem to want to get that involved. She says she is too busy with school right now to get involved in a relationship. She wants to keep it casual."

"Okay," Carlisle commented. "So how long you planning to casually hang out with Monica?"

"'Til something better comes along, I guess," Milton said. "I like her; I'll wait for a while. She's teaching me patience," Milton laughed.

"Zen and the seduction of Monica," Carlisle joked.

Carlisle's radio squawked. There was an accident south of town on a gravel road. A pickup truck had come around the corner and run into the back of a wagon full of corn being pulled by a tractor. No serious injuries were reported. Carlisle got those kind of calls a lot during harvest time.

Carlisle keyed the mic but did not remove it from the holder. He leaned toward it with a mouth full of fries and replied, "Ten-four, seventy-six." He looked over at Milton. "Gotta go," he said as he moved his lunch from the dash into the briefcase that sat open on the passenger seat of his patrol car. "Talk with you later. Tell Monica hi, and tell her I'm still interested in taking her out if she ever decides to dump you."

"Yeah, I'll be sure to tell her that," Milton called out as Carlisle pulled away.

Chapter 12

Tuesday

Milton followed Carlisle out of the truck stop and went back on patrol. He was driving a utility car. His job was to drive aimlessly around town doing routine patrol duties, but mostly backing up area cars and filling in wherever needed. It was a job usually reserved for senior officers with experience, but on day shift, some of the more experienced officers chose to work areas, where they could hide out and push their calls off on the utility cars, so even though Milton was low on the day shift seniority list, he worked utility more often than not.

Milton liked working days well enough. He didn't like getting up early to make the six forty-five briefing, but he liked getting off at three in the afternoon. He liked having the run of the town, not being bound by an area. One thing he didn't especially like was his days-off schedule: five days on, two days off, then six days on, three days off. It meant that he got one full weekend off every six weeks, but then he got a three-day weekend every six weeks as well, so that made up for it a little. But that was how it was, and that is how it would be as long as he worked patrol, so he had learned to live with it. Still, his schedule made it hard to go out on a weekend night with Monica and their friends, then crawl out of bed at five forty-five the next morning.

Everything was quiet. There had not been more than a few calls for service all morning. The area cars were all in hiding, so he wasn't running back and forth across town to back them up on traffic stops like he had done when he worked utility on the evening and night shifts. But Milton got bored easily on days. He had thought about bidding for three-to-eleven shift in January. He could get into a little more action on three-to-elevens. He could sleep as late in the mornings as he wanted. He could take classes at the college. There were a lot of things he could do if he worked three-to-elevens. At this point he had enough seniority to bid whatever shift he wanted to work. The only thing holding him back was Monica. If he worked three-to-elevens he would never see her, except on his days off. But lately things hadn't been going so well. Monica had been standoffish. Milton wasn't sure where he stood with her anymore.

Milton migrated west. He ran his radar as he drove, set to sound an alarm if he met any speeders going ten over. But the radar was silent. Milton came to a four-way stop and waited for his turn to proceed through the intersection. No one moved. Everyone was waiting for him. Milton looked from one car to another, then slowly pulled through the intersection, anticipating someone getting nervous and jumping through it with him. There was always confusion for the other drivers when there was a patrol car present. No one wanted to do something that might be construed as illegal. A lot of times if Milton was following them, drivers would keep slowing down. That was especially annoying when he was in a residential area with a twenty-five mile per hour speed limit. Sometimes the cars that he was following would slow to twenty miles an hour—five miles under the speed limit—just in case. Milton would poke along behind them, wishing they would just go the speed limit at least. As Milton pulled through the intersection and proceeded down the street, not paying particular attention to how fast he was driving, he came up behind a car. He noticed the brake lights flicker as the driver slowed to thirty-five in a forty-five mile an hour speed zone. Milton rolled his eyes. "Christ, I wish people would just drive," he thought.

Milton drove past the G&B Detective Agency. He noticed that Monica's car was parked in her reserved space directly in front of the door. Max's yellow Mustang was parked next to Monica's car and Skip's Mercedes was parked across the lot in the shade of a tree that Skip had planted there specifically for that purpose. Milton drove into the lot and parked his patrol car on the other side of Max's Mustang. As he got out of his car, Milton switched on his portable radio instead of calling out with dispatch. Somewhere there was a rule against doing that, because dispatch liked to keep track of where everyone was, but it was common practice to get out of the car without calling out. No one took much notice of it.

Milton walked through the door and into the reception area of G&B Detective Agency. Monica was sitting at her desk, looking at her computer screen. Max and Skip were standing behind her, looking over her shoulder. They were all laughing at something. They looked up as Milton came in.

"Hey Milton, take a look, your girlfriend is getting hit on by a bunch of cowboys on a dating site," Max called out.

Milton walked around the desk and shouldered Max out of the way. Max had been Milton's training officer when he had first come to the police department. The two had developed a father-son relationship that existed for the whole time that Max had been on the department. It was a relationship that most officers feel with their training officers. But since Max and Skip had won the Powerball jackpot, resigned from the PD and stared up G&B Detective Agency as a place to hang out, the relationship between him and Max had developed more of a big brother-little brother feel.

Max, who wasn't small, pushed Milton back, but he couldn't move the big man. Milton peered over Monica's shoulder.

"What's lonelyfarmers.com?" Milton asked, clearly recognizing an online dating site on the screen.

"A dating site for farmers," Monica answered, noting the annoyed tone in Milton's voice. "It is part of an ongoing investigation," she added, looking over her shoulder at Milton. "By the way Max, you owe me thirty-five bucks. I had to pay to get past the introduction."

"Why didn't you use the G&B card?" Max asked.

"Yeah, right," Monica laughed. "A detective agency card wouldn't be a red flag for a dating site."

"There isn't anyone actually checking the name on the credit cards," Max replied.

"Just fork over thirty-five bucks," Monica responded.

Milton was reading through the comments and emails that Monica was receiving. There was one from Clint Eastwood.

"Clint Eastwood?" Milton pointed at the screen.

"Just a user name," Monica answered him. "No one uses their real name."

"You used Moni," Milton fired back.

"Okay, almost no one uses their real name."

Milton grumbled something under his breath.

Monica looked back over her shoulder again. "Look, what difference does it make? I danced under my own name. It's no big deal."

Milton did not respond.

"You could have used Calamity Jane," Max interjected. "That would have been a good one. Look," he pointed at another reply, "this guy wants you to ride him into the sunset," Max laughed out loud. "Does anyone really think that line is the way to get a woman to go out with them?"

"It isn't doing anything for me," Monica laughed.

Max could see that Milton was becoming aggravated. He decided to move things along. "Did you find anything that might actually help us?"

"I found this one," Monica said, pulling up a page. "Professional woman sitting alone at night. Looking for a friend I can talk with, share with and spend time with," Monica read out loud. "Yada yada yada yada. Lonely and left at home."

Monica looked around. "Here's the picture: that her?"

"Yep," Skip said. "That's her ten years ago, probably."

"Right now she is inactive, which I guess means that she's found someone. I mean, they all have their own ways of doing things, so I'm guessing that she found someone to talk to and share with."

"You've been on a lot of these sites, to know that they are all different?" Milton snapped.

"No," Monica snapped back, "I haven't been on a lot of them, but I know things."

"Would you two save it for later?" Max said.

"Anything else?" Skip asked.

"Well, the men are sneaky," Monica replied. "I'm thinking that there are a lot of married guys here who plan to stay that way, and they have to be careful. I have a couple of guys that look like they could be your man Proctor."

Monica pulled up another page. "So here's this: Farm Manager, looking for a secure woman with a good job in agriculture. Someone who doesn't need 24/7 care. Just looking for a friend right now, but anything could happen with the right woman."

Monica stopped reading. "What do you think?"

"That's him," Skip replied looking at the picture. "What does 'anything could happen' mean?"

"Like he is leaving the door open, but not making any commitment," Max said. "That's him."

"Shit fire, woman," Max exclaimed. "Good job. You ought to work for a real detective agency."

Monica turned and smiled at Max. She narrowed her eyes at Milton, then smiled at him, too. She reached around and tried to pinch him, but just got ahold of his bullet proof vest.

"You been working out or something?" she asked playfully.

Milton didn't respond.

"I need to go," Milton said as he stood up straight and headed toward the door.

"I'll walk you to your car," Monica rolled her chair backwards over Max's foot. He jumped back and let her get up.

The two went out on the sidewalk. Milton turned around.

"You're not real happy with me getting on that lonelyfarmers.com, are you?" Monica said.

"I don't find it as entertaining as the rest of you seem to," Milton replied.

"Listen," Monica said, "Max asked me if I would join the site and look around for Peggy and Proctor. Nothing more. I'm going to delete my account as soon as we're done. I promise."

"Do what you please," Milton replied.

"Don't be that way," Monica said. "Why don't we go out for ice cream? You, me and Essie? I'll pay. How often do you get to go on a date with two good-looking women?"

"I don't know," Milton responded.

"So what, you're going to sit at home and be grumpy instead?"

"I just wish we could have a little alone time, you and me," Milton replied. "When's the last time we had some time together?"

"Yesterday," Monica replied. "When we drove around in the 'Stang."

"You know what I mean," Milton said.

Monica stood looking up at Milton. "Let's go someplace the next weekend you have off. We'll go to Omaha. Mom can take care of Essie. What do you think?"

"I might have to work a football game," Milton remarked.

"No, you don't have to work a football game," Monica said. "What's better, a little overtime, or a little nookie?"

"I guess nookie," Milton smiled.

"See, nothing like a little nookie to get a guy smiling again."

"Maybe I could get a preview beforehand?" Milton suggested.

"Maybe we could work it into our busy schedules," Monica teased. "But this evening it's you, me and Essie, and ice cream."

"Okay," Milton agreed.

"Milton got into his car and backed out of the parking space. He drove out of the lot and onto the street toward downtown and the police station.

Monica went back into the agency. Max was sitting at her desk, and he and Skip were checking out the lonelyfarmer.com site.

"Looking for hookups?" asked Monica.

"I can't afford it," Max quipped. "The woman I have is all I can handle right now. This is crazy, though." Max looked up from the screen. "You two okay?"

"We're fine," Monica answered. "Just going through a rough spot."

"I know," Max said. "Follow your heart."

"Yeah, right, follow Mr. Love Connection's advice," Skip snorted. "He knows all about it."

Max was peering at the screen. "I'm looking to see if there's someone I might know on here."

"Me, too," Skip replied.

"Hey, I thought I saw your picture back there a ways," Max laughed at Skip.

"Yeah," Skip shot back, "I thought I saw yours back there in the ugly, bald and desperate column."

"Get out of my chair," Monica interrupted. "You two are like children."

Max reluctantly got out of Monica's chair. She squeezed past him and sat down. She closed the lonelyfarmers site on her computer.

"We weren't done," Max said.

"You owe me thirty-five dollars," Monica demanded.

"Take it out of the petty cash box," Skip said as he headed down the hall toward his office.

"I already did," Monica replied back. "I just wanted you to say that it was okay." She looked up to see Max looking over her shoulder like he expected the lonelyfarmer.com site to come back up. "Can I help you with something?"

"No," replied Max, "I'm going." He turned and followed Skip down the hall.

Monica sat back in her chair. She was troubled about Milton. She knew that she was falling in love with him, and that he loved her. But she wondered how their love would survive in the long term. She wondered about her own history, whether her own circumstances would eventually drive a wedge between them. Furthermore, she really didn't know much about Milton. He seldom talked about his family or his past. She didn't even know where he came from before he became a police officer. Maybe a weekend in Omaha was exactly what they needed. Monica just knew that she couldn't make another mistake. She owed it to Essie to keep her act together; she owed it to Max, to Skip, to her mother, and she owed it to herself.

Max stopped at the bar and mixed himself a rum and Coke on the way to his office. He sat down and waited for his email to load. The little blue dot in the middle of the screen kept turning.

"You know something?" Max called across the hall to Skip. "Who said that money can buy you happiness? Is this the best they can do? I mean, I paid a fortune for this damned piece-of-shit computer, and it does nothing. It just sits here spinning."

Skip did not respond to Max's computer tirade. Max and technology had been locked in mortal combat since the beginning of time.

"What's the plan?" Max asked, calm again.

"I'm thinking that we call it a day. Peggy's going to just go home after work, just like she always does when Travis is home. Tomorrow night is the night. That's the first night that Travis is gone, and I think that Wednesday is her big night out. At least it is her first opportunity for a night out. I say that we plan for a late one tomorrow."

"What about lunch?" Max asked. "We gonna go have lunch with her again tomorrow?"

Skip thought about that for a while. "I think so," Skip replied.

"Should Ben have lunch with her again, if no one else shows up?"

Skip thought again. "I don't think so. Let's just walk in and sit down like we're working together. See what happens. See if she says anything to us."

"What if Proctor comes in and she says something like, 'look, there's your old buddy Ben Ralston'? Then what?"

"You'll think of something," Skip said. "You've got a knack for wiggling out of that kind of thing."

"Right," Max responded. "I just love being put on the spot."

"I know you do," Skip laughed again.

Max's computer loaded his email, and he worked his way through the messages. Skip was lost in his own thoughts.

"You know something? That might not be a bad thing," he called over to Max.

"What might not be a bad thing?" Max asked.

"If Proctor had a little competition," Skip replied. "I wonder what he would think about that."

"Maybe we'll find out tomorrow," Max replied.

Chapter 13

Wednesday

Peggy drove down Dakota Ave to the interchange with New Highway 30, took the on ramp and merged with the early morning traffic eastbound toward Nevada. She and Travis had spent the evening like they always spent their Tuesday evenings: she made supper, they ate in silence, then Travis went to his office to prepare for the class on Wednesday. Peggy cleaned up the dishes and the kitchen, then went down to the family room and turned on Netflix. Travis called it the family room; Peggy called it the TV room. She and Travis didn't have a family. It was just them. Usually Travis would join her later, halfway into a show. Sometimes she wondered why they had such a big house. They could certainly get along with something smaller. Maybe a townhouse. Maybe Travis liked a big house; they had never even talked about it.

Peggy pulled through the gate and into the nearly empty employee parking lot at BioForce. Peggy liked to get to work early. Travis was always still sleeping when she got up. Usually he would get out of bed and come down to eat breakfast before she left, but lately he had been staying in bed. She wondered if he was seeing someone else. She wondered if he was just using his classes as a reason to get out of the house and away.

Peggy walked through the employee entrance and up the flight of stairs to the hallway that led to her office. Sandra, her receptionist, wasn't in yet. Peggy looked at Sandra's desk to see if there was anything that needed her attention, but the desktop was empty except for the October issue of *Cosmopolitan* and a Nora Roberts novel.

Peggy unlocked the door to her own office, turned on her computer and waited for it to boot up. The plan for the day was to go over the contracts that were coming up for renewal. Allan's was one of them. Even though Allan didn't like to talk business at their lunch dates, today she would at least broach the subject of renewing the contract with him. Maybe hint that she was taking other bids. Remind him that she had a little bit of pull, that she wasn't just there for his convenience.

Peggy pulled up the contract and gave it a quick scan. Then she sighed and closed the contract. She would worry about it later. She pulled up the janitorial contract instead.

Peggy was almost finished reviewing the janitorial contract when she heard Sandra come in and go to her desk. Peggy kept working. There were days when she and Sandra hardly talked. Sandra's true title was Office Manager, but for some reason Peggy still thought of her as "the receptionist."

Peggy's office phone rang. She picked it up. "Yes," she answered.

It was Sandra. "There are some people from the state here to talk to you."

"Do you know what they want?" Peggy asked.

"No, I don't. They want to talk to you." Peggy thought that the receptionist's tone was a little tart.

"Okay, I'll come up." Peggy put the phone down. She could hear Sandra down the hall telling them that she was on her way.

Peggy walked the short distance from her office to the reception area. A man and a woman were waiting. They had not taken chairs. Peggy thought that they looked quite official standing there. The man was dressed in a suit, the woman wore a DNR uniform. She had a gun belt around her waist, a pistol at her side. Peggy wondered what it would be like to go to work every day wearing a gun.

Peggy extended her hand to the two. "Peggy Bentley," she introduced herself. "Can I help you?"

"Bill Rossman, from the State Environmental Department," the man said as he shook her hand. "This is Virginia Broward from the Department of Natural Resources.

Peggy shook Broward's hand. It was firm, like a man's hand shake. Peggy was fascinated by her, and a bit intimidated.

"Yes, I think you can help us," Rossman continued in a casual tone. "We need to talk to you about the cleaning water that you use in your tanks, how and where it is being disposed of."

"Let's go to my office," Peggy suggested. The man and the woman followed her to her office.

"Please, sit down," Peggy said. They both took seats.

Rossman got right to the point. "We are just checking with the different ethanol plants in the area. We aren't investigating anyone right now," he reassured her, "just getting some information and documentation gathered up."

"Anything," Peggy replied. "Whatever you need. We want to cooperate with the authorities in any way that we can. We take compliance to the regulations quite seriously here."

"I'm sure that you do," he continued. "We found some pollution in a waterway that goes through Story and Polk counties. It has been identified as possibly some kind of industrial cleaning chemicals. We're going around to all of the industries in the area who are registered with the state to use certain regulated cleaning agents, and we're collecting copies of their documentation."

"That sounds pretty serious," Peggy remarked.

"It's just routine," Rossman reassured her. "We don't have any idea where the contamination is coming from at this point. But right now we are eliminating everyone that we can. We simply need to review your documentation for the disposal of your cleaning water so that we can eliminate you from our investigation."

"We contract out the cleaning," Peggy told them. "I'm sure that the cleaning company has all the documentation on file. I don't have anything here. I'll have to contact someone there and have them send it to me."

"Do you know where the cleaning wastewater is being disposed of?" Officer Broward asked the question. Peggy thought that her tone was a little accusatory. "Do you know if it is going to an approved disposal facility, and where that facility is located?"

Peggy felt her heartbeat quicken. "I don't know specifically, but I do know that it is being taken by tanker truck to a facility in Princeton, Missouri."

"And how do you know that?"

Peggy most certainly heard the accusation in the DNR officer's voice this time. "The CEO of the cleaning company told me," Peggy answered.

"Who might that be, and what is the name of the cleaning company?" the woman asked as she pulled a notebook out of her breast pocket.

"The company is Cleanguard. The CEO and owner is Allan Proctor," Peggy answered, trying to sound authoritative.

Broward was writing the information in her notebook "Thank you," she said as she wrote, the tone a little less accusatory than it had been.

"If you can just get that documentation, scan it and send it to my office, I would appreciate it," Rossman jumped back into the conversation. "Before the end of the week would be fine. Just routine," he said reassuringly.

"I can do that," Peggy said in what she meant as a lighthearted voice, hoping that her panicked feelings didn't show. The tone of the DNR officer had unnerved her. Peggy had the feeling that there wasn't anything routine about the visit.

"Thank you for your time," Rossman stood up and handed her his card. "Law enforcement," the man tilted his head to indicate the DNR officer, who was already walking out the door. "They're always all business." He smiled and walked out of the office. Peggy stood at her desk, holding his business card and listening to their footsteps as they left.

The two state officials walked out of the building and into the parking lot. "What do you think?" Rossman asked the DNR officer.

"I don't know," she replied. "She was kind of nervous."

The man laughed. "You make me nervous."

The woman laughed as they got into her pickup with the DNR insignia on both doors. "Where to now?" she asked.

"Next ethanol plant," he answered.

"We'll just have to see what she gets back to us with," Broward remarked. "Probably nothing there, but we'll see. I'm going to check out this Cleanguard guy, though," she continued. "See what his deal is."

Peggy sat down at her desk. She fished her personal cell out of her purse and saw a missed call from Allan. He hadn't left a message. She started to push the recall button, but instead put the phone back in her purse and picked up her office phone. Allan's cell phone rang six times, then went to voicemail. Peggy ended the call without leaving a message.

Peggy got up and walked to the reception area where she found Sandra absorbed in the *Cosmo*. She looked up at Peggy.

"Mr. Proctor called while you were in your meeting and said that he could not make the luncheon meeting again today, for the same reasons as yesterday, but he plans to meet with you later on today as planned."

Peggy was a little annoyed, and she showed it.

"Don't you have something to do?" she asked the receptionist, who was taken aback by the question. Peggy had never expected anything more than someone to answer the phone and take messages. Sandra didn't know what to say.

Peggy went back to her office, leaving Sandra stuffing the magazine into a drawer. Peggy called Allan's phone again. She waited for the six rings, then left a message.

"Allan, I need to talk to you ASAP. It's business and it's important. Please call me back on my office phone."

Peggy ended the call. She didn't know what else to do. She reassured herself that all was good. Allan was a good businessman. He ran a good business. Gordon was a good man, too. Other than the issue of the illegal laborers, which she understood even if she wasn't comfortable with it, Allan didn't cut corners. Peggy was sure of that. The DNR wouldn't deal with aliens, would they? But Peggy couldn't get the official visit out of her head.

Peggy went back to reviewing contracts. Twice more she tried to get in touch with Allan, but he would not answer his phone. Peggy looked up to see Sandra standing at her door.

"I'm going to lunch, if that's okay," she said.

"I'm right behind you," Peggy tried to address her in a nicer voice. She felt bad that she had snapped earlier. Sandra left without a comment. Peggy got up from her desk and gathered her purse and phone. She looked around to make sure that she wasn't forgetting anything. As she walked out, she locked the door to her office and then the door to the reception area. She walked down the stairs to the parking lot and drove out onto the highway.

Skip had shown up at the office in a late model Chevy Impala. Max was already there, waiting. Skip was sitting in the car with the window down as Max came out of the building and locked the door.

"What is this?" Max exclaimed.

"Enterprise," Skip replied. "Got us an undercover car for the day. What do you think?"

"Reminds me of those Impalas we had one time for patrol cars. Back when Ford got out of the Police Interceptor business for a while," Max said.

Max climbed into the passenger side of the Impala and hunkered down in the seat. "Man, is this a blast from the past?" he said. "Weren't we driving Impalas when we won the Powerball?"

"I don't remember what we were driving," Skip answered. "Maybe."

Skip pulled out of the parking lot and drove to New 30, then toward Nevada. Skip was in a hurry and put the accelerator to the floor. He let it up at eighty. He wasn't Max, so he had no desire to see how fast the Impala would go. Besides, there was a lot more traffic on New 30 than there had been on the Maxwell blacktop. Skip wanted to get to the café and seated before Peggy got there. As he passed the ethanol plant he looked toward the parking lot.

"Still there," Max said. Skip turned his attention back to his driving.

They got to the West Café just a few minutes before noon. The parking lot was nearly empty, mostly farmers' pickup trucks, getting there before the lunch crowd from the ethanol plants and the businesses around the area. Skip parked the car and the two got out. Skip went through the door with Max right behind him.

"Take a seat, boys," the waitress said as she passed by.

The two found a booth where they could see most of the others in the restaurant without drawing attention to themselves. Just as they sat down, Peggy came in and took a seat in the same booth that Max had shared with her the day before, and Proctor had the day before that.

"Creature of habit," Max remarked.

"Aren't we all?" Skip replied.

The waitress came to their table with water. The two detectives were ready to order without looking at the menus.

"Hot beef sandwich and a hamburger," she said before the two could order. She pointed her pen at each of them as she said it. "Coke and Diet Coke," she continued, pen poised over her pad.

"You're good," Max commented.

"It's my job," she smiled. "That it today, boys?"

"For now," Max replied.

Max glanced over toward Peggy's table and caught her looking their way. He waved, and she waved back. Max got up and walked across the restaurant to sit down in Peggy's both.

"Having lunch alone again?" Max asked.

"Probably," Peggy answered. "I'm supposed to meet someone. He cancelled on me this morning, but I left him a couple messages and I'm hoping he shows up, anyway."

"Business?" Max asked.

"Yes, it is," Peggy answered tersely.

"Allan?" Max asked.

"Yes."

Max sat for a moment, but Peggy didn't say anything more. The waitress came to take her order.

"Well, I'm over there with one of my associates," Max said, pointing toward Skip. "You're welcome to come over and eat with us. We're talking business, though."

"No, thank you," Peggy said. "I'll just wait here for Allan, if he shows up."

Max smiled at Peggy, slid out of the booth and walked back to the table with Skip.

"She's stood up again," Max said in a low voice. "She really needs to talk to him, too. I think that he is trying to avoid her."

"She tell you that?" Skip asked.

"Well, not in so many words, but I can read between the lines, and she has that body language going on. She's in a panic."

"We'll see what happens," Skip said.

The two got their food and started eating. Peggy's chef salad arrived about the same time. She picked at it a bit, but spent much of her time watching the door. Max and Skip were eating and chatting, talking about the same things that they always talked about, which was pretty much nothing important.

Max looked up to see Peggy getting out of her seat. She had paid and was leaving. Max and Skip still had half-full plates in front of them.

"She's leaving," Max tapped Skip's arm.

Skip frantically looked for the waitress. She was taking an order on the other side. Skip tried to get her attention, but to no avail. She put in an order at the window and stood talking to the cook.

"Come on, come on, come on," Skip was saying under his breath.

Finally she turned around and Skip got her attention. She came over to the table.

"Say, we got a phone call and we need to get going," he told her.

"I'll get the ticket," she said.

"How much is it?" Skip asked.

The waitress was looking at the two plates and started adding it up in her head.

"More than forty bucks?" Skip asked.

"No," she laughed, "more like twenty bucks."

Skip was pulling two twenties out of his billfold. He handed them to the waitress as he got up.

"Here," Skip said as he placed the bills in her hand. "Keep it, we need to get going."

"It'll only take a minute," she protested.

"It's okay, we gotta go," Skip said. "Besides, we'll expense it out."

Max was already heading out the door. Skip crossed the parking lot to the Impala where Max was waiting for him to unlock the door. "Like that didn't draw any attention," he said to Skip over the roof of the car as they were getting in.

Meanwhile, Peggy was on New 30, driving past the ethanol plant. She had to think. She continued west toward Ames. Right then, all she knew was that she wanted to talk to Travis.

Chapter 14

Wednesday

Skip took the quick route out of town, heading west on Old 30. Just past the city limits he turned the Impala south on Airport Road. When he got to New 30, he turned west again and drove past the ethanol plant. He slowed down as they passed the parking lot.

"She's not there," Max commented.

"Where is she?" Skip asked.

"Not here," Max shrugged. "Maybe she went looking for Proctor."

"Think so?" asked Skip.

"I don't know," Max replied. "Maybe she went to get gas? Who knows where she went? Turn around and drive through the lot."

Skip pulled over at the next drive and turned around. He went back to the employee lot and drove in. It was not a huge lot, just four rows of parking. They checked the lot with one quick drive through and Skip pulled back onto the highway.

"Where to?" Max asked.

"If she's looking for Proctor I would say that she's heading down toward Maxwell."

"What if she's not?"

"Then after we check out Proctor's places, we'll come back."

"Sounds good," Max agreed. "I mean, we're grasping at straws."

Skip pulled back onto New 30 and proceeded east, through and past Nevada. When he got to the Maxwell blacktop he turned south and accelerated. The miles clicked by. Max watched up ahead for Peggy's car, but the road was empty.

"How fast ya going?" Max asked.

"Hundred," Skip replied.

"Kind of childish, isn't it?" Max responded.

"No, a hundred-twenty is childish," Skip quipped.

As the two detectives flew past Proctor's house, they saw the white Silverado parked in front. "She's not with Proctor. His truck's there, but her car's not," Max noted.

"We'll backtrack," Skip said. "See if we got in front of her somehow. Maybe we'll still meet her coming this direction."

"Let's do it," Max replied.

Skip pulled off the blacktop and turned around at the next gravel intersection. They drove back past Proctor's house.

"I don't think that she's going to come here," Max reflected. "I mean, I don't see her confronting him for standing her up for lunch right there at his place. She doesn't seem the type to go on a rampage."

"I agree." Skip continued to the intersection with New 30, crossed through and continued north to Old 30. He turned toward Nevada and drove into town on Lincolnway. They continued through, past the West Café and out of town again. Skip took the same route that he had when they left the café just a half hour earlier. As they drove past the ethanol plant for the second time, Peggy's car still was not in the employee lot.

"Now what?" Skip asked rhetorically.

"She went home," Max suggested.

"In the middle of the afternoon?" Skip asked.

"Maybe she didn't feel good," Max suggested.

"Maybe," Skip replied.

Skip continued west on New 30, bypassing most of the city of Ames as he drove. At County Line Road, the blacktop that marked the line between Story and Boone counties, Skip turned north. They passed under the Union Pacific Railroad overpass and continued north, into the country. After a few miles, Skip turned into a rural housing development on the Boone County side of the road.

"Know which house is theirs?" Max asked.

"That one up there with Peggy's silver Lexus convertible in the drive," Skip replied nonchalantly.

"Good one," Max snarked back at him. "What now?"

"Let's hunker down for the long haul," Skip said. "Might as well get serious with this stakeout."

Max nodded. Skip drove to the end of the concrete street where it turned into a circle. An unpicked cornfield lay beyond that. He turned the Impala around so that it was facing back down the street toward Travis and Peggy's house. There were four houses on the circle, each with a Realtor's sign in front of it. They all looked unlived in.

"Spec houses that didn't spec out?" Max observed.

Skip moved his seat back as far as he could get it, then lay back in it, resting his head on the headrest. Max was squirming around.

"I gotta pee," he finally said.

"Cornfield right there," Skip replied. "You're a farm boy."

Max climbed out of the car and walked into the field.

When Peggy had gotten home, Travis had been in his office working. As she came in she heard him call out, "Who's there?"

"Just me," Peggy had replied.

Travis had come up from the lower level of the house, where his office was. "What's wrong?" he asked. Peggy was sitting in an easy chair in the front room, looking out the window at the countryside. She didn't answer.

"Are you okay?" Travis asked.

"I'm fine," Peggy answered with a sigh. "Rough morning, so I just decided to take a long lunch and get away for a little while. I need to decompress."

"What's going on?" Travis asked, taking a seat in the chair opposite from her.

"State investigators found industrial cleaning chemicals in a river somewhere, and they are going around to all of the ethanol plants and asking for documentation on wastewater disposal. So they paid me a visit this morning, wanting ours."

"What's wrong with that?" Travis asked. "You have documentation, don't you? No big deal."

"Well, yes and no," Peggy explained. "The contractor that does all the cleaning has them, and I can't seem to get him to answer his phone."

"So how soon do you have to get it to them?" Travis asked.

"Friday," Peggy answered.

"Well, that's three days," Travis said. "It's early. He's probably busy and can't answer his phone right now."

"He's always busy and can't answer his phone," Peggy snapped. "I can't ever get ahold of him."

Travis was taken aback by her tone. He didn't say anything.

"I'm going to sit here for a while and take it easy, then I'm going back to the office," she said.

"Anything I can do?" Travis asked.

"Just be around," Peggy said in a quiet voice. "Just be here."

"I can do that," Travis said as he got up. "Okay if I go down and keep prepping for my class tonight?"

"Sure," said Peggy, again with a sigh.

Travis went back down to the office in the lower level. Peggy sat looking out the window, lost in thought. A silver car drove by with two men in it. One was looking toward the house. It looked like Ben Ralston and the guy that he was having lunch with. She wondered what they were doing. Probably checking on one of the cornfields that surrounded the housing development. She looked at her phone to see if she had missed a call or a text from Allan, but there was nothing. Peggy dozed off with her phone in her hand. Peggy had a history of depression, and sleeping was one of the ways she coped with it.

Peggy woke up an hour later to find Travis talking to her.

"Are you okay?" he was asking.

"What time is it?" she asked him.

"Two o'clock," Travis said.

"I have to go back to work," Peggy said, getting up out of the chair. She gathered up her purse and put her phone inside it, fishing out her car keys at the same time.

"I'll be home around ten, maybe before," Travis was saying.

"That's fine," Peggy said.

"You want me to call you when we take a break?" Travis asked.

"No," Peggy sighed. "I'm already exhausted. I'll probably be in bed asleep when you get home."

Peggy went out to her car. She noticed the car that had gone by earlier was parked at the end of the street. She couldn't tell whether anyone was anyone in it or not. "It probably wasn't even those insurance guys," she thought. "Maybe something is finally happening with one of those empty houses that has been on the market for so long." Peggy got in her car, backed out of the drive and drove toward County Line Road.

When Peggy came out of the house, both Max and Skip scrunched down. Max got so low that he could not see out the windshield. Skip peered through the steering wheel and over the dash. Skip knew that from that distance, he wouldn't be visible if he kept his head below the seat back. The only way she could see him was if he was silhouetted through the windows.

Peggy pulled out of the driveway and drove to County Line Road. As soon as she turned onto the blacktop, Skip fired up the Impala and followed her, keeping as much distance between them and Peggy as possible without losing sight of her. A car pulled off a side road and onto the blacktop between them. Skip relaxed. It gave him a little bit of cover to work with. He sped up and got behind the car, closer to Peggy.

Peggy turned onto New 30, eastbound toward the ethanol plant. The car following her went straight. Skip slowed and waited for Peggy to get a half mile down the highway before he turned and followed.

"She's going back to work," Max guessed.

"Maybe," Skip replied. "I wonder what that was all about."

Max didn't answer.

They followed Peggy until she turned into the parking lot at the ethanol plant. The two drove by and watched her park. Skip continued a mile down the highway to the intersection with Airport Road, turned around and went back.

"Hunker down?" Max asked.

"Looking for a place to set up," Skip said. "I don't want to sit in that implement dealership lot again. Too visible sitting there for so long, but I don't see anywhere else."

"Just go in there and sit as long as we can get away with it," Max suggested. "What are they going to do, call Carlisle again? If we get chased out, we go somewhere else."

Skip was already turning into the implement dealership. Max was right, the dealership was as good as it was going to get for the time being. Skip pulled up between the same two combines he had parked between on Monday, trying to hug one of them so he wasn't quite as visible from the dealership windows. The two detectives lay back in their seats and got ready to wait.

"I hate stakeouts," Max remarked.

"You ever notice that on TV they don't show the hours and hours that cops sit on stakeout while nothing happens?" Skip asked.

"I'm going to snooze a little," Max replied, and closed his eyes.

Peggy called Allan's cell phone twice more after she got back to the office, and both times she got his voicemail. Both times she left him a message to call back. She continued to busy herself going over the security contract. Allan had mentioned one day that maybe he could take over that contract as well as the cleaning contract. Peggy had asked what he knew about security, and he had told her that he had run a security company before he married Brenda. He said that with a little capital, it wouldn't be hard for him to get something up and going. She had hesitated when he first suggested it, and he had let it go. But lately he had started asking when the contract was up.

Peggy's work phone rang. She picked it up. It was Sandra.

"Mr. Proctor on the phone," the receptionist reported. Peggy picked it up.

"Hey, what's so urgent?" Allan asked in a curious tone.

"Where have you been?" snapped Peggy.

"Working," Allan shot back. "I'm pretty busy. I just got your messages and I called you right back. What's up?"

"Do you have the documentation for the wastewater that you're taking down to Missouri?" Peggy asked.

"Sure," Allan said. "Of course I do. Why?"

"Because I need for you to get it to me as soon as you can," Peggy explained. "The state is doing some kind of investigation because they found chemicals in some water somewhere, and all the ethanol plants have to send in their documentation. I need it."

"No problem," Allan said. "I can get it to you next week."

"I need it today," Peggy replied. "I've got to have it in to them by Friday, and I want to make copies for my own files. I should have been keeping a file all along, but it just never occurred to me that anyone would come looking for it. I need that documentation today."

"Take it easy," Allan tried to calm her over the phone. "It is all fine. I'll bring the paperwork tonight, when I meet you at the lake." Peggy didn't respond. "Is that okay?" he asked. "Is that soon enough?"

"I guess so," Peggy said, resigned.

"It will be fine," Allan reassured her. "So, how did you find out about this investigation?"

"A guy from the State Environmental Agency and a woman officer from the DNR came by the office this morning," Peggy explained.

"And what did they say?" Allan pressed.

"Just that they were doing an investigation and they need that paperwork."

"No, what exactly did they say?" Allan asked, his voice sharpening.

Peggy did not respond for a moment. "I'll talk to you about it tonight," she said.

"Six-thirty," Allan changed the subject. "You stop by the grocery store and pick up some hot dogs, buns and some chips. I'll bring a bottle of wine and some dip. We'll start a fire in the shelter house and have a little picnic, together. It will be nice and cozy. It will be fun."

Peggy still didn't say anything.

"And I'll bring all the papers and documentation with me."

"I'll see you then," Peggy finally replied.

Allan ended the call. For some reason that she couldn't put her finger on, Peggy was beginning to wonder about Allan. Something didn't feel right. At home that afternoon, talking to Travis, that had felt right. Even though they seldom talked anymore, she knew that when she needed someone, she could find Travis. Talking to Allan, she suddenly realized, was always dictated by Allan's terms. Allan was around when he wanted to be around. At first Allan had been exciting. He was someone new, so much different than Travis. He had listened to her every word, and she had listened to him. But over time, the relationship had turned into a fling, like a couple of high schoolers, not even a real affair. They always talked about a future together, but if Peggy was honest with herself, she knew that's all it was: talk.

But Peggy wasn't honest with herself very often. She sneaked around with Allan, catching fleeting kisses and feeling each other up in a car, usually her car, parked like a couple of teenage kids on a date, giggling and laughing while Allan fumbled around the back of her bra trying to get it unsnapped. It was far from satisfying. Peggy was an adult, not a high school girl. She didn't want to go steady, she wanted a real relationship, and this was no real relationship. She could see that there never was going to be one. But at this point, whatever it was, Peggy didn't know how to get out of it.

Peggy sat in her office the rest of the afternoon, lost in thought. Outside and across the highway, Max was snoring, while Skip was fighting not to close his eyes and join him.

Chapter 15

Wednesday

Milton had been cruising all morning. Slowly he was working his way toward the truck stop. Earlier he had been up in area one, taking routine calls and covering for the area one officer while she took a half dozen reports of vandalism to a motor vehicle. Milton had done a drive-by to check on her while she took one of them, and he had stopped in the middle of the street to see if there were any leads that he could follow up for her, but there was nothing. It looked like some teenagers had shot out some car windows with a BB gun overnight. It happened more than most people knew, which just made it routine for the patrol officers. There was nothing to go on yet, but shooting out car windows with a BB gun was addicting for kids, and Milton knew that once they got started, they usually couldn't quit until they got caught. In the meantime, the night shift officers would start watching for patterns. The utility officers would start patrolling the residential streets with their headlights turned off, watching for cars full of teenage boys (the culprits were inevitably boys) roving around the dark, empty residential streets. Two, three, maybe even four nights of this routine, and eventually the night shift officers would narrow it down to a place and a time, and then they would converge on the area and nail the offenders. At the same time, the School Resource Officer would monitor her social media. The kids loved to connect with the School Resource Officer on social media—they thought it was cool—but they didn't realize that information was going both directions. Right now, the School Resource Officer was looking at all the chatter, watching for someone to say something about the vandalism. But for now it was just a matter of how much restitution they would rack up for their parents to pay.

Milton let his mind wander. He and Monica had taken Essie to Cold Stone for ice cream the evening before. It had been nice. While they stood in line, Essie sat on Milton's foot with her arms wrapped around his leg, riding on his foot as he walked through the line. Several times he lifted his foot off the ground and swung her back and forth like a swing. Monica kept telling her to get off the dirty floor, but it was too much fun for her, and the only thing that finally pried her off Milton's leg was a chocolate ice cream cone with sprinkles.

Monica had bought, like she promised. Milton had insisted that he could pay, but Monica insisted louder, and Milton had relented. They had gone outside to sit at a table, taking advantage of one of the last warm evenings before the frost would start to set in. He and Monica had sat at the table chatting, while Essie ran around dripping melted ice cream all over. When they were done, Milton took Essie's sticky hand in his, led her to the restroom and held her up over the sink while he ran tap water over her hands to wash them clean. When they walked out, Milton pretended that he was her father. At least he hoped the people thought that he was her father.

Milton thought about his own father. Milton had grown up in Sioux City, a river town on the banks of the Missouri River. His father was a machinist, a job skill that he had learned in the navy. His mother worked at the State Farm Insurance Agency. Milton's dad had worked at the same job for Milton's whole life. Doing the same thing every day, eight to five, Monday through Friday, for decades. His mother had gone back to work when he and his sister were teenagers. Before that, she had stayed at home taking care of the kids and making sure there was supper on the table when Milton's father came home from work.

Milton's parents were Christian, but Milton wasn't sure what kind of Christians. They went every Sunday morning to services at the House of Christ. Milton and his sister had attended services with them until they left home for college. And even after that, when they came back home to visit, Milton's parents insisted the whole family attend together.

Milton did not know how to describe the House of Christ. It was a church that was loosely affiliated with some other churches. It wasn't a big church. Maybe they were Fundamentalists. He didn't know. Fundamentalist was such a broad term. What he did know was that the Christ who lived there was not the Christ that Milton wanted to believe in. The Christ who lived at House of Christ Church was judgmental. The Christ who lived at the House of Christ Church did not like the Mexicans coming to Sioux City to work. The Christ who lived at the House of Christ did not like people who wanted to celebrate their love for one other if they were the same sex. His parents' Christ only loved babies born of parents who weren't mixed in some way. In their Christian faith there were strict rules, and Milton's parents thought like the Christ who lived in their church instructed them to think. He was their teacher. He was their savior and they were special in His eyes. They were chosen, and their lives were pure. Their reward would be everlasting life. And every week the preacher reminded them of how they were to live, how they were to think, and most of all, who would be judged unworthy. He spoke for the church's Christ, and the people listened. They were God fearing people, or at least they were Christ fearing people.

Milton's father and mother did well. They were not rich, but his father made a good wage, and between him and his wife, they provided for their family. And while Milton's father liked to point out how well he had done without a college education, he encouraged both of his children to go to college, even though he strongly warned them to be careful not to be indoctrinated by the liberal educational system that was taking over the country. He reminded them to be strong in their beliefs, which he also reminded them were the ones that they were instructed to believe by the House of Christ church.

But when Milton's older sister Judy went off to college, she met a Vietnamese boy. He was first-generation American. His parents had named him Charlie, because that was an American name, and no one would mistake him for anything but an American with a name like Charlie. Charlie's mother and father had fled war-torn Vietnam in the seventies. They had been brought to the US as refugees. Charlie was the oldest of their four children, born just two weeks after his parents arrived on American soil. His mother had carried him in her belly as they escaped. Charlie fell in love with Milton's sister, and over their four years of college, their love blossomed. When they graduated, he with a degree in geology, she with a degree in public administration, the two had married in a traditional Vietnamese wedding ceremony. Milton's parents had chosen not to attend. Milton had. It was beautiful.

It was after the wedding, at the reception, that Judy told Milton that she had wanted to have a wedding ceremony at the House of Christ Church, and then have the Vietnamese ceremony after their honeymoon, but that their father had told her that she could not marry a Vietnamese man in their church. And so they had done the Vietnamese ceremony only. She also told Milton that the pastor at the Lutheran church that had sponsored the refugees when they came to the United States, and where Charlie's parents attended services, was the official performing the Vietnamese ceremony. "It was all just trappings, the Vietnamese part," his sister had told him, defending herself to the only family member there. But she didn't have to defend her choice to Milton. Milton could see she was happy, and he was happy for her. Judy and Charlie had moved to Oklahoma where Charlie got a job with an oil company. Judy found a job in a school, and now they had two kids of their own. Milton made it a point to stay in touch.

So now Milton wondered how he was going to explain Monica and Essie. Would his parents accept them? He didn't think so. Would they put on a good front? He didn't think that they would do that, either. They would judge her and him. They would even judge Essie. Milton knew that they would, and he knew he would not hold his tongue when they judged Essie. Milton could walk into bar full of bikers and clean house; he carried a gun to work every day, and he was willing to lay his own life on the line to protect others' lives, but he was afraid to tell his parents about Monica. That was a problem.

Milton drove along the street that ran beside the truck stop. Carlisle was parked in the corner. Milton skipped the drive through and drove up alongside the deputy's patrol car, rolling down his window.

"Was wondering if you were going to make it," Carlisle remarked.

"Just out patrolling," Milton said. "Anything going on out in the county?"

"Same old crap," Carlisle answered between bites. "People running into farm equipment. Couple of kids ran into the back of a tractor last night after I got off. Killed one of them. The other's in the hospital. They don't think he's gonna make it."

"That's too bad," Milton said. "Lucky you didn't have to go investigate that one."

"No shit," Carlisle replied. "It was a mess, they said." Carlisle stuffed some fries in his mouth. "Guess what?" he said as he chewed. "The state's sending a biologist over to look at those dead fish on Friday. Ten o'clock. I'm going with him to check what's going on back there behind Higgins's place."

"Sounds good," Milton replied. "Gonna do a little fishing, just not in the river, huh?"

"Yep," said Carlisle. "I'm off tomorrow and Friday, but I got the sergeant to authorize a little OT. He's always talking about 'interagency cooperation.' I told him this was going to be a good chance for interagency cooperation."

"Sounds like it to me," Milton laughed. "That's why I come over here and watch you eat every day."

"Don't you eat?" Carlisle asked.

"I bring my lunch, but I already ate it," Milton replied. "I don't like eating fast food every day."

"Health nut," Carlisle shook his head.

Milton chatted with Carlisle. It was just small talk, mostly shop talk. Carlisle was much more busy out in the county than Milton was in town. Not that Ames didn't have crime, but it went in waves, and lately they had been having a stretch of good luck and a bit of a low crime wave. He was enjoying it while he could. Things could change fast, and they were bound to change.

"Okay," Milton finally said, "I need to do some crime fighting today. At least write a speeding ticket or something."

"Catch ya later," Carlisle said as Milton pulled away.

"Good luck on your fishing trip," Milton called back.

Milton drove up the street, across Old 30 and toward the north part of town. He wound around past the softball fields and River Valley Park, past the golf course, past the parking lot where Higgins had planned to collect the ransom for Tucker back in early summer, and he finally found himself at the mall. Milton parked his car on the yellow curb in front of the entrance, picked up the radio and called out.

"Ames, one-twenty-six, I'll be out at the mall doing some foot patrol. I'll be on portable if you need me."

The radio squawked when the dispatcher answered. "Ten-four, one-twenty-six."

Milton got out of his patrol car, turned on his portable radio. He locked the door and closed it. Out of habit he looked across at the passenger side door to make sure it was locked, and pulled up on the handle of the rear door to check it as well. Milton walked through the entrance and into the mall. Shopping on duty was against the rules and regulations, but getting out into the public and being seen was encouraged by the administration. It was called community based policing. Max had taught Milton well. It was all about the spin. If you wanted to get out and buy a new pair of shoes on duty, you didn't go shopping for them. You got out of your car on foot patrol, and then you did a little community based policing at the shoe store, chatting it up with the salesperson, acting like you were interested in shoes, and then you just sort of bought them. That was the grey area. The other side of it was hustling out to the patrol car and throwing the shopping bag in the back seat before anyone figured out that community policing and shopping on duty were one and the same. But most shoppers didn't give it much thought.

Max had explained the power of community policing to Milton when he had just started on the police department and was still in training. Max told him about an officer who had gotten a two week suspension without pay for taking off his gunbelt one evening, locking it up in his patrol car and playing basketball with some kids in the park. That was before community based policing came along. That same officer would get a commendation for doing the same thing these days, and probably get a video of it posted on the internet, where everyone would comment on what a great guy he was for playing basketball with the kids, instead of arresting people or writing tickets. "Gotta flow with the times," Max had told him. "It's not about the crime, it's about the dime," Max liked to say. Milton had no idea what that meant. He didn't know if Max was saying that it was about money, or if it was just Max making up some random rhyme, which he often did. It didn't make any difference: Milton got the idea. It was all about the city's priorities. The cops with their own personal agendas, especially those cops whose personal agendas were in conflict with the city, were destined to leave the department after thirty years still at the entry level. Just like his father had been a machinist all his life, there were cops that would come in an area patrol officer and be an area patrol officer their whole careers. Officers who wanted to move up in the organization worked with the city, not against it. Milton made sure that he was on the right track.

Milton walked into the jewelry store just inside the main doors. He wandered along the display cases looking at the watches.

"Can I help you find something, sir?"

Milton looked up at the woman behind the counter. She looked friendly, like she really wanted to help.

"I'm just getting out of the car to stretch my legs," he said. "Thought that I might stop in and see what you have for rings, while I'm here." He felt a little awkward.

"What kind of rings are you looking for?" the woman asked.

"Um, engagement rings, I guess," Milton replied.

"They're over here." The woman moved down the line of display cases and stopped behind one of them, opening it up. "Do you have anything in particular in mind?" she asked. "Are you looking for a wedding set or just an engagement ring?"

"I don't know. I guess just an engagement ring," Milton answered as he scanned the displays. He spotted a gold ring with one diamond. It was simple. Milton liked things simple. He didn't like clutter. "Let me take a look at that one." He pointed at the one that had caught his eye.

"That is a nice one," the woman remarked. "It is a solitaire. Can't go wrong with a nice solitaire. Just about any wedding band will go nicely with it."

Milton had not thought about a wedding band. He just wanted to get engaged; he wasn't sure he was ready to get married. The woman handed the ring to Milton. He turned the little tag attached to it and looked at the price. He had to control himself not to gasp. "The nice thing about a solitaire is that we can change the diamond out to something a little bigger if you like." Milton was barely listening to the woman. "We don't charge you for doing that, we just charge you for the difference in the cost of the diamonds," she added.

Milton stood looking at the ring. He liked it a lot, but he was thinking that he needed to look around more. He couldn't just take the first viable option. This ring had to be special. Plus, he hadn't realized that an engagement ring was going to cost more than he made in a month. Actually, more than he made in two months, before he paid his bills.

"All our settings are guaranteed for life," the woman continued. "Just bring it in twice a year for cleaning and we check the setting to make sure that it is not bent and that nothing is coming loose."

Milton handed the ring back to the saleswoman. "I need to think about it," he said, as she took the ring from him. "I was just looking." He stood up straight to leave.

"Well, let us know if we can help you," the saleswoman replied. She put the ring in the display case. "Anything else that you would like to see?"

"Not right now," Milton responded, feeling a little whipped.

Milton left the jewelry store and strolled through the mall. There were two other jewelry stores, one of them right across from the one that he had just left, but Milton did not go into them. First of all, he didn't want to look obvious, and besides, his mind was all over the place. He walked out of the mall and into the sunlight. He went to his patrol car, unlocked the door and got in. He squirmed around in the seat, buckling his seatbelt and adjusting the Toughbook computer that sat on a pedestal mount next to him. He picked up the radio mic and brought it up toward his mouth.

"Ames, one-twenty-six is ten-eight."

"One-twenty-six, ten-four," the dispatcher responded.

Milton pulled away from the curb and drove out of the lot and onto 24th Street. He adjusted his radar to ten over the speed limit as he drove. Milton needed to get Monica out of his brain for a while and concentrate on his work. It would be hard to support a wife and kid without a job, but then Milton never knew anyone who ever got fired from the PD for thinking about marrying a girl too much.

Milton was coming up over a rise when his radar alarm went off. He glanced at the readout. The car that was coming toward him was doing forty-two in the twenty-five mile an hour speed zone. Milton locked it in and hit the red lights before the car was even past him. As he made a U turn in the middle of the street, he saw the car pull over to the side to wait for him. The driver knew that he was caught. Milton resolved to write him for ten over and cut him a little slack. It always went better if he wasn't a hard-ass about it. Another lesson from Max.

As Milton was pulling around he thought that maybe he should call his sister later on. He needed to talk to her. She would know what he should do.

Chapter 16

Wednesday

Allan finally called Peggy from his home office. She had been trying to call him all afternoon, leaving messages. Allan could hear the stress in her voice. As he ended the call, he leaned back in his chair and closed his eyes. He had to think. Allan wasn't about to panic: he knew that he was smarter than most. He had been a con artist his whole life; he liked outsmarting people. Allan had always loved those movies where they got together a team of expert criminals and con men, then concocted a big scam to steal millions. To him, the con was simply being smart. He had a great con going with BioForce that was making him a lot of money for very little work. Allan didn't seriously think that some paper pushers from the state were going to pull one on him. He just had to figure out how he was going to get around them and leave them behind. It was no big deal.

Right now, Allan had two things to deal with. The first was the chemicals migrating out of the ponds. Somehow he needed to drain those ponds, maybe spread the muck somewhere. Maybe that gal who lived down the road from him, Elizabeth what's-her-name. He had sold her that moldy hay; maybe he could convince her to let him spread the water out of the ponds on her pasture. He would tell her that it was pig manure, good fertilizer. After all, there was pig manure mixed in with it. Manure was environmentally friendly, unlike chemical fertilizers, and ol' Elizabeth seemed like a Mother Earth type. He could make it sound good to her. She would probably jump on it. But that could wait a little while.

The second thing was the documents. Allan couldn't remember when the last time was that Gordon had been able to make the round trip down to Princeton. Maybe three months ago, maybe four. He remembered the tanker truck breaking down. So they had documentation up to whenever that was. Allan had some ideas. He just had to iron them out and see what would work.

Allan dialed Gordon's cell. The phone rang three times, then Gordon picked up.

"Hey Allan, what's up?" Gordon asked. "Have you come down to look at this shit yet?"

"I have," Allan replied. "I got an idea for that, but right now I got a bigger problem."

"A bigger problem?" Gordon exclaimed. "What's bigger than polluting the aquifer with cleaning chemicals?"

Allan did not answer. He also did not appreciate Gordon's tone. "You have the documentation somewhere for the trips you made down to Princeton before the truck broke down?"

"Sure," replied Gordon, wondering what was going on.

"Okay, I need those right now," Allan told him.

"Okay," Gordon said. "I can swing by with them tomorrow—"

"I need them right now," Allan interrupted. "Get 'em and bring them up here right now. I'm at home."

"Okay," Gordon replied.

"Another thing," Allan continued. "Did you dump the tanker from Monday yet?"

"No," Gordon replied. "I thought that I better not do that until you got a look at the situation down here. I didn't want to add to it."

"Good," Allan said. "Don't dump it, I got a plan for it."

"What's going on?" Gordon asked.

"I'll tell you when you get up here," Allan replied. "Make it quick."

Allan ended the call. He had a plan alright. A good plan. Allan sat up and leaned over his desk. He took the computer mouse in his hand and clicked on the lonelyfarmers.com tab. He looked to see if there were any new women on it, putting his problems aside as he scrolled down the page. As he was doing so, he heard the school bus stop at the end of the drive, and he heard his kids yelling at their friends as they got off the bus.

It wasn't fifteen minutes after that before Gordon pulled into the drive.

"Gordon's here," Allan heard one of his kids call out.

"Thanks," he called back.

Allan heard Gordon come clomping into the house and chatting with the kids. The kids liked Gordon. He always had time for them. He was always trying to teach them Spanish, and they would run around the house repeating whatever Gordon had taught them. Gordon walked into Allan's office and tossed a dirty manila folder on his desk.

"Here's what I have," Gordon said.

Allan took the documents out and studied them.

"How many tanks have you dumped down at the farm?" Allan asked.

"Probably five or six," Gordon replied.

"I wonder if we could take these and copy them, but change the dates to fill in for those five or six loads," Allan mused.

"I don't know. So what's going on?" he asked again. Gordon was getting tired of Allan asking all of the questions and not giving him an answer to his.

Allan didn't respond. He kept looking at the documents, one after another.

"I don't know if we can do that or not," Gordon replied to the question. "The thing is, the date and time are stamped on them by a machine. Look here." Gordon pointed to the embossed stamp.

Allan looked along the border of the documents. The font was designed to make it hard to reproduce, and he could see where Gordon was pointing to some kind of seal that was stamped over the writing.

"Also, the number of gallons is different on each one of them. You would have to change a lot of things, so I don't think it is just a whiteout, typeover, print kind of thing, if that is what you're thinking about. I don't think that we can do it right here, right now. Maybe if we had some time I could find someone who could do it."

Allan pondered what Gordon told him. "We don't have that much time," he said as he took one of the forms, lifted the lid on the printer and placed the form over the glass. Allan punched in the number six for the number of copies and pushed print.

"Allan, tell me what is going on," Gordon demanded.

Allan looked up as if he had not even been aware that Gordon was standing in the office. "Peggy has to send them in to the state. I need to get them to her tonight," he explained.

"I thought that the state never looks at those," Gordon remarked.

"Well, they do when they are investigating chemicals leaked into the river," Allan said matter-of-factly.

"That's not good," Gordon said.

Allan put the copies from the printer on his desk. Then he took the one that he had copied and put it with the other documents in the manila folder.

"Here's what we're going to do," Allan said. "I'm going to give what I have here to Peggy tonight." He held up the manila folder. "I'm going to tell her that the rest of the documents are in the truck." Allan pointed at the copies sitting on the desk while he dug around looking for another folder. He came up with one, put the copies in it and handed it to Gordon. "You're going to put these behind the seat, and first thing tomorrow morning you are going to haul that load of water down to Princeton."

"Won't make it," Gordon shook his head.

"You don't have to make it," Allan replied. "You're going to drive it as far as you can. Get in the machine shed, there's a rasp in there somewhere. Take that rasp with you, and when the truck craps out, get under the hood and rasp the fuel line so that it looks like it wore on the block or something. Then get back in the truck and crank the motor over until it won't crank no more. Get gas all over everything. Then, just light it up with a lighter. Not a match, a lighter. Then let it burn."

Allan stopped and looked at Gordon. He expected a big smile. It was a brilliant plan. They would tell the authorities that the rest of the documents burned up in the truck. It couldn't be better. Gordon wasn't smiling.

"That's arson," Gordon said. "Like, people go to jail for arson. They just get fined for illegally dumping cleaning water. Just saying. You really want to do this?"

"We aren't going to go to jail," Allan replied, "and we aren't going to get fined. Proof, my man, proof! It's the American way: they got to prove it! It's going to look like the truck broke down and burned—quite a plausible explanation, by the way. That truck is a piece of shit. The only way this doesn't work is if one of us talks. You say nothing. Just shrug your shoulders and say nothing. You don't know what happened. You were trying to get it started, and it just caught on fire. You barely escaped with your life. The truck burns to the ground, and they find the charred documents in a folder behind the seat. Too bad, so sad."

Allan waited to see if Gordon was getting the idea yet.

"I don't know about this," Gordon said. "Too many things could go the wrong direction with this idea."

"Yes, you do," Allan coaxed him. "It is do or die time. Look, you got as much to lose here as I do. You been running those illegals in there, you been dumping that shit in the pits and the pond. You got a lot of skin in this game."

Gordon had been looking at the folder filled with copies in his hand. He looked up at Allan. "You aren't pinning all this shit on me."

"Look," Allan went on, "it was your idea to empty the tanker in the pit."

"It was our idea," Gordon countered.

"I'm remembering that it was your idea," Allan replied. "And when we burn that truck, the only trace of these documents is gone, too. We just sit tight and let everything blow over. I'm doing this for you, Gordon. I'm saving your ass here." Allan waited for a response. Gordon said nothing.

"Okay," Allan said, "Take those down with you and put them in the truck. Don't freak out on me. Get up early and drive south. Simple as can be. Don't take the interstate. Drive the piss out of it until it blows up. The plan is foolproof. Just do it."

Gordon was still quiet. He looked at Allan, who had a big grin on his face. There was no changing his mind. Gordon was stuck. He turned and walked out of the office without a word. As he walked through the house he was confronted by Allan's boy, Jason. He was a tall, skinny kid, probably ten or so.

"*Como esta usted*?" he shouted at Gordon. How are you?

"*Estoy cansado y el culo me duele*," Gordon replied without enthusiasm.

Jason looked back at Gordon, confused. "What does that mean?"

"It means that I'm tired and my ass hurts," Gordon replied.

Allan's son squealed with delight. "How do you say that again?" he asked as he followed Gordon to his truck.

"Later," Gordon replied. "I'll tell you later."

Gordon got into his truck and started it up. He pulled out of the driveway. He could see the boy through his rearview mirror, watching him drive out to the blacktop. Gordon felt a little sick. The illegals, Gordon could make them disappear. They were just nameless ghosts that showed up, did the job and got paid in cash. They didn't even exist. But Allan was right, it had been his idea to dump the chemicals into the pit. He had to admit that. But also, he had had every intention to pump it out of the pit and haul it down to Princeton as soon as the truck was reliable enough to make the trip. Gordon had actually thought that Allan would buy a new truck before it got to this point. He couldn't remember whose idea it had been to pump the wastewater into the ponds once the pits were full. Deniability: Allan always talked about deniability. Gordon could see now that Allan had all of the deniability. Gordon had nothing.

Allan wandered from his office to the dining room and selected a merlot from the wine refrigerator. Then he took two wine glasses from the rack above the refrigerator. He dug a clean dishtowel out of a drawer in the kitchen, wrapped the bottle, then carried it and the glasses out to his truck and placed them on the seat. As he was doing that, he saw Brenda's car coming down the drive. She pulled up and parked her car next to the truck.

"What's up?" she asked.

"Nothing," Allan replied. "Got a Pork Producer's meeting tonight."

Brenda looked at him a little exasperated. "I thought that's where you were last night."

"Last night I was getting ready for tonight," Allan explained.

"Are you going to be home for supper?" she asked.

"Probably not," Allan replied. "Probably have food there."

"At a Pork Producer's meeting?" Brenda said.

"Yeah," Allan responded. "They usually do."

"It would be nice if you could find a little time to spend at home with your wife and kids," Brenda suggested.

"I know, baby," Allan replied with resignation in his voice. "Maybe later this fall, when things get quieter, but right now I got to make a living."

"I'm getting a little tired of waiting for you to come home every night," Brenda remarked.

Allan shrugged his shoulders. "Maybe you need to find someone to hang out with."

Brenda never knew whether Allan was serious or not when he said things like that. She had no doubt that Allan liked to play around with the ladies. It used to bother her, but over the years she had come to accept it, and at this point, she just hoped that Allan wouldn't do something or get caught with someone that would embarrass her or the kids. But she was still hurt when he was so bold.

Brenda walked into the house. Allan followed her in.

"I'm home," Brenda yelled to the kids. She could hear the TV blaring in the basement. Brenda threw her jacket on a chair and opened up the refrigerator to look for something to make supper.

"I was going to grill pork chops," she said to Allan, who was looking out the window toward the road. "I was going to bake some potatoes, too. I think that I'll save them for tomorrow night, if you're going to be here?" She looked at him, questioning.

Allan looked away from the window. "Yeah, sure, I'll be around tomorrow," he answered. "We can all have supper together. We haven't done that for a while."

"Yes, I know," Brenda remarked. "I'll just make mac and cheese tonight instead."

"I'm gonna get going," Allan said. "I want to get there early so that if there's anything that we need to discuss before the meeting, we can."

"Whatever," Brenda said sarcastically. "Have fun with whoever's at your Pork Producer's meeting."

Allan wasn't listening. He walked out the door and got into his truck. When he got to the blacktop he turned south toward Maxwell. Allan wasn't paying much attention to his driving. A couple of times he drove across the center line, but luckily there was no one coming from the other direction. Once he drove off onto the shoulder. When he arrived at the intersection, he turned toward the farm. He drove past Elizabeth's house. It looked to Allan like she was out doing chores. He drove on to the farm, a quarter mile farther down the gravel road, and pulled into the yard. Gordon's pickup was nowhere to be seen.

Allan parked the Silverado and got out. First he went to the empty hog confinement building. He could smell the chemicals in the water being stored in the pit underneath the floor. Then he went out back and stood on the bank above the ponds. He could tell by the dead grass that the polluted water had moved even farther toward the creek below than it had been the last time that he looked. Allan wondered if it was actually migrating into the creek, or if it was just going that direction. Maybe it wasn't his ponds that were responsible for the state's investigation. Maybe it was someone else, he thought. But even if it wasn't his chemicals that caught the state's attention, he could very well be swept up in the investigation. He needed to get more information. He would pump Peggy for everything she knew about it. The last thing that Allan needed was to get caught illegally dumping wastewater. Allan looked over toward Elizabeth's place. He would pump it all out and spread it over there on her property and no one would know the difference.

Allan walked back to his truck to leave. Still there was no sign of Gordon. Allan hoped that Gordon hadn't skipped town on him. But then he thought that it might be easier if he had. It would be a lot easier to pin all this on someone who wasn't around to defend themselves. No, now that he thought about it, it wouldn't be bad at all if Gordon just disappeared.

Chapter 17

Wednesday

Peggy's receptionist left, but Peggy kept working. She revisited the security contract for the third time. She hadn't heard of any complaints or problems with the current contractor. The security people she had met seemed friendly, at least. The only one she had any real contact with was the fellow who came down the hall every evening around six and checked to make sure all of the office doors were closed and locked. That was a policy with BioForce: offices were not left unlocked and unattended. Most of the time Sandra locked the doors on her way out at five, but sometimes if Peggy was still in the office, she left the door unlocked. On those occasions the security guard would come wandering back to see if anyone was working late before he locked the door himself and noted it on his security log. When Peggy had first started at BioForce, she had not been particularly security conscious. One evening she left the door unlocked and went home. The next morning her boss told her in no uncertain terms that it would not happen again, and Peggy made sure that it didn't.

Peggy retrieved her duffel and a jean jacket from the closet next to the restroom. She brought it back to her office, took one last look at her email, then took her purse and the duffel in one hand, draped the jacket over the same arm and made her way out of the office, locking up as she went. She walked down the hallway to the stairs that led to the ground floor, then took a hallway that went back into the building. She met the security guard on the way.

"Mrs. Bentley," the guard acknowledged her.

"How are you tonight?" she replied.

"Fine," was all he said as he passed by her.

Peggy turned into the women's locker room. She had a locker there, but she seldom kept anything in it. Peggy changed out of her suit and heels, into a pair of jeans, a sweater, wool socks and a pair of canvas shoes. She carefully folded the pants suit and put it into the duffel. Then she put on the jacket and took the duffel back out into the hallway.

When Peggy walked out into the parking lot it was almost dusk. It was getting dark earlier every day. Soon daylight savings time would end and it would be dark when she left the office. She walked to her car and started it. She backed out of her parking space, drove out to the highway and turned toward Nevada.

Peggy was a Nevada girl. She had grown up in Nevada. He father was one of two veterinarians who had practices there. When she was younger, her father had been the large-animal vet. He carried most of the medical equipment that he needed in an old pickup truck with a topper. The only thing that Peggy remembered about that truck was that it was so cluttered that there was only room for her father in the cab. He drove from one farm to the next, vaccinating herds of cattle for shipping fever, dehorning the Herefords and the shorthorns that came to the feedlots that sat two or three for every square mile from the vast ranges west of Iowa, to be fed out and fattened for market. At any sign of sickness, the farmers would call her father and he would rush out as if he were on an emergency and squash whatever ailed the cattle.

Peggy's father lived to be a large-animal vet. He wore cowboy boots, a cowboy hat and a wide belt with a big buckle. He looked the part of a cowboy. The farmers around Nevada depended on him, and he was highly respected. Every farmer knew him by his first name.

Peggy's mother was a socialite. She worked as a receptionist for Peggy's father, but being a socialite was her calling. She belonged to every club and group in the Methodist church where Peggy and her parents attended services every Sunday. She belonged to the bridge club and a group called Questors. She spent her days going from one meeting or event to the other. And there was no fundraiser or community project that she was not a part of. Peggy's mother was as well known as her father.

As time went on, there came a point where the cattle lots were no longer profitable. Giant feedlots popped up out west, closer to the ranches, and the packing plants moved closer to the western feed lots. For Iowa farmers, grain became the commodity. Farmers took out the fences that surrounded their farms so they could plant an extra row of corn where the fences had been. They plowed up their feedlots to plant more soybeans. And after a few short years, there were few cattle feeding setups left. The ones that stayed grew into large corporate businesses that didn't call the hometown vet to vaccinate or dehorn their cattle, but did it all themselves. Peggy's father found himself with fewer and fewer patients.

Peggy's father had seen the writing on the wall, and he knew that he had to change his practice if he were to survive. He talked about pulling up stakes and moving west, but Peggy's mother would have nothing to do with that. She had too much to do in Nevada, being a socialite. She could not just pull up stakes and start over. Peggy's dad was getting older, too. He didn't have as much drive as he used to.

At the same time, there were hog confinement setups popping up where the feed lots used to be. Hogs were easier than cattle. They could be confined in a smaller space. The buildings that they lived in were low affairs, crowded so close together that just a tractor and spreader could make it through. Peggy's father started to gear his business toward the pork industry, but his heart wasn't in it. He loved cattle and horses; pigs were not his cup of tea. So Peggy's father had abruptly turned his practice into a small-animal clinic. He turned the garage into an examining room, built a kennel to board dogs and cats out back and started attending to people's pets. His reputation in the community, and Peggy's mother's as well, turned his small-animal practice into a gold mine. And even though he missed the feedlots and the cattle until the day he retired, he got rich taking care of dogs and cats.

Peggy did well in school growing up. She was a star athlete on the basketball and track teams, mostly because she was young, thin and active, and being a big fish in a small pond made her destined for Nevada Cubs greatness. But the influences of her father and mother didn't hurt, either. When Peggy was in her senior year, she had had to make a decision: just eight miles west of Nevada was Ames, home of Iowa State University. It had one of the best vet med programs in the nation, not to mention a prestigious engineering department. It was her father's alma mater. Then there was the University of Iowa, two hours east, in Iowa City. The Iowa Hawkeyes were bitter enemies of the ISU Cyclones. Families were divided by the rivalry, which was not always very friendly. While U of I was mostly known for its medical school, the hospital that came with it and the law school, U of I also had a good business curriculum. A lot of people thought of U of I as a much more liberal university than ISU. It was Peggy's mother's alma mater.

While there were other schools that Peggy could have attended, such as the University of Northern Iowa, Drake, Simpson and any number of small colleges scattered across the state, Peggy's parents expected her to attend either ISU or U of I. Peggy chose U of I. She didn't think that her father ever truly got over his disappointment, but he hid it well.

Peggy started out in the pre-law program, but after the first year she changed her major to business. Two years into college, she met a senior majoring in pre-med, Travis Bentley. Peggy got along well with Travis. He was a kind and thoughtful young man. They had a lot of mutual friends, and whenever those friends were doing stupid college pranks that would probably land one or more of them in the city jail for the night, Travis would be the voice of reason. He kept everyone out of trouble.

Peggy dated Travis probably a dozen or more times. Then they were steady for close to an entire semester. When Travis graduated, he enrolled in grad school. Two years later they both graduated, Peggy with a Bachelor's in Business Administration, Travis with a Master's in Psychology. Peggy went back home and Travis started working toward his doctorate.

Peggy soon found a job at Wells Fargo Bank in Ames. She was happy there. It wasn't challenging, but it was a good job. It was like the small animal clinic was for her dad: it was how she made a living. One day she was working in her office with its glass walls when she saw a familiar face in the lobby. It was Travis. She had not seen nor talked to him in over three years. He looked lost. Peggy came out of her office and called to him. They hugged. Travis told her that he had taken a job with the clinic there in Ames. He had

G&B Detective Agency

continued his studies and become a psychiatrist as well as a psychologist. They had supper that night, and Travis joked that he had run out of classes to take at U of I and had to finally get a real job. The two started dating again.

Peggy didn't know if she had ever really loved Travis or if he had just been there at the right time. She had often questioned whether she was heterosexual, homosexual or just not sexual at all. She had not had a serious relationship with a man or a woman in her life. Travis came along when she was most trying to figure it all out. One day he proposed, and she said yes. She just wanted to put all the questions of her sexuality behind her and not think about them anymore.

Over the years of their marriage, Peggy had been satisfied. She and Travis seldom argued. They seldom even talked. They lived together in harmony. They had no children. Peggy didn't know if the problem was her or Travis, or if it was just that they seldom had sex, but she didn't really care. She and Travis had talked about it in passing a few times, but neither seemed very interested. It felt more as if they were each trying to see whether the other really wanted kids or not. They had each come to the conclusion individually that probably neither of them did. And so life went along smoothly and uneventfully for Peggy and Travis. As their careers moved laboriously along, they had changed slowly. Peggy moved from Wells Fargo to an implement manufacturing company, and then to BioForce. Travis went into private practice and found out that he made a better psychologist than he did a psychiatrist. So it went, a very convenient life for both of them.

Then one evening, while Travis was off tending to some substance abuse class that he was leading, Peggy looked back, something she seldom did. But that evening she asked herself, what if she had done things differently? What if she had actually tried to have a relationship with someone, instead of just waiting until Travis showed up? So that night she joined a dating site and looked at people who were seeking a relationship with someone else. That was where she had found Allan.

While her evenings came and went, over the course of weeks Peggy talked to Allan, first online, then in person. She had found someone who was not passive, like Travis. Someone who showed her how to be intimate. At first it had been exciting, and she had loved this new world she was living in, but when the newness wore off she realized that she was who she was. She wasn't someone's lover. She wasn't someone's mistress. But by then Allan was talking about a life together, her and him. He was ready to leave his wife and family for her. He loved her. He wanted her. Peggy didn't know what to do about it, so she just lived her double life, the same Peggy with two completely different kinds of men.

Peggy sighed as she drove out of the parking lot. She was tempted to just go home, but she needed to get the documents from Allan, and she knew that if she didn't get them tonight, he probably wouldn't bring them tomorrow. She had no choice but to meet him.

Chapter 18

Wednesday

"She's moving," Max startled Skip awake.

"What?" he said, trying to find his bearings.

"You were sleeping," Max said.

"I thought that you were sleeping," Skip replied.

"I was, but your snoring woke me up," Max responded.

"Are we getting old, or what?" Skip shook his head as he started the car.

"I think that we're just getting lazy," Max observed. "We're just too used to taking naps in the afternoons."

"Jeez," Skip exclaimed as he backed out from between the two combines. He saw the headlights, then Peggy's car come by on the highway as she went east.

"Step on it," Max urged.

It was dark as they drove out of the implement dealership. As Skip turned onto the highway he could see the taillights of Peggy's car up ahead. He accelerated to get a little closer so he wouldn't lose her.

"What do you think we should be doing about Higgins?" Max asked.

Skip had almost forgotten about Higgins. "I suppose we should go down and do some snooping around," Skip replied. "Maybe in the morning?"

Max didn't respond for a moment as he watched the car in front of them continue past the first and second exits that would take her into Nevada.

"Where is she going?" Max asked.

"Beats me," Skip replied.

"Are we, like, working this case 24/7?" Max asked as he looked at his watch. "Pretty soon Gloria and Marjorie are going to be on some lonely-dot-com site themselves if we're not careful."

"It's just a week," Skip replied. "Besides, how long did they sit at home while we were out and about when we worked at the PD?"

"They had jobs and kids to take up their time back then," Max said.

"This is the last case," Skip replied. "This one and Higgins," he added.

Max picked up his phone and dialed Gloria's number. The phone rang once and she picked up. "What are you doing?" she asked.

"Working this case of Skip's," Max said.

"Are you coming home sometime?" she asked.

"Well, I think so," Max answered her. "We're on stakeout."

Gloria laughed. "So you'll be home at four in the morning?"

"God, I hope I get home before that. I can't do that anymore. We both fell asleep sitting in the car while we were watching her car in the parking lot across the road for four hours. What are you doing?"

"I'm talking to Marjorie," Gloria answered.

"Okay," Max said.

"She stopped by the agency and no one was there, so she came over here. We had a glass of wine, and now we're on the internet looking at Jimmy Choos."

Max turned to Skip. "Your wife is at my place, and they're looking at shoes that cost seven hundred dollars a pair."

"Tell your wife to quit giving my wife ideas."

Gloria laughed again. "I heard that. You boys have fun playing detectives. We'll try not to spend all your money. I'll see you when I see you."

"Love ya," Max said as he ended the call.

"She's going to the grocery store," Skip exclaimed as they followed Peggy into the Fareway parking lot.

"Why drive all the way out here to get groceries?" Max asked.

"That's what I'm wondering," Skip replied as he parked in the corner of the lot, away from Peggy's Lexus, but where he still had a good view of it. The two waited while she went into the store.

"So Marjorie and Gloria are up to no good tonight," Skip observed.

"I guess so," Max replied. "I don't want to think about it. So back to Higgins: what are we going to do with that?"

Skip thought for a while. "I guess we go down there tomorrow and follow the river upstream until we don't see any more dead fish."

"I think we should stop by the office and bring up a satellite view and see what we can see," Max suggested.

"That's probably a good idea," Skip agreed.

"Actually, I think I can do that on my phone," Max said, turning on his phone and looking at the three navigation apps that were installed. "Why do they think I need so many map programs on this stupid thing?" Max complained.

Skip didn't reply. Max kept working on his phone. "This thing makes me mad," he said in a frustrated voice. "I can do this on the computer; I do it all the time."

"We'll do it tomorrow," Skip said. "She's coming out."

The two detectives watched Peggy come out of the store and get into her car.

"One bag, and it doesn't look like there are many groceries in it," Max observed.

Peggy drove out of the parking lot, onto the street and back to New 30. She took the on ramp eastbound again.

"Okay," said Skip. "Now where?"

"She's going someplace," Max observed. "Maybe down to Proctor's?"

"That might be interesting," Skip said. "If she does go to Proctor's place, there isn't any way for us to get in close enough to see anything."

Skip followed Peggy's car east on New 30, past the Maxwell turnoff.

"Nope," Skip observed as he continued east.

Skip stayed back far enough not to draw attention to himself, but it was a four lane highway and there was enough traffic that it would have been hard for anyone to notice that the nondescript silver Impala was following them. Plus, it was getting darker. Several miles past the Maxwell turnoff, Peggy put on her signal to turn right.

"I think she's going to the lake," Max said.

"Or someplace around there," Skip agreed.

They followed her over the bridge on the east end of the lake, and then back west along the south side. They were on a two lane blacktop now. Skip held back a little. The two detectives watched her turn into the entrance for one of the picnic areas that were spaced around the lake.

"Snow Bunting Lodge," Max remarked as they passed the entrance to the parking lot.

"You know it, or you just reading signs?" asked Skip.

"I know it," Max said. "We used to go back in there when we were kids. Pretty popular spot for high school kids to park and make out."

"Can we drive in?" Skip asked.

"Not without being seen," Max answered. "It's just a parking lot, one way in and one way out, some picnic tables and a lodge with a fireplace."

"Lodge with a fireplace?" Skip observed.

"Yep, they might be going in there, but it has some windows, so they can look out and see the parking lot. I wouldn't go in; we don't want to spook them."

"What do you think, then?" Skip asked.

Max thought for a moment. "We passed a boat ramp back there. We could park there and try to make our way down the path that goes behind the lodge. But it is pretty dark back in there," Max suggested, remembering his younger days.

"Let's give it a try," Skip said.

Skip turned the Impala around at the next picnic area and went back the way they had come. Max pointed out the entrance to the boat ramp, and Skip parked on one side, out of the way. The two got out of the car. Max had his camera with him.

"Is that camera going to take pictures in the dark, or are you planning to use a flash?" Skip asked.

Max reluctantly threw the camera back in the car and Skip locked the doors.

"Where's this path?" Skip inquired.

"Over this way somewhere." Max was walking toward the lake trying to get the flashlight to work on his phone.

"Can we just walk along the road?" Skip asked. "I mean, it's a hundred yards, if that."

Max stopped and turned around. "That's probably a better idea."

The two walked out to the road and proceeded west toward Snow Bunting shelter. Except for one car that drove by, the road was deserted. When they got to the drive, they hugged the shoulder of the pavement, close to the tree line, ready to duck in at the first sign of anyone. As they came around a corner, Max made out Proctor's Silverado with Peggy's Lexus parked beside it. Both vehicles were dark. As they walked a little farther, the shelter came into view. They could see light shining through the window, and they got a whiff of smoke coming from the chimney. The two stopped and hunkered down.

"Wanna be the window peeper?" Max whispered to Skip.

Skip scanned the parking lot. There were no other cars. "I guess," Skip sighed.

Max moved into the shadow of the trees and found a big boulder to sit on as Skip worked his way toward a window on the wall that did not have a door. Skip didn't walk right up to the window to peer in, where he could be seen. He stayed back and maneuvered himself one side to another, visually dividing the interior into pie-shaped segments, getting a glimpse of each section before moving to the next. Max was watching him, keeping an eye out for anyone else on foot or cars that might come into the lot and shine their lights on his partner, who had stopped moving and was concentrating on the window.

What seemed like a long time passed while Skip peered through the window, before he ducked down and came back to where Max waited.

"They're having a picnic," Skip said. "Nice and cozy. They've got a fire going, the table's set and they're sitting in there roasting hot dogs over the fire. That's it."

"No making out and playing stinky finger?" Max asked.

"Nope," Skip replied.

Max moved to one side to make room on the boulder for Skip.

"They're just talking," Skip went on. "And they're drinking a bottle of wine."

"Good wine?" Max inquired.

"I don't know what kind of wine it is," Skip exclaimed. "What difference does that make?"

"Well, that sounds kind of romantic," Max observed. "It doesn't sound like it's a business meeting."

"Still, could be old friends catching up," Skip remarked. "I mean, I think that they have something more going on, but we've got nothing that proves it. It could be something else."

The two sat looking at the shelter house.

"I'm gonna take a look," Max said.

"Be my guest," Skip replied.

Max bent low and crept to a spot near where Skip had done his observations earlier. He stood up until he could see the two occupants through the window. He moved just as Skip had, cutting the inside into pie shaped segments. Skip was watching him from the boulder. All of a sudden Max moved in closer. Skip wanted to call out to warn him to stay back so that he didn't get spotted, but he knew that he would draw more attention making noises than Max would make moving in closer. Besides, Max knew what he was doing.

Max ducked down and scrambled back to the rock where Skip was sitting. "They're making out. He has his hand up under her sweater and he's feeling her up. I think she's giving him a hand job," Max whispered. "It's heating up, anyway."

Skip stood up from the rock, bent down and ran to where Max had been. He stood up slowly and looked through the window for a moment. Max watched him duck low, then make his way to the corner of the stone building where he wouldn't be seen from the window. Skip stood there for several minutes, apparently listening, then ducked back down and hustled back to the rock.

"They're not making out anymore," Skip said. "It looks to me like they're arguing. At least like they're having some kind of serious talk. I can't hear. The walls are too thick."

Max got up and worked his way to where he could see through the window. He paused a minute before going to the corner of the building and listened through the wall. As he came back to where Skip was sitting, he stopped to peer through the window again. Skip was watching him move quietly. Skip had to admit that even though Max made him nervous scurrying around like he did, Max was good. All of a sudden Max ducked his head, turned toward Skip and motioned for him to come quick. Skip got up and hurried as quietly as he could toward where Max was now standing and looking through the window. Max kept turning toward him and pointing two fingers toward his eyes, then shifting them toward the window. When he got next to Max, Skip looked in the shelter to see Peggy laying on the table with her trousers down around her ankles, legs spread. Allan, with his back to the widow, was thrusting himself into her. The two detectives watched. After what seemed like minutes, Skip pulled on Max's arm and nodded his head toward the rock. The two turned to make their way back, but Max took one last look through the window.

"That pretty much makes the case," Max said as they reached the rock.

Skip didn't reply. The two sat down on the boulder.

"What do you think, should we stick around?" Skip asked Max after looking toward the shelter.

"And what?" Max asked him back.

"We saw what we saw," Skip said. "What else is there? Travis's wife is fucking Proctor in the shelter house at the lake on a Wednesday night while he's working. Open and closed. At least for tonight."

"I still wish that I could get some pictures," Max said.

"Well, I don't think that's going to happen tonight," Skip replied.

"So are you ready to call it a night?" Max asked.

Skip didn't answer. The two sat watching the light through the window for a while longer, saying nothing.

"Wanna go look again?" Max asked.

"Not really," Skip replied. "I'm just not a good window peeper. It makes me feel like a pervert."

"Let's get out of here then, and go home before those girls buy shoes," Max suggested. Skip agreed, and the two got up to make their way back to their car.

"Are you going call Travis and tell him what we saw tonight?" Max inquired as they walked back to the car.

Skip thought about it for a moment. "Not yet."

"So we aren't done with it now? We're going to keep watching her?" Max asked.

"I think that we keep watching for a few more days. I told Travis that we would go for a week on it." Skip replied. "I think we need to give it a little more time."

"What about Higgins?" Max asked.

"Let's get those satellite pictures, then go out there in the morning and look around," Skip suggested. "We've got some time now. We don't need to follow her every move at this point."

"Agreed," Max replied.

The two detectives reached the car and Max stood next to the passenger door waiting for Skip to unlock it.

"I'm kind of bummed over this," Skip remarked to Max over the hood of the car. "I don't like these kind of cases."

Max shrugged his shoulders. "Let's not do any more like this, then."

The door unlocked and the two detectives climbed into the car. As they did so, Max saw Allan's white Silverado speed past on the road.

"That was quick," Max observed.

Skip stayed parked, and the two watched for Peggy's car to come by. They didn't have to wait long. Skip gave her a minute to get down the road, then pulled out of the boat ramp and followed her taillights as she wound around the east end of the lake and proceeded to New 30. When they got on the highway, Skip closed the distance between the two cars. Peggy drove straight toward home. The two detectives followed as far as the exit that took them to the agency and pulled into the parking lot.

"Tell Marjorie that I'm heading home, if she's still at your place," Skip told Max as he was getting out of the Impala.

"Will do," Max replied. "What time tomorrow?"

"Make it eight," Skip replied.

"Make it nine," Max came back. "Eight is awful early."

"I'll be here at eight," Skip said. Max could tell that Skip was feeling down. "You come in when you want."

Chapter 19

Thursday

Max got up early. Seven o'clock early, just for the record. Max was not an early morning person, but he knew that Skip would be at the agency before eight, and he didn't like the idea of Skip waiting for him. So Max dragged himself out of bed, made Gloria get up with him and the two had breakfast before he left. Max arrived at the door of the agency at a quarter before eight. Skip's Mercedes was already there. Max put his hand on the hood as he walked by. It was warm, but not warm enough that Skip had just arrived as well. Max estimated maybe forty minutes. The door was locked, so Max unlocked it and went in.

"Hey," he hollered.

"Hey," he heard Skip call out from his office down the hall.

Max walked to Skip's office and stopped at the door.

"What time did you get here?" Max asked.

"I don't know," Skip replied, looking up from the satellite photos on his desk.

"No," Max said, "What time did you get here? I'm serious."

"Zero-seven-o-two," Skip answered. "And thirty seconds."

Max looked at his watch. "Knew it," he exclaimed.

"What did you know?" Skip asked.

"I felt the hood of your car and figured from how warm it was that you parked it there forty minutes ago. It's exactly ten till." Max stood with a look of self-satisfaction on his face.

"Exactly ten till?" Skip remarked.

"Close enough to ten till," Max responded. "Forty minutes, with an error margin of plus or minus two minutes." He was still smiling with self satisfaction.

"That's fifty minutes, give or take two minutes," Skip corrected.

"Dang," said Max, "you're right."

Skip was looking at the satellite images that he had printed earlier. Max walked over to his desk and stood beside him, examining the images himself.

"First one," Skip said, pointing at the photo on the far right. "This one is Higgins's place. You can actually see the beaver dam."

"Are these real time?" Max asked.

"Don't think so," Skip answered. "Looks like the old tractor with the flat tires is in this picture. It was gone when we were down there the other day. Also the place looks junkier in the picture, like it was before he cleaned the place up."

Max didn't respond.

"There isn't anything between Higgins and the road that goes out of town there," Skip pointed, "except for the rodeo grounds and the baseball field. But no big structures or businesses to speak of. Then you can go north here, and the road goes clear out there to the west of the river before it goes north again, and there's these two places here," Skip pointed at two farmsteads that could be seen in the photo. "But they're on the other side of the road, and there's a lot of land between them and the river."

Skip placed another image on top of the one they had been looking at. "So continue north, and the road kind of parallels the river a little bit, but the river starts twisting around and getting closer to the road as it goes north." Skip was following the road with a pencil as a pointer. "Then we keep going, and there's nothing." He paused as he picked up another photo.

"Just a minute," interrupted Max. "Look here. Here's a road that goes back to the river and dead ends there." Max was pointing at it with his finger. "Wouldn't be real hard to drive back there and dump something. Maybe go back there and set up a meth lab—it would be a perfect place for a meth lab. We should check it out."

Skip looked at the road. "So how do you explain the dead fish upstream?"

Max shrugged his shoulders but didn't say anything. Skip put the third photo on the pile.

"Hey," the two heard Monica coming in the front door.

"Hey," Max shouted back.

Skip continued. "Going north, you come to Proctor's place. The creek's getting pretty close to his place. He has these two hog sheds and these two ponds back there." Skip was pointing with his pencil again. "Hog manure?" He looked up at Max.

"Beats me," Max answered. "I've heard about hog manure spills and such, but I don't know what they do. Do they kill all the fish like that?"

It was Skip's turn to shrug his shoulders. "I don't know."

"I'd think there would have been evidence of hog shit and straw and stuff if that were the case," Max observed. "I would think that the water would be all shit brown if it was manure. It didn't look shit brown to me."

"I don't know," Skip replied. "If it filtrates through the ground and into the water, is it still brown?"

"Wishful thinking?" Max asked.

"Well, it couldn't happen to a more deserving guy," Skip said. "But also there's the dead fish that we saw from the bridge up here," he pointed to the bridge with his pencil. "And then we got your friend here," Skip pointed at Elizabeth's place. "But then nothing past her place until that bridge."

Skip picked up a fourth photo and put it on the pile.

"Moving on, we wind around and we wind around, and there are a few places that back up to the river, but the road goes back away from it here, so those places get farther and farther away, and then the river turns east there and runs under the blacktop. And we didn't see any dead fish when we looked there."

"What about that place?" Max pointed at a farmstead that sat on a hill before the creek went under the blacktop.

"Downstream from the bridge, just barely, but it is pretty close to the road, and as I remember, you could see it well. I would think that if they were dumping chemicals, someone would notice from the road."

Max agreed with him. "Let's just drive down there and look around again."

Max looked up and saw that Monica was standing right behind him looking at the photos.

"You snuck up on me," he exclaimed.

"That's 'cause you're not as quick as you used to be," Monica teased. "You're getting old, Max."

Max gave her his evil eye look.

"Just kidding," Monica said.

"I saw her come in," Skip spoke up.

"Right," Monica laughed.

"So this is the Higgins case that you're working on now?" Monica asked.

"Yeah," Skip replied. "We pretty much wrapped up the Travis case last night. We have a few loose ends to follow up, but we pretty much saw what we needed to see."

"Catch her doing the naughty?" Monica asked in a conspiratorial tone.

Skip didn't answer.

"Yes, we did," Max said.

"That sucks," Monica replied.

"It does," Skip said. "I feel really bad about this whole case."

"Is that your feminine side showing?" Monica asked.

Skip didn't answer again.

"That's okay," Monica said. "It is good for you to be sensitive. It shows that you are emotionally balanced."

"You learn that in school?" Max asked.

"I did learn that in school," Monica answered.

"Okay," Skip changed the subject away from his sensitivity. "We might as well get out of here and start sorting some of this out." He was getting up out of his chair and gathered his printouts.

Max went into his office and got his .38 special and a couple of speed loaders out of his drawer, where he kept them locked up.

"Packing?" Max called across the hall.

"I guess," Skip called back.

When they had all their gear together, the two detectives walked up front, toward the reception area where Monica was sitting.

"Monica," Skip addressed her, "can you do something for me?"

"Yes, I can, I work for you," she answered him. "Provided it doesn't get in the way of my classes," she added.

"Can you get on the internet and look for some real-time satellite photos of where Indian Creek runs through Maxwell, and if you can, see if you can get them up river for four or five miles?"

"Sure," said Monica. "I'll do that."

"You seem pretty happy today," Max said as they got ready to go out the door. "You and Milton getting along better?"

"We're getting along fine," she reassured him. "But I just feel good today, that's all. I have good days and I have bad days, just like everybody. This is a good day."

Skip had hurried out the door and was standing by the passenger door of Max's Mustang.

"Where's the Impala?" Max asked.

"Dropped it off last night," Skip replied.

"Don't you want to drive?" Max asked.

"The 'Stang?" Skip asked him back.

"No, your car," Max replied.

"I don't want to get it dirty on the gravel roads. I just washed it this morning on the way in."

Max laughed and shook his head. He unlocked the doors and they got in the car.

The two drove toward Maxwell, a trip that was beginning to be routine. They said little. Max had the radio on 100.3, The Bus, and had the volume cranked high enough that it discouraged conversation. As they drove past the BioForce ethanol plant, Max and Skip both looked over at the parking lot. Peggy's car was parked in its usual place. They continued past the outskirts of Nevada and back out into the country.

At the Maxwell blacktop Max turned south. They spotted Allan's Silverado parked in front of his house as they passed. A few miles later they dropped into the river bottom. Skip shouted over the music for Max to stop at the bridge so that he could get out and look for dead fish. Max pulled halfway onto the shoulder again to protect them from traffic, took a quick look in his rearview mirror, then got out and went with Skip out on the bridge. The two looked over the rail. There were no dead fish, and the water was clear as it flowed under the bridge. A deadfall lay up against one of the pilings on the other side. The detectives crossed the bridge and inspected the fallen trees.

"If there was anything coming down stream here, some of it would surely get caught up in that and we would see it," Skip remarked.

"You'd think so," Max agreed.

They walked back to the Mustang and got back in. Skip turned and looked up at the farmstead that sat on the hill above the creek.

"You got your binoculars?" Skip asked Max.

Max reached back and took a rucksack from the back seat. He fished out a pair of Burris eight powers and handed them over to Skip. Skip scanned the farmstead.

"That isn't even a farm," Skip observed. "It's more like an acreage. They have some horses, it looks like, but no machinery or anything. Looks like someone's hobby farm."

"Damn townies," Max joked. "Buying up all the farmland."

"You trying to sound like Higgins?" Skip asked.

"Trying," Max replied.

"I'm ready," Skip said.

Max checked his rearview mirror again for traffic. He was always checking his rearview mirrors, a habit from his years on the police department. More cops got killed when they were picked off by cars in traffic, than anything. Max used to think that the most dangerous thing a cop did was get in and out of the car. That and directing traffic.

Max pulled back onto the highway and started south again toward Higgins's place. When they got there, they were met at the gate by the two Dobermans, Pete and Repeat. The two dogs trotted alongside the car as Max pulled into the yard and parked.

"You first," Max said to Skip.

"They aren't going to bite you," Skip said. "They are nice dogs now."

"You make sure they still are," Max suggested.

Skip opened his door, and the two dogs ran around to his side of the car. They stood there panting and wagging their little stubs of tail. Skip got out and extended his hand. The two dogs sniffed his hand, then ran back around to Max's side of the car as he opened his door as well.

"We probably should have called," Max said as they got out.

"Probably should have," Skip replied.

"Howdy," they heard the call from the direction of the barn. Both men turned to see Higgins standing in the doorway. The first thing that Max noticed was that he had the Browning Highpower 9mm stuck in his waistband.

"You guys come up with anything yet?" he asked as he walked toward them from the barn.

"Not really," Skip replied. "We went up north the other day and checked every bridge that goes over the creek, and we saw dead fish for about two or three miles. Then that was it."

"Well, that ought to narrow it down," Higgins commented.

"I don't know if it does or not," Skip responded. "You know a guy named Allan Proctor?"

"Nope," Higgins responded.

"He has a hog confinement up north of here. I'm wondering if there's a chance that his manure pits are leaking into the creek," Skip explained.

"Still don't know him, and I don't think it is manure. It doesn't smell like manure. Besides, I seen manure get into the water before, and it doesn't kill the fish like that. I mean not so many of them," Higgins said. "Besides, you can see manure in the water."

Skip didn't respond.

"Still hoping, aren't you?" Max commented.

"Let's go back down there to the beaver dam and look around again," Skip suggested.

"Let's go," Higgins agreed.

The three headed on foot toward the gate to the pasture. As they walked, Pete and Repeat either trotted along behind them or ran out into the pasture chasing birds and a rabbit that they flushed out of the clumps of grass. As they got near the fence that separated Higgins's property from his neighbor's, Max looked over toward the marijuana grow that was still standing. Higgins noticed.

"Cousin's gonna take that out of there tomorrow after the dew dries off it." Higgins said.

"That's good," Max replied. "One less thing you need to worry about."

"Yep," said Higgins. "I told him he needed to do something with it."

"Why not wait until tomorrow, when he gets it out of there, then just call the DNR and tell them about the beaver dam and all the dead fish, and just let them take over?" Skip asked.

"Because there's a restraining order that says I can't be on this here property, and if I was to call it in, they would know that I was over here violating the order."

"Okay," Max paused for a moment. "Call it in and just don't tell them your name. Have Bonnie call it in for you, and she doesn't have to give her name, either."

Higgins kept walking. "I don't want nobody snooping around, even if I don't have anything that I need to keep on the down low. Besides, he's gonna hang it in the barn so it can dry. Last thing I need is someone to get wind of that."

Skip laughed out loud. "Higgins, you take the cake. I thought that you turned over a new leaf."

"I did," Higgins shot back. "Pot ain't a crime, it's just pot. It doesn't make you a bad person. They just make it illegal so they can put people in jail. It is all about giving the cops something to do, because they ain't got anything better."

Max and Skip did not respond for a moment, both of them digesting Higgins's words. Finally Skip spoke up. "You got that pretty well pegged," he said.

Higgins stopped, turned around and looked at Skip, looking for an explanation.

"No," Skip went on, "you're right, it is all about politics and money. It's all about getting grants and hiring more people."

"So you're agreeing with me?" Higgins asked.

"Yes, I am," Skip said.

Higgins turned around and started walking toward the creek again. "I knew you were stand up guys," he said over his shoulder.

Long before the three arrived at the beaver dam, they could smell the dead fish. As they looked over the bank and into the river, the stench was overpowering.

"See? There ain't no manure smell," Higgins stated, "just that other smell, that chemical smell."

"I can't smell anything but dead fish," Max said, holding his nose.

"Me neither," Skip agreed.

"Well, I can smell some kind of chemicals," Higgins said. "And that water has more of a blue tinge to it than it usually does. Look where it goes over the beaver dam over there. Look at the foam: it's almost turquoise."

Max and Skip could see what Higgins was saying. Skip was nodding his head.

"Let's get out of here," Max suggested. "I can't take this stench anymore."

The three men turned away and walked the path back to the fence. The path was well worn, and Max could see where someone doing an investigation back there in the woods would naturally follow the path to see where it went. It was pretty evident that Higgins was violating the restraining order on a daily basis.

Higgins held the fence while Skip and Max climbed through, then Skip held it for Higgins. They walked across the pasture, through the gate and to Max's car. Skip opened the door, took out his satellite photos and spread them out on the hood. A light breeze threatened to blow them off. Skip found a rock about the size of a golf ball and put it on the first photo to keep it from blowing away.

"Don't scratch my car," Max protested.

"I'm not going to scratch your car," Skip replied.

"Nice car," Higgins observed. "I thought that it was a nice car first time you guys came down here looking for Tucker, by the way, even if I didn't want to say it."

"Thanks," said Max.

"Okay," Skip started, "look at this, Higgins: here's your place."

Higgins and Max bent over the hood of the car so that they could look down on the photos.

"The creek goes up here, and there aren't any farm places close to it," Skip was pointing with his finger. He took the next photo out of his hand and traded it for the one that they were looking at. "Then it goes up here, and it gets closer to the road, then you got this little dirt road that goes back toward the creek."

"Been down there," Higgins said.

"So what's there?" Skip asked.

"Just a dead end," he answered. "A little place that you can turn around, that's all."

"Good place for a meth lab?" Max asked.

"I suppose," Higgins said. "I don't do meth, and I never have, so I'm not a meth lab expert. I don't even know how they make it."

"We aren't, either," Max replied. "I mean, I know that they use chemicals to make it, but enough to pollute a whole river and kill all the fish? I can't imagine."

The three looked at each other, but none of them had an answer.

"I thought that you guys used to bust people for that," Higgins said.

"We used to bust people for having it, but we never busted anyone for making it," Skip explained. "Anyway, we might have to drive down that road and check it out. Who knows what can go on back there?"

Max was imagining driving down that road in the Mustang, and how many scratches the car would get when he did. He was resigning himself to the fact that they were probably going to check it out as soon as they left Higgins's place.

"So here's Proctor's place," Skip continued.

"Been by there," Higgins said. "Never knew who owned it."

"It's pretty close to the river there, especially those two ponds," Skip remarked. "Then we have Elizabeth's place, on the other side of the road."

"Horse lady," Higgins commented. "Been by there, too."

"Then you just go a long ways," Skip was placing one photo after another on the hood, holding them down with his hand, "then you end up where the creek goes under the Maxwell blacktop. And then I don't know."

"It goes all the way up to the lake," Higgins said.

Max, Skip and Higgins looked at the photos. Higgins picked one up from under Skip's hand and examined it. "I don't know," he muttered. "It sure doesn't look like hog shit to me, but maybe there's something I don't know about hog farming."

"Well, that's three of us," Skip agreed.

They stood there a little longer, looking out over the pasture toward the river. Max thought that he could get a whiff of the dead fish in the breeze.

"I think it's a good idea that your cousin get that stuff out of there as soon as he can," Max said. "And I think that he should get it off your property and go dry it somewhere else."

Higgins nodded in agreement. "But he's not going to though, b'cause he don't have nowhere else to take it."

Skip was getting back into the car. "We're going to check out that dead end road, and then go from there," he said as he opened the door.

Max turned to get in as well.

"Thanks, you guys," Higgins said earnestly. "I really do appreciate it. I just appreciate you guys looking into it for me, whatever happens."

Max started the Mustang, backed around and drove to the road. Pete and Repeat escorted them as far as the gate, then trotted back to Higgins, who was watching them leave. Higgins felt good that someone cared enough to pay attention to his problems and help him out a little. He was glad that they had all ended up being friends after the Tucker case.

Chapter 20

Thursday

Peggy carried the documents that Allan had given her across the parking lot to the building where her office was located. She was later than usual. She had gotten up early enough, but unlike her usual routine, she had waited for Travis to get up and shared breakfast with him before leaving for work. She had every intention of confessing everything about Allan to Travis; she wanted to come clean, tell Travis that it was over between her and Allan. That it had never really amounted to anything, anyway. She wanted to tell Travis that she wished that they could make a new start together. To somehow get closer, to save their marriage. But she hadn't done that. She had made breakfast, chatted about things so unimportant that she could not even remember what they were, and when Travis went down to his office in the basement to prepare for the class that he was leading that evening, Peggy had left for work.

But Peggy knew one thing for sure: she was going to end it with Allan. She had known that even before last evening, but last evening solidified it. Last evening the curtain was raised and she saw Allan for what he was: just some self-serving ass who was using their relationship for his own gain. She knew that Allan never planned to leave his wife and family for her, or for anyone. His whole existence was centered on using other people, and Peggy had realized that the evening before, laying on her back on a picnic table in a smoky shelter house, wishing that Allan would just get done and get off her. She had not wanted to have sex with him in the first place, but he was always so persistent. He wore her down. And Allan had been happy to do just that—get done and leave. When he had finished, he promptly told Peggy that he had a Pork Producer's meeting that he had to go to. Then he took his two wine glasses and left her to clean up the mess.

Peggy walked into her office. Her receptionist looked up, but did not comment. Peggy could see that she had been wondering where Peggy was. It was unusual for Sandra to come in before Peggy and have to open up the office. In fact, it had never happened before. Peggy did not acknowledge her. She walked down the hallway, took off her coat and put it in the closet that sat next to the coffee room, then went into her own office. She sat down and opened the large envelope that Allan had given her, pulled the documents out and got them ready to be scanned. She was anxious to send them off to the fellow from the state. She wanted to get it taken care of so that she could concentrate on the contracts, something she had not been able to do the last couple of days.

Peggy started to organize the documents on her desk. It was something that she could have passed off to her receptionist, but she did it herself. There was just something about Allan that told her in the back of her mind that she needed to make sure the documents were all in order. She noticed that Gordon had been making two, sometimes three trips a month to Princeton earlier in the spring. She carefully went over each document. She noticed the date and time stamped on the margins, and jotted them down on a note pad as she worked. But the documents from mid July to the present were missing. Peggy was furious. She had known that Allan would screw it up. She needed to get ahold of him and have him find the rest of the documents and get them to her immediately. She was getting real tired of Allan.

Peggy called Allan's office. After several rings, it rolled over to voicemail. Peggy left a message. "Allan, there are no documents here past the fifteenth of July. You need to hunt them down for me, wherever they are, and get them over here so I can send them in." She hung up the phone. As soon as she did, she picked up the receiver again and dialed Allan's cell phone. Like his office phone, it rang several times then went to voicemail. "Allan, there's nothing here after July fifteenth. Go find the rest of them and get them over here to me so that I can send them off with the rest." Peggy got ready to end the call, but before she did, she spoke into the phone again. "Listen, Allan, I'm not dicking around here, I need them ASAP. So find them, or you can explain to the state where you're dumping your wastewater." She emphasized the words "your wastewater," then ended the call. She was becoming more and more angry, which was as unusual for Peggy as it was for her to come into work late.

When the call came in on Allan's cell, he was in his Silverado headed toward the farm. He looked at the screen while he was driving. Peggy. Allan didn't answer. He had been trying to call Gordon all morning, but Gordon wasn't answering his phone. Allan liked to keep track of Gordon and Gordon seldom missed a call from him unless he was at the plant and couldn't hear it. Gordon was supposed to be on his way south with the tanker truck this morning, not at the plant. Allan had a hunch that Gordon hadn't left yet. Something was holding him up, and Allan needed to see what was going on. He tossed the phone in the passenger's seat of his truck and let it ring.

As soon as Peggy ended the call, she started looking for Gordon's number. She seldom talked to Gordon directly, preferring to speak to Allan, which was what Gordon told her to do almost every time she talked to him, but she had Gordon's number somewhere. She hoped that if she couldn't reach Allan, that Gordon could find the documents and bring them to her. The phone rang several times, then rolled over to voicemail. Peggy was getting tired of leaving messages. "Gordon, this is Peggy Bentley. I need to get ahold of Allan as soon as possible. It is important. He was supposed to get some documentation to me and he only gave me half of it. If you have a way of getting him, please have him call me ASAP." She got ready to end the call but stopped. "Gordon, when you get this, call me. Please." She ended the call.

Peggy sat back and looked over the documents spread across her desk. She started thinking that perhaps she should have been making Allan more accountable all along. She should have made him turn in the documentation every time they made the trip, or at least every month. Peggy would talk to him about that. She sat for a moment thinking about it.

Suddenly, Peggy had an idea: perhaps both Gordon and Allan were back in the plant! Maybe they had some guys cleaning, or maybe they were working on equipment and the noise was so loud they couldn't hear their phones. Peggy got up, took her pass key to get her through the layers of security doors to the back of the plant and started for the door.

"I'm going back in the plant," Peggy told Sandra. "I need to see if anyone from Cleanguard is back there. They aren't answering their phones. If anyone from there calls, tell them that I will be right back." Peggy stopped and turned at the door. "In fact, if anyone from there calls, keep them on the line until I get back, don't let them off." The receptionist nodded. Peggy went out the door.

Peggy worked her way through the plant, negotiating her way past the tanks where the corn was processed to make the ethanol and alongside the pipes that carried it to the area where the ethanol was separated from the byproduct. When she finally made it to the back of the plant, where two huge overhead doors stood open, she found two plant workmen, but no one else. She did not recognize either worker. She held up the nametag that hung around her neck from a lanyard.

"You guys seen anyone from Cleanguard this morning?" she asked.

Both men shook their heads no. One of them spoke up. "Haven't seen anyone from there since Monday. They had a couple of wetbacks in here cleaning a tank, but no one else has been here."

Peggy glanced over toward the doors, where Allan's cleaning equipment sat along one of the walls. "Nobody has been working on the equipment or anything like that?"

"Not that I've seen," the worker answered.

Peggy stood for a moment. The two men waited to see if she had any other questions.

"Thanks," she said.

As she turned to leave, the other man spoke up. "Mrs. Bentley, I think those guys are using illegals to clean those tanks, and that Gordon is paying them in cash. We think that they're playing a little fast and loose with the OSHA regs, too."

Peggy looked at the two men. They were nervous. "I think you are right," she sighed. "That's one of the reasons I'm back here. If they are, we'll be looking for another company to contract with," Peggy reassured the two. They both smiled with some satisfaction. Peggy was the first person who had acknowledged their concerns.

As Peggy turned and walked back the way she had come, one of the workers looked over at the other. "I think she means business."

The other man shrugged his shoulders. He was a little less certain. "We'll see," he replied.

Peggy worked her way back through the plant to her office. As she walked through the door, her receptionist looked up. "No one called," she said as Peggy came by.

"Don't take any messages from them," Peggy instructed. "Make them stay on the line until I can talk to them."

While Peggy was back in the plant, Allan drove down to the farm. He found the tanker truck sitting where it had been the day before. Gordon's Dodge Ram was gone. Allan got out of his Silverado and went to the tanker truck. He opened the door and pulled the seat forward. A quick glance showed him that the folder with the copied documents was behind the seat. Allan looked around the interior of the truck. It was the usual clutter, nothing out of the ordinary. He closed the door, went to the back of the tank and climbed the ladder to the top. He opened the hatch and looked down into the tank. It was probably three-quarters filled with caustic smelling cleaning water. He closed the hatch quickly and climbed back down.

Allan walked to the first hog confinement building and went inside. It was full of grunting and squealing hogs, fighting each other to get their snouts into the feed trough, which was full of feed. Gordon had fed them before he had left to go wherever he had gone. Allan checked the automatic watering troughs and the feed hoppers out of habit. Both were full.

Allan went to the other building, which was empty. He peered down into the pit beneath the floor. It was full of water with the same pungent smell as the liquid in the tanker truck. There wasn't enough room remaining there to dump the tanker. He went out the back of the building where he could see the holding ponds below. The dead grass now reached all the way to the trees that sat as a fringe buffer at the creek. Allan looked up at the sky. If those idiots from the state flew over, they would be able to spot the dead grass. Even if there was a frost and the grass went dormant, they would be able to see it.

Allan walked to the house and tried the door. It was unlocked. He pulled it open.

"Gordon," Allan yelled through the open door. "You in there?" Allan knew that he wasn't; his pickup was gone. But Allan called, anyway. Maybe Gordon had some of those Evergreen Mexicans living in there. Maybe he had some Evergreen Mexican woman living in there with him. Allan was just making sure that he wouldn't have any surprises.

No one answered. Allan went in and looked around. It looked much the same as it had when he and Brenda had lived there. Those were good times, he thought. Allan rummaged around Gordon's personal items. He had started to wonder if Gordon might have taken off on him, but it looked like a lot of his stuff was still in the house. Allan wondered where he might be.

As he walked out the back door and into the yard, Allan looked over toward his machine shed. He could see the rolled bales of alfalfa beyond the shed, almost out of sight. When he had bought them, he had planned to sell them to the Beckman woman down the road for twice what he had paid. But he had kept them instead, and taken her some older bales from one of the previous year's cuts. But those were moldy, and before he got around to taking the good ones over to replace the moldy bales, he had come across the bales of brome grass.

These alfalfa bales were still green. They would stay green, even when they dried. Allan got an idea. He would spread the alfalfa over the brown grass from the ponds. The long grass would probably hold it in place. If it didn't, he could water it down so that it wouldn't blow away. Maybe he could empty the water from the pit over it. That would make the dead grass harder to spot from the sky. But first he had to find Gordon and get him moving in the tanker truck. As soon as he got Gordon on the road, he would come back and spread the alfalfa. Allan smiled at his ability to come up with a good plan, no matter what came up. He was pretty clever that way, he told himself.

Allan walked around to his truck. If he didn't find Gordon pretty soon, he was going to have to come up with an alternative plan. He was rolling ideas around in his head as he left the farm and made his way past Elizabeth's place. She was exercising one of her horses. Allan made a mental note to talk to her about spreading some of that water from the holding ponds on her pasture. He wanted to get that done, but he could talk to her later. First things first, Allan drove to the Maxwell blacktop and turned north. He thought that maybe Gordon had gone to the plant for some reason. That was the only thing that he could think of. Where else would Gordon go? The more he thought about it, the more Allan was sure that was where he would find him.

Chapter 21

Thursday

Max and Skip took the same route out of Maxwell as they had the day before, checking for dead fish floating in the water at each bridge over the creek. As Max had feared, Skip insisted that they drive on the dirt road that they had discovered in the satellite photos. Max had thought about suggesting that they walk along the road instead, but didn't. He pulled onto the road and slowly worked his way toward the river, wincing as the dry fox tails that lined the road passed over the paint on both sides of the Mustang.

The road was narrow and rutted. In places the undercarriage dragged on the ground, and Max would deftly turn the wheels to get out of the tracks made by four wheel drive trucks and jeeps that probably used the road just for the challenge during the wet months.

"We could have parked and walked down," Skip observed.

"Thought about it," Max replied.

Skip did not respond.

"I always wanted to see how far I could take this thing before I got it stuck," Max joked. "Maybe we'll have to get someone from triple-A out here if we get her in there and can't get her out."

They arrived at the end of the road, a small clearing just inside the tree line that was barely big enough to turn around. Max parked the car and the two got out. There was a distinct odor of dead fish in the still air. They walked the short distance to the riverbank and peered over. There was a deadfall on the far side of the river, and dead fish were caught up in it. They could also see a couple of fish floating belly-up in the slow current.

"What do you think?" Skip asked.

"I think we got dead fish here," Max answered. "Do you smell chemicals?"

"I don't smell anything but dead fish," Skip observed.

The two stood looking across the creek at the downed tree on the other bank for a moment.

"I think, though, that I can see that blue in the water that Higgins was talking about," Skip observed.

"Yep." Max agreed. "Nice out here," Max said as they turned and walked back to the Mustang. "I mean, if it didn't smell like dead fish."

Max checked out the sides of his car as Skip was opening the door and climbing in. Other than some brush marks in the dust that was clinging to the car, Max couldn't see any real damage. He got in, started the motor and began the slow trip back over the rutted path. Eventually he arrived at the gravel road that would take them north past Proctor's place, and then past Elizabeth's. Max waited for a lone pickup truck to go by, then turned onto the gravel. As he drove he could hear the rocks in the road being thrown up into the wheel wells from the tires. He drove slowly; the pickup truck ahead pulled away. "I really don't like this road," Max said.

As they slowly drove past Proctor's place, Skip took it in. The tanker truck was still sitting where it had been the last time that they had driven by. Other than that, there were no vehicles in the yard. Max was almost at a standstill while they scanned the farmyard. Max noticed the No Trespassing sign and the No Solicitors sign on the post that marked one side of the driveway.

"What do you think?" he asked.

"Pretty quiet," Skip answered. "Nothing suspicious that I can see."

"Want to turn in?" Max asked.

"I don't think so," Skip responded, eyeing the signs.

Max picked up some speed as he went past the driveway, but he was still only doing forty miles an hour. When they got close to Elizabeth's place, Max slowed and turned into her drive. Elizabeth came out of the huge Butler building that housed the horse stalls and the indoor riding arena to see who was coming in. She smiled and waved as Max stopped the car. The two detectives got out, just as Elizabeth was coming near.

"You guys still poking around out here?" she asked.

"Yep," Max replied. "Just thought that we would give ol' Proctor another drive-by."

"Well," Elizabeth said, "you just missed him. He was over there for a while this morning, but he came barreling by about fifteen minutes ago."

"What about the hired hand?" Skip asked.

"I don't know about him," she answered. "I don't know whether he's over there anymore or not. Honestly, I don't really pay that much attention to them, it just looks like I do."

"Didn't look like anyone is there now," Max observed. "Pretty quiet over there."

Elizabeth just shrugged her shoulders and looked toward Proctor's place in the distance down the road.

"Elizabeth," Max said, "you've got my card, don't you?"

"No," she answered.

Max dug out his billfold and removed a card. He turned to the car and rummaged in the console looking for a pen, which he finally found. He wrote a number on the back of the card and handed it to Elizabeth. "I don't want to impose on you and all, but if you see anything strange going on over there, would you give me a call? I wrote my cell number on the back there."

"Sure," said Elizabeth, taking the card. "I'll be your neighborhood watch," she laughed.

"Seriously," Max said. "I don't want to put you out, I just have a bad feeling about Proctor and that place."

"It's no problem," Elizabeth assured him. "Liven up things a little. Contrary to what I just said, I'm kind of a suppressed gossip, anyway." She smiled at Max.

"Okay," said Max. "We probably better get back to work." He returned the smile.

The two detectives got into Max's car. Max started the engine, backed around and drove toward the gate and the road.

"You ever feel like she just has some big joke going on in her head that you aren't smart enough to get?" Skip asked.

"All the time," Max answered.

Max turned back onto the road. When he got to the intersection he turned toward the Maxwell blacktop. As they neared the next bridge over the creek, he slowed and stopped as close to the rail as he could. Skip looked down into the water from the car window.

"See anything?" Max asked.

"Yep," Skip replied. "Looks like maybe one or two that I can see from here."

Max drove off with Skip looking out the window and watching the countryside go by. "Why didn't you tell Elizabeth about the fish kill investigation?" he asked.

"I was thinking about it," Max replied. "I don't know, I guess I didn't want to say anything that we weren't sure of. I hate to get the neighbors all up in arms over something unless I know there's something for them to get all up in arms about. Besides, I don't want to get blindsided by someone getting wind of it and calling DNR before we're ready."

When Max got to the blacktop, he turned north toward Nevada. Max waited to see if Skip wanted to stop one more time at the bridge where the blacktop went over the creek, but Skip didn't say anything, so Max continued north. As they drove past Proctor's house, they saw that his Silverado was not in the yard.

"You know something?" Skip asked as they drove up the blacktop.

"I know a lot of things," Max replied.

"For some reason I think that Proctor has something to do with this fish kill thing," Skip went on, ignoring Max's remark.

"Still wishful thinking?" Max suggested.

"No, I don't think so. I think he is somehow involved with it, and I think it is right under our noses." Skip said. "I'll figure it out."

"I'm sure you will," Max replied.

Max stopped at New 30 and waited for traffic before he entered the intersection. He had his turn signal on to turn left.

"Go north and through town," Skip instructed him. "I want to see if we can find Proctor somewhere in Nevada."

When Max got a break in traffic, he punched the accelerator and the Mustang leaped through the intersection. He proceeded north for a mile, then turned west onto Old 30 toward Nevada. When they got to the city limits, Max started cruising the streets, anywhere he could imagine that Proctor might be at that time of the day. He and Skip scanned every parking lot, every side street and every alley that they passed. They were experts at locating suspect vehicles. For more than half an hour, Max crisscrossed every street in town, but the Silverado was nowhere to be found.

"What now?" Max asked.

Skip looked at the clock on the dash. It was eleven-thirty. "Go out and see what Peggy's doing," Skip said.

"We back to watching her now?" Max asked.

"There's some connection between her, Proctor and those dead fish," Skip mused. "She's our connection to Proctor and Proctor has something to do with those fish."

Max shrugged his shoulders and proceeded through town to county road S-14, and took that south to New 30. He waited for a chance to merge into traffic, and when there was an opening he turned onto the four-lane highway toward the ethanol plant. As they drove past the plant, they saw Peggy's Lexus in the parking lot. Max drove on past, and took the first gravel road north. When he came to Old 30, he turned right, back toward Nevada.

"Figured that we were going to lunch at the West Café?" he suggested.

"Might as well," Skip agreed.

Max proceeded back into Nevada. When he got to the West Café, he drove past. It was still just a little early for Peggy. They drove around town again, as they had been doing before. Finally Max took a round-about route to the café, pulled into the lot and parked.

"Let's go on in," Skip said.

The two got out of the car, went into the café and found a seat in their usual booth. It was just a few minutes before noon, and the café was almost empty. The waitress came up to the table with her pen poised over her pad.

"Hot roast beef sandwich," she said, nodding toward Max, "and a burger with fries?" she continued, nodding toward Skip.

"I think we might want to change things up a little today," Max said. "Could we see some menus?"

"Sure thing," the waitress answered. "Anything to drink?"

"Coke," replied Max.

"Diet Coke," said Skip.

The waitress jotted down the drink order on her pad and left. Max and Skip settled into their seats to wait.

"So you think that Proctor's got something to do with Higgins's dead fish, while he's fucking Travis's wife, and that coincidentally both of our cases are related?" Max asked.

"I do," Skip replied. "I do, and I don't think it is coincidental, either. I think there is something going on here that ties everything together, and I'm close to putting a finger on it. I just am not there yet."

"Okay," Max said. "If you think that there is a connection, I'm going to think that there is a connection, too. So we'll just say that there is and see where it takes us. I'm going to go along with you on this for the sake of discussion."

"Fair enough," Skip replied.

The two sat in silence, each in their own thoughts. Max knew from experience that you don't solve cases by telling other investigators that their suspicions aren't worth investigating. Max didn't know how Skip's hunches were going to pan out, but he was certainly willing to entertain them. But Max was looking at two cases, and the dots weren't connecting. Skip was looking at one big case, and his dots weren't connecting, either.

The waitress returned with their drinks and two menus. She put them on the table in front of each.

"I'll come back in a little while," she said. Customers were starting to fill the booths. Farmers, construction workers, workers from the three ethanol plants, all locals; the West Café was a busy place on weekdays at lunch. At five after, Peggy came through the door and took a seat in her usual booth. She looked over at Max and gave him a curt nod, not smiling.

"Order me a hot beef sandwich," Max said to Skip, getting out of his seat. Max walked across the restaurant and sat down across from Peggy.

"How we doing today?" He smiled as he sat.

"Not so good today," she replied.

"Say, I'm trying to get ahold of Proctor. I can't seem to get him to answer his phone, and I can't find him anywhere," Max said. "You don't know where he is, do you?"

"Matter of fact," Peggy replied, "I'm looking for Allan, myself."

"Hmm," Max muttered, "I was hoping we'd catch him here for lunch."

"I'm thinking that he won't be here," Peggy said in a particularly sarcastic tone. "I'm pretty sure that he's avoiding me."

"Maybe he's avoiding both of us," Max suggested. "What have you got going on with him that he doesn't want to talk about?"

"Business," Peggy replied bluntly without elaborating.

Max nodded as he dug into his billfold and pulled out another one of Ben Ralston's cards. He pulled the pen out of his pocket and wrote Skip's cell number on the back. "This is the number of one of my associates," Max said. "If you see Allan, would you give him a call? I really need to get ahold of him, and I'm thinking he's not returning my calls for a reason. Call my associate there, not the office." Max held the card out to her.

Peggy didn't answer for a moment while she thought about it. "Sure," she finally said, taking the card and looking at it.

Max got up from the seat and went back to the table with Skip.

"I ordered for you," Skip said.

"She is pissed," Max observed.

"What about?" Skip asked.

"I don't know," Max went on, "but he's got her mad at something. She thinks he's avoiding her, and she's not happy about it."

"Did she say why he's avoiding her?" Skip asked.

"Nope," said Max, "but I gave her your cell number and she's going to call you if she finds out where he is."

"You gave her my number?" Skip exclaimed.

"Well, I didn't want to give her my number," Max said defensively.

"So you gave her mine?" Skip said again.

Max took bite of his roast beef sandwich. "These are good. When we get done with this case, we might have to come over here regularly. You think the girls would like this place?"

"Do you really think Gloria and Marjorie would like to eat here?" Skip asked.

"Why not?" Max replied. "They've got good food, and it's pretty cheap, considering."

"Yeah, and the atmosphere is so great. Especially if you like eau de pig," Skip said as he took a big bite out of his burger.

The two detectives ate their lunch without talking any more. Max watched Peggy out of the corner of his eye as she ate her salad. Her phone lay on the table beside her, and occasionally she would swipe the screen. Max couldn't decide if that meant that she was waiting for a call from

Proctor, or if she was just noodling on it. After she finished eating, she paid the bill and walked out, giving Max a half-hearted wave.

"Okay," said Max. "We'll see where this goes."

Skip had finished his burger and was trying to get the waitress's attention.

"Eat up," he said to Max.

Max dug into the last fork fulls of mashed potatoes and savored them while Skip paid the bill.

"I think that the girls would like this place," Max repeated as they walked out. "I really do."

Chapter 22

Thursday

Allan turned into the service drive at BioForce and stopped at the gate. He could see the guard on the phone through the window in the guard shack. He honked his horn to get the guard's attention. The guard looked up at Allan, frowning, and held up one finger. Allan was annoyed with the wait. Finally, the guard put down the phone and stepped out of the shack. Allan did not recognize him, and thought that he must be new. As he approached the open window of the Silverado with his clipboard in hand, Allan noticed his shiny new nametag: D. Moss.

"Yes, sir?" Moss addressed him.

"Allan Proctor," Allan humored the guard. "I own Cleanguard. I have the cleaning contract for the equipment inside."

"You got any ID, Mr. Proctor?"

"Listen…" Allan began.

"Sorry, Mr. Proctor, but until I learn who's who around here, I'm going to have to see some kind of identification."

Allan dug for his billfold to find his driver's license.

"So you're new?" Allan said more as a statement than a question. It was obvious that he was new.

"Yes, sir," Moss replied as he took the license from Allan and looked at it. "Sorry for the inconvenience." He wrote Proctor's name on his clipboard, then pushed a button on a fob that was attached to it. The gate went up.

"How long have you been working here?" Allan asked, suddenly interested in Mr. D. Moss, trying to find common ground to cement some kind of working relationship with the new guard. Allan was always ready to shake a hand and make a new friend, especially when that new friend ran a gate that Allan might need to sneak something through someday.

"This is my first week," Moss answered. "I'm retired navy, Chief Petty Officer. I got tired of sitting around the house, so I came out here and got a job. I'm gonna be here three days a week."

"Retired navy," Allan remarked. "I was in the navy."

"What rate?" Moss asked.

Allan was confused. "I was on a battle ship," Allan hurriedly replied, trying to sound genuine.

"What rate?" Moss asked again. Allan didn't answer. The gate came back down in front of Allan's truck. Moss was waiting for an answer.

"I can't remember," Allan said.

"What ship were you on?" Moss asked.

Allan quickly tried to think of a name. "Titanic," Allan replied.

A smirk came across Moss's face. He hit the button to raise the gate again.

"By the way, Mr. Proctor, Mrs. Bentley's receptionist called down and said that if you came through to tell you that she needs to talk to you before you leave. That was her I was talking to when you drove up. You want me to call and tell her that you're here?"

"No need, no need at all. I'll go up and see her first thing," Allan said as he started to move forward through the gate. Allan made a mental note to fire D. Moss as soon as he got the security contract.

Allan drove back to the rear of the plant. Gordon's red Dodge Ram was nowhere to be seen. Allan had meant to ask Moss if Gordon had been in, but he had forgotten with all the stupid navy talk. Allan parked, got out of his truck and walked into the building. There were two fellows working on one of the tanks that the Mexicans had cleaned on Monday. Allan approached them.

"What's up?" Allan asked.

The two men looked up. "Transfer valve is stuck. Puttin' in a new one while it's empty," one of the workers said. "You guys flushing these things out good?"

"I'm sure that we are," Allan said.

"Well, that cleaning water is corrosive, and if it sets in these valves, it mucks them up," the worker went on. "You gotta flush them out good with fresh water."

"I'll talk to Gordon about that," Allan reassured them. "I'll make sure he gives them more attention."

The two men didn't respond.

"You haven't seen Gordon this morning, have you?" Allan asked.

Both men shook their heads and turned their attention back to the valve that they were replacing. "Mrs. Bentley was down here looking for one of you guys just a little while ago," one of the workers said as he was placing a wrench on the valve. Allan pretended not to hear. He walked out of the building and back to his truck.

Allan drove out of the plant onto New 30, headed back toward the farm again to see if Gordon had returned. As he drove through the gate, he waved at Moss. Moss had his clipboard in hand and was writing on it as Allan passed. "Writing down the time I left," Allan thought. This guy was really playing it by the book. Time in and time out. Now there was an official record of the visit. Allan didn't like official records. Moss had to go. He would talk to Peggy about it later. As he drove by the parking lot, he looked for Peggy's car. It was parked in her usual spot. He continued toward the farm.

Gordon had gotten up early and gone out to the tanker truck. He put the forms that Allan had given him behind the seat. He had gotten the rasp from the shed and put it in the cab as well, like Allan had instructed him. But then he didn't get in. Instead he went to his own pickup truck and drove out on the gravel road that ran past the farmstead, turned south and drove to Maxwell. As he pulled into town, Gordon stopped, got out and looked at the water running under the bridge. He could plainly see a half dozen or so dead fish floating under the bridge.

Gordon got back in the truck and drove into town. He stopped at the Casey's and filled up, paying at the pump. Then he drove down Main Street and continued over the next bridge that went over the creek that wound itself through the town and the countryside beyond. On the other side of the bridge there was a pulloff, just a small dirt parking area that gave access to the river for kayakers and canoers. Gordon pulled in and parked his truck. He got out and walked to the riverbank, looking across the water. He saw two dead fish. Gordon wondered why there were so few of them below the town, and so many above. Gordon got into his truck and drove back toward town.

Gordon was not very familiar with Maxwell, but he had been coming into town for gas and beer while he was living out at Allan's place. He often filled the tanker truck at the Casey's as well. Gordon started exploring every street that went toward the creek. The first two made a loop near the woods that bordered both sides of the creek. The third one actually dead-ended at the woods. At the dead end Gordon noticed a path into the woods and a faded No

Trespassing sign nailed to a tree. Gordon looked around. There were no houses close by. Gordon got out of the truck and walked down the path, ignoring the sign.

The path was well worn, and it took Gordon straight to the riverbank, only thirty yards or so from where the road ended. There were beer cans and empty packages littering the bank. It looked like the area was frequented regularly. One path went upstream and another went downstream. Gordon looked at the water. He didn't see any dead fish at first, but then he spotted what he thought were a couple of them bobbing in the eddy currents across on the other bank. Gordon turned and took the path upstream.

The going was rough. In some places the path was well traveled. In others, it was nonexistent, and when Gordon was convinced that he had lost it completely, he would find it again. Gordon had no idea how far he had walked. He had climbed through or over several fences to get where he was. He came to a new barbed wire fence that crossed the path and ended close to the riverbank. The path went through the fence and continued. Another No Trespassing sign was posted on the barbed wire over the path. Gordon stopped for a moment. The fence and the sign looked new. Much newer than the one that he had ignored when he first entered the woods. Gordon decided to forge on. He climbed through the fence and continued.

Gordon had not gone far when he started to smell the dead fish. The stench got worse and worse with every step upstream. Finally the path came to a clearing. Below the riverbank there was a beaver dam. Gordon tried not to breathe through his nose. There were hundreds, maybe thousands of dead fish held in the slow current by the dam. Gordon could make out what looked like a couple of dead beavers bobbing in amongst the dead fish.

Gordon was disturbed by what he had discovered. He looked around. The path that he was on continued upstream. There was another path that went away from the river. It looked well traveled. Gordon decided to see where it went. It was not a straight path, like the first one he had taken from his truck to the river. This one wound through the woods for a hundred yards, where it came out at another new barbed wire fence, beyond which lay a pasture. Gordon stayed inside the shadow of the woods, looking at the acreage across the pasture. There were more houses on the south side of it. North there was nothing. It looked to Gordon like he was on the north city limits. He was tempted to just walk through the pasture to the road, but then he spotted two big Dobermans trotting around the yard. Then he noticed what looked like a marijuana grow along the woods, in the corner of the pasture. It made him nervous and he quickly looked around for anyone who might be observing him. He knew that marijuana grows were often booby trapped. He looked back at the house beyond the pasture and tried to get a location on those two dogs, which he couldn't see anymore. He backed into the trees and hurriedly worked his way back the direction that he had come.

When Allan got back to the farm, there still was no sign of Gordon. The tanker truck sat parked in the yard just as it had earlier. Allan parked the Silverado and thought about it. He climbed out of his pickup, walked over to the tanker and got in. The keys were in the ignition, as they always were. Allan had told Gordon once that the best thing that could happen to that truck was for it to get stolen, so Gordon always left the keys in it. The rasp was laying on the passenger seat. It looked like Gordon had gotten ready to go, and then something had taken him away. Allan wondered if some cops had come by and arrested Gordon for something. Maybe for running illegal aliens? That probably wouldn't be good. Allan would have to distance himself from that, if it was the case. Allan started thinking about the illegal aliens.

For no reason, Allan turned the key in the ignition. The motor ground as it turned over, seemingly fighting to stay dormant, but after a couple of tries, it caught and started. Allan put the truck in gear and drove it around the farmyard and out the drive onto the road. It was running, Allan thought. He continued down the road. As he passed Elizabeth's place it looked empty, but he waved, anyway, just in case. When he got to the Maxwell blacktop he turned south. He would just burn the truck himself.

As he drove into Maxwell he slowed down, then pulled off to the side of the street and stopped. He had forgotten about Peggy's call. He squirmed around, fishing his phone out of his pocket, and dialed his voicemail. He pushed buttons as he was directed. Allan often wondered what the woman who gave the directions looked like. He wondered if she was a real knockout, or if she was some old lady that they got to do it. Voice talent, they called those women. The Pork Producers had done some online training courses with a company, and they had used Allan as voice talent for the course. They hadn't paid him anything for it, because they were trying to save money with the courses, but there were people who did get paid for it. Allan had inquired about doing more and getting paid. They had taken his name and number, but he had never heard anything more of it. When he got all this wastewater bullshit cleared up, he thought that he should look into it some more. There might be a whole new career there, with easy money.

Allan heard Peggy's recorded voice over the phone. "Allan, there's nothing here after July fifteenth. Go find the rest of them and get them over here to me so that I can send them off with the rest." After a short pause, she continued, "Listen Allan, I'm not dicking around here, I need them ASAP. So find them, or you can explain to the state where you're dumping your wastewater." Allan played the message back again.

"This isn't good," Allan thought, Peggy threatening him like that. He hadn't thought she was one to make threats. Allan wondered what had gotten into her. He thought that he had her pretty much under control, but now she was threatening him. Allan put his phone on the passenger seat next to the rasp, and put the tanker truck into gear. He went around the block and started back to the farm. He really needed to find Gordon and find out what was going on with him before he did anything else.

Gordon took the back roads to the farm. When he got there, Allan's Silverado was parked in the yard. The tanker truck was gone. Gordon wondered what was up with that. Was Allan going to go burn it himself? That didn't make much sense to Gordon. He knew Allan well enough to know that when that tanker burned, Allan would want to be as far from it as he could be, with a solid alibi. It wasn't like Allan to let himself be connected in any way. Gordon looked at his phone. There was a missed call and a message from Peggy Bentley. Gordon was curious; Peggy never called him. He listened to the message.

"Gordon, this is Peggy Bentley. I need to get ahold of Allan, as soon as possible. It is important. He was supposed to get some documentation to me and he only gave me half of it. If you have a way of getting him, please have him call me ASAP. Gordon, if you get this, call me. Please." Gordon deleted the message and frowned. Something was going on. Gordon started thinking about packing up his stuff and leaving. Allan owed him some money, but Gordon was beginning to wonder if it was worth it. He felt like things were coming unhinged. It might be a good time to disappear.

Gordon looked down the road. He could see and hear the tanker truck coming back. He waited as it came closer and turned into the yard. Allan got out. He was controlling his rage, Gordon could see that. Allan didn't scare Gordon. He was all mouth, but whenever he went off, it still wasn't pleasant. But usually Allan held it in, not wanting to lose control of himself, and Gordon could see that was the case today.

"Running late?" Allan asked in an even clipped voice.

"Guess that I am," Gordon replied. "Where've you been?"

Allan didn't answer.

"I took a little drive down by Maxwell," Gordon broke the silence. "I went down there and hiked up Indian Creek. There's a big beaver dam up there on the north end of town. Gotta be a thousand dead fish piled up behind it, and some dead critters as well. It is a wasteland, literally a wasteland. I think we got a bigger problem than we thought we had, and I don't think burning the truck is going to do anything to change that."

Allan was half listening to Gordon. He was changing his plans in his head while Gordon was talking.

"I think you're right," Allan answered, much to Gordon's surprise. "What we need right now is to buy some time." He thought for a moment. "Forget the tanker truck. Take the tractor and get some of those alfalfa bales back there and spread them out over that dead grass below the ponds. Do whatever you need to do to keep it from blowing away. The last thing we need is for someone to fly over in a plane or a helicopter, see it and then pop in on us before we're ready."

"Sounds good," Gordon agreed, relieved that Allan had decided not to burn the truck.

"When you're done with that," Allan continued, "pump the honey wagon full from one of the holding ponds. I'm going to figure out somewhere we can spread it. I'm thinking the neighbor lady over there. I might be able to talk her into it."

Gordon looked skeptical. "How many loads you think are in there?" he asked.

"As many as there are," Allan snapped. "Just get the first load topped off, and I'll find someplace to get rid of it, if not up the road, somewhere else. Then we go from there. Worse comes to worst, we'll haul it up to the other place and spread it on that forty acres of bean stubble."

"You don't want that stuff up there," Gordon said.

"We'll do what we gotta do," Allan shrugged.

"Okay," Gordon said.

"Another thing," Allan said. "Don't be running off again. I might need you. Keep your phone close."

"I got shit for reception down here," Gordon said.

"Well, then just stay here where I can find you." Allan snapped.

Allan left Gordon to get to work, got into his truck and drove out toward Elizabeth's place. He drove through the gate and into the barnyard. Elizabeth had a hammer in her hand and looked like she was trying to fix one of the doors on her huge Butler building. Allan got out of the truck and walked over to where she was standing.

"Need some help?" he asked jovially.

"I need a new door," Elizabeth shook her head. "What are you hatching up now that brings you over here?"

Allan chuckled. "Nothing much. But I was thinking just this morning that my holding ponds are getting full and I need to haul some of the manure out of there and spread it. Best fertilizer there is. Green, no phosphates. It's good for the environment. Pure pig manure and water. I was thinking that maybe you and I could strike up a deal. I could come over and dump a load or two on your pasture, you could pay me a little for overhead, and we would both come out ahead." Allan smiled.

"The pasture is already eaten down, and I don't think it would grow a lot between now and snowfall, anyway," Elizabeth replied. "What I need is that alfalfa hay that you keep telling me is coming."

"It's coming," Allan assured her. "Should be able to pick it up in the next couple of weeks. I'm behind a little, but I'll get it to you." Allan paused for a moment. "You still got some bales of that brome, don't you?"

"I won't for long," Elizabeth answered. "The horses eat that and it goes right through them. There's not a lot of nutrition in that stuff."

Allan continued. "I feel bad about this hay thing. It isn't my fault, but I feel like it is, because I said I would get you some. Right at the moment I'm having trouble getting my hands on it, is all. But I will get some. But here's the thing: why don't I just have Gordon come over here and spread some of that natural fertilizer on your pastures? It's good to get it down in the fall. Then it can work all those nutrients into the soil during the winter, under the snow. You don't owe me anything. Just a good faith gesture on my part because of the hay and all. In the meantime, I'll find some alfalfa for you."

Elizabeth didn't answer. She could see that Allan was up to something. He never came over unless he had some deal that was going to benefit Allan, and Elizabeth was wondering where the profit was in this deal. Probably it was just the convenience of a place close by to get rid of his manure, and if that was all, she didn't see any harm. But Elizabeth was wary. She didn't trust Allan.

"Let me think about it."

"No, I insist," Allan replied, pushing a little to see if he could get her to agree, wanting to get it done and over with. "It is the least I can do." Allan was heading to his truck as he spoke. "I'll have Gordon spread a load or two this afternoon. If not this afternoon, tomorrow morning."

Elizabeth tried to speak up, but Allan got in his truck and shut the door. He drove back to the farm. Gordon was headed toward the ponds with a bale of alfalfa on the back of the tractor. He stopped and idled it down as Allan drove up with his window down.

"When you get done with this, you get a load in the honey wagon, go over to Beckman's place and spread it in that far pasture, as far from the buildings as you can."

Gordon frowned. "She's got horses out there," he protested. "You dump that shit out there, you could kill them. At least make them sick as hell."

"Just do it," Allan ordered. "It's not gonna kill the horses. Who knows? Maybe it's good for the grass. Maybe after it sits out there all winter, she'll have grass six feet high in the spring. Monsanto's made billions of dollars spreading chemicals on farmland."

Allan pulled away before Gordon could argue, drove out of the farmyard and onto the road.

Chapter 23

Thursday

It was a quarter after three. Monica was working at her desk at the agency when she saw a city patrol car pull up in front and Milton unfold from the passenger door. He stood for a moment saying something to the driver, laughed, then flipped off the driver as he closed the door. He was still chuckling to himself when he came into the agency.

"What's so funny?" Monica asked.

"Not something I want to talk about in mixed company," he laughed.

"Mixed company in what way?" Monica narrowed her eyes.

"Mixed company, in that I don't say things like that when there are refined ladies around."

Monica laughed at that. "You really know how to wiggle out of things, don't you?"

Milton was still in uniform. Often he would call dispatch in the mornings to ask if there was a patrol officer close by who had time to run him into the PD for his shift. Milton felt like he was saving a little on gas, but mostly he was saving a space in the always overcrowded city employee parking lot. The down side was that he had to mooch a ride home at the end of his shift, and sometimes no one was going in the direction of his apartment and he would have to wait. This time he had been able to get a ride out to G&B.

"Will you take me home when you get done?" Milton asked.

"Sure," Monica answered.

"What are you doing?" Milton asked.

"Research for the two master detectives," she answered.

"You on that dating site?" Milton asked.

"No," Monica answered. "I'm looking up about water pollution, particularly creeks and rivers."

Milton went to the conference room, got a chair and rolled it next to Monica's desk, cozied up next to her and watched her search. "You like Google?" he asked.

"Most of the time," Monica answered.

"I like Yahoo," Milton said.

Monica didn't answer him. She was clicking on different sites, scanning them, then closing the tab and going to the next site. Some sites she read more carefully.

"You ever think about this?" Milton asked, "'Milton and Monica,' our names go together don't they?"

Monica was reading and did not respond. When she was done, she closed the tab and looked up. "'Monica and Milton,' they do go together nicely. Sort of rolls off the tongue."

"So what's with the case?" Milton asked. "What does water pollution have to do with some gal messing around?"

"Nothing," Monica answered. "This is a different case. This is Higgins's case."

"Higgins the dognapper?" Milton exclaimed.

"Yeah, they actually took on a case for him. Evidently his creek is polluted, and he wants the guys to find out who's doing it."

"No one told me about this one." Milton sounded hurt that they had not included him. "Well, I've got a little bit of scuttlebutt on that."

"What's that?" Monica inquired.

"Well, the DNR has been out testing the water around down there, because they already have an investigation going on, and Carlisle is going out with them tomorrow to do some snooping around back behind Higgins's place."

"So the DNR is doing an investigation?" Monica asked.

"Yep," Milton answered. "And here's another thing: Carlisle thinks that Higgins is up to something, and he's going to use this as a reason to take a look at Higgins's place from the back side, to see what he can see." Milton ended on a note of satisfaction that he knew something that Monica didn't. "Pretty good knowing a cop, don't you think?" he added.

Monica thought about it a moment. "You know something? That might just solve the case for Higgins, too. I wondered why they didn't just call the DNR to start with. I think that they were just doing it for him to be nice."

"What do you think about Carlisle going back there?" Milton asked.

"I don't think he's going to see anything," Monica answered. "What I hear is that Higgins has changed his ways. He was in here the other day, and he was just as nice as could be. I don't think he has anything to hide. I hope not, anyway," Monica said, a bit worried.

Milton shrugged his shoulders. "Maybe so, but Carlisle has a hard-on for him, I know that. He doesn't think the new Higgins is so squeaky clean."

Monica was bookmarking a page.

"Do you have Gloria's cell number?" Milton asked.

"Yes," Monica answered. "You want it?"

"I need to talk to her, get some advice on something."

"Oooooh, a surprise for Max?" Monica asked, raising her eyebrows. "What are you going to do? I love surprises."

"Why do you think it is a surprise for Max? I just want to ask her something."

"Why can't you tell me?" Monica teased. "'Loose lips sink ships?' You think I'll tell him what you're up to?"

"You'll be the first to know, I promise," Milton said.

"I better be," she countered.

"When are you getting out of here?" Milton asked, changing the subject.

"I was waiting around for the guys to get back. But I can take you home and then come back," Monica replied.

"Only if it's not any trouble," Milton answered.

"For you, it isn't any trouble," she said. "But don't be pushing your luck."

Monica got up and gathered her things. Milton went out to the parking lot and stood by her car while he waited for her to lock the agency door. The two got in her car and Monica pulled out of the lot. Milton asked what Essie was up to, and they talked about her and preschool. Monica pulled into the parking lot at Milton's apartment complex and parked next to Milton's Jeep Wrangler in front of his building.

Milton got out of the car, then bent down to ask through the open door, "Wanna come on up for a little while?"

"What do you have in mind?" Monica countered.

"I don't know," Milton said with a grin on his face. "What do you have in mind?"

"Well, if you don't have anything in mind, I suppose that I better get back to work so that I don't miss the guys," Monica teased.

"I got something in mind," Milton replied hastily.

"I figured that you did," Monica said as she reached for her purse and started to get out of the car.

"This isn't going to take the place of us going to Omaha or anything, right?" Milton asked as they walked into the apartment building.

"Preview of coming attractions," Monica answered.

Monica made her way back to the office. It was later than she usually stayed at work. After she left Milton's place, she had run by her townhouse and picked up Essie. On the way she had called Max, and he had told her that he and Skip had done routine patrol all afternoon, which Monica knew meant that they were out driving around aimlessly. Now they were on the way back to town. She told them that she had bookmarked some sites on the internet that they might be interested in. Max told her that they would meet her back at the agency.

When Monica pulled into the parking lot, Max's yellow Mustang convertible was parked in front. Monica had never seen it so dirty. Max was pretty particular about his car. She wondered if the mud spattered on the top would stain it. She thought that if it were her car, she would just ask Milton to take it to the carwash. She was pretty sure that he would be happy to do it for her. Lately he had been keeping up the maintenance on her car, something that Monica let slide. She liked having Milton doing it for her.

Monica parked her car, got Essie out of her carseat and took her hand, leading her through the doors and into the agency's reception area. As soon as Monica let go of her hand, Essie ran down the hallway toward Max and Skip's offices. Monica heard the guys hollering at her and chasing her around. Essie was squealing as she ran away from them. Soon Monica heard Essie's little footsteps in the hall as she ran back toward the waiting area, and Max and Skip clomping along behind her yelling, "We're gonna get ya, we're gonna get ya!" The three arrived at Monica's desk.

Essie ran around to the other side of her and tried to hide, giggling. Max and Skip showed up red-faced and puffing.

"Everybody done getting my daughter all riled up and out of control?" Monica gave Max a stern look.

"What did I do?" Max asked defensively.

"She started it," Skip said. "Hey, Essie, do you want a Mountain Dew?"

Essie came out from behind Monica's leg and looked up expectantly toward Skip.

"No Mountain Dew," Monica said firmly. "Look here," she said, bringing up a page on her computer screen. "I started searching ethanol plants and cleaning, considering that Proctor does the cleaning at BioForce, and guess what? Ethanol plants are getting fined for improper disposal of cleaning water. It is like the biggest hit when you do a search on cleaning and ethanol."

Max looked over Monica's shoulder. Skip went around to the other side, grabbed up Essie, turned around and put her behind him, and looked over Monica's other shoulder.

"Click on that one," Max pointed.

Monica clicked on the headline, "Iowa Ethanol Plant Fined."

"That one's five years ago," Monica said, as she clicked on it. "It was a big one."

"Anything on our plant?" Max asked.

"BioForce?" Monica asked.

"Yep, BioForce."

"Nothing on BioForce specifically," Monica said. "But here's the thing: the cleaning water is very corrosive and toxic, and there are both federal and state regulations for the disposing of it." Monica let Max and Skip read. "If you read down there, the cleaning company that was cleaning the equipment for this other plant was dumping it on a field. It got into the ground water, contaminating the wells for a several miles around it. Both the plant and the cleaning contractor got major fines."

Monica let them read a little more. Neither were commenting.

"I think that Monica has just come up with our connection." Skip muttered. "Proctor's got that farm, right upstream from Higgins's place." He thought for a moment. "But one thing doesn't fit: what about the fish upstream from there?"

The three stood in thought for a minute. "Fish swim upstream," Max said suddenly, as if he just had a revelation. "I mean, back in my fishing days, we'd catch catfish just below the dam because the fish would go upstream until they got stopped by the dam. And their snouts would be all buggered up from bumping into the dam, trying to get up above it. So maybe a fish swims through the chemicals, then it continues upstream a ways before the chemicals do it in. Then it dies and floats back down."

Skip looked up at Max. "How far upstream?"

"As far as it can get before the chemicals take effect," Max replied.

"I knew it," Skip exclaimed. "I knew that Proctor was involved in this."

The two continued reading over Monica's shoulder. When they were done, they had Monica go to another article, then another.

"One other thing, though," Monica said after they had read a couple of her bookmarked articles. "Did you know that the DNR is already investigating a fish kill down near Maxwell?"

"What?" Skip stood up.

"Higgins's creek," she said. "Carlisle ran into a DNR guy who was taking water samples, and he told Carlisle that they were down there investigating chemicals in the water."

"That's interesting," Max said.

"Turn it over to the DNR: case closed," Monica said.

"So where did you get that little piece of info?" asked Skip.

"Milton was in here earlier, and he told me," Monica replied. "He said that Carlisle told him that tomorrow the DNR guy is going to walk up the creek behind Higgins's place and see if he can find out where the dead fish are coming from. Carlisle's going to tag along so that he can get back in there and spy on Higgins."

"Why does Carlisle want to spy on Higgns?" Skip perked up.

"Because he thinks that Higgins is up to something," Monica replied.

"Shit, shit, shit," Max exclaimed. Skip had a worried look on his face.

"You know what time they're going to go down there?" Skip already had his phone out of his pocket and was dialing Higgins's number. It started ringing. Max and Skip waited. There was no answer. Skip looked up from his phone. "Mailbox is full," Skip said incredulously.

"Let's just drive down there," Max said.

"What's the deal?" Monica asked, realizing that things were getting serious for some reason that she was not privy to. "Why are you guys so edgy all of a sudden?"

"Because," Max replied, "Higgins has turned over a new leaf okay, but his stupid cousin hasn't. His cousin has a marijuana grow out there in Higgins's back pasture. You can't see it from the road, but you can't miss it from the back."

"That's why you didn't call the DNR in the first place," Monica observed.

"That's why," Max said.

"Okay," Skip said, "let's get going."

"You want me to stay?" Monica asked. "Because I can."

Skip stopped at the door. "I don't think so. There's nothing you can do." He turned before he went out the door. Monica was watching them leave with a worried look on her face. Skip stuck his head back through the door. "Good job on the wastewater disposal thing," he said. "That explains a lot. Good teamwork." He hesitated a moment. "Glad we got a heads-up on the DNR investigation, too."

Monica was a bit dazed as Skip turned and hustled to the car.

Max already had the motor going. "Call Milton," Max said as Skip climbed in. "See if he knows what time Carlisle and the posse are going to go back there."

Skip took out his phone and found Milton in his speed dial. The phone rang four times, and Skip was sure it was going to voicemail when Milton answered.

"Hey, Skip," he said. "I was just talking to Monica."

"Jeez," Skip exclaimed. "Like, we left two seconds ago."

Milton didn't reply.

"Do you know what time Carlisle is going to meet those guys to go back in there behind Higgins's place?" Skip asked.

Milton still didn't reply.

"Milton, what the fuck?" Skip said.

"That's the second time I've ever heard you say fuck," Max remarked as he drove out of the parking lot. "First time was when we won the lottery."

Skip ignored him. "Milton, it's just a grow. It isn't even Higgins's grow. It belongs to his stupid cousin. But if Carlisle gets wind of it, Higgins is going to jail, not his cousin." Skip waited. "Higgins is not some big drug lord; he's just a hillbilly."

"Ten," Milton finally said.

"Thanks," Skip said into the phone, but Milton had already ended the call.

"He's not happy," Skip said to Max.

"I'm sure he's not," Max replied.

Max put his foot into it, rocketing down New 30 to the Maxwell blacktop.

"We've been flying through here so much lately that the sheriff's going to put a radar trap out here to catch us one of these days," Skip remarked.

"Yep," was all Max said.

Max made short work of the drive to Maxwell and Higgins's place. When they pulled through the gate and stopped, the two dogs came charging out of the barn, barking and growling. The rest of the place looked deserted.

"Apparently the dogs don't recognize the car," Max said, as the two lunged at the window, barking and snarling.

"Honk the horn," Skip said.

Max honked the horn and waited. The dogs became even more enraged.

"Pete! Repeat!" Max shouted through the glass. "It's me and Skip. Calm down. We're friends." The dogs kept growling and barking. One ran around to Skip's side of the car. They had it surrounded.

"Honk the horn again," Skip said.

Max honked the horn.

"I have an idea," Skip said after a moment. "Let's go to Casey's and see if Bonnie is there. She probably knows how to get ahold of him."

Max was backing out of the yard before Skip had finished talking. He drove the five blocks to Main Street and pulled up to the door of the Casey's convenience store. Skip jumped out and ran inside. Max kept the motor running and waited. Soon Skip came running back out and got in the car.

"Bonnie's not working," he said as he got in. "The guy behind the counter wouldn't give me her phone number. He said that he would call her and have her call us back, but I don't think that he is really going to do that. I gave him my card. We'll see. He wasn't too impressed that a couple of private detectives were trying to find one of his friends."

"What now?" Max asked.

"Go back over to Higgins's place," Skip replied.

Max backtracked the way he had come and stopped in the street outside Higgins's gate. The two dogs stood in the yard, challenging them to come back in.

"Those dogs are not friendly without Higgins," Max observed. The two sat watching the dogs, who were watching them intently in turn.

"Go on home," Skip said. "I'll keep trying to call him tonight. If I don't get him, we'll come down first thing in the morning."

"Sounds good," Max replied. "Want to go past Proctor's place and look around as long as we're down here?"

Skip thought for a moment. "No," he finally said. "Just go home. We'll help Higgins get that weed out of there in the morning before Carlisle and crew get there, and then we'll let the DNR take care of the rest. Nothing we can do about it at this point. It isn't our jurisdiction. Maybe we just call the DNR first thing tomorrow and let them know that we suspect Proctor is dumping his cleaning water illegally. Point the finger at him."

Max agreed.

Milton went back to Monica on his phone as soon as he was done talking to Skip. "It was Skip wanting to know what time Carlisle is going to go take a peek at Higgins's place tomorrow."

"Did you tell him?" Monica asked.

"Yes," Milton answered.

"I'm sorry," Monica said quietly. "I shouldn't have said anything to them about it."

"You don't need to be sorry," Milton said. "Max and Skip are as much your family as anyone. You can't walk around all the time worrying about what you say to them. I always say, you can choose your friends, but you can't choose your family. I don't want to come between you guys."

"You're not," Monica said.

"Besides, I've known them longer than you have," Milton said. "Well, I told them, and that's going to blow Carlisle's case, and I just don't feel good about that," Milton said. "There is a confidentiality issue here."

"Carlisle didn't have a case," Monica offered. "He was fishing. You told me that. You can't blow a case that he didn't have."

Milton was quiet for a moment. "Why is it that I always feel better about things after I talk to you?"

"Maybe because I'm so smart and worldly?" Monica answered.

"I'm sure that's it," Milton laughed.

Milton and Monica ended the call. Milton thought for a moment, then went to his contacts and found Judy in his speed dial. He hit call. He waited while the phone rang, and then he heard the familiar voice of his sister.

"Milton, to what do I owe the pleasure?"

"Hey," Milton responded, "what are you doing?"

"Well," she said thoughtfully, "hauling kids around, juggling a career, making supper and washing clothes for an unappreciative husband." She stopped for a moment. "I shouldn't really say that; he's kind of appreciative."

"Sounds good, actually," Milton said. "How's the kids?"

"They are doing fine," Judy replied. "Everything is good here."

Milton paused for a few seconds, trying to form his words. "I've got a question for you," he said.

"Okay," Judy replied.

"So when Charlie proposed, did he show up with an engagement ring and ask you to marry him like they do in the movies, or did he ask you first and then take you shopping to pick out one that you liked?"

Judy didn't answer right away. "Are you thinking of getting engaged?" she finally asked.

It was Milton's turn to say nothing for a moment. "I guess that I wouldn't be asking you that question if I wasn't," he said matter-of-factly.

"We talked a lot about getting married before we actually got engaged. We made a pretense that looking at rings was 'just on a whim,' but I knew pretty much what I wanted and what I was getting."

"Okay," Milton said.

"In retrospect," Judy continued, interrupting him, "I wish that he had just picked the ring and popped the question."

"Really?" Milton responded.

"Yes, really," she answered. "So tell me about this poor girl that you are going to ask to spend her life putting up with you. How long have you known her? Why haven't I heard about her before now?"

"We've been dating about five months. She is just a very nice person. She's the receptionist for those guys that I know who won the lottery and started that detective agency. She's going to college to get a degree in psychology."

"Sounds like I need to meet her," Judy remarked.

"She's African American," Milton said.

Judy didn't answer for a moment. "Have Mom and Dad met her? That's going to be interesting," she chuckled.

"She has a little girl," Milton added.

"That's getting real interesting," Judy said, her voice showing her excitement.

"She used to be a stripper," Milton said.

"Man," Judy replied, "are you just trying to start trouble?" She was laughing out loud. "I'm going to be the golden child again."

"I'm very serious about this girl," Milton said defensively. "I'm not trying to do anything, I'm falling in love and I don't have any control over it anymore."

Judy got serious. "I know you are. I can tell. I can hear it in your voice. I'm sorry to tease you. After everything that I've been through with Dad, I am just listening to you and thinking that this is going to be a big adjustment for him. We're ganging up on him," she said in a conspiratorial tone.

"I don't want to gang up on him," Milton replied, "I want him to just deal with it and not make everyone uncomfortable."

Judy didn't say anything for a moment. "So does this girl have a name?"

"Monica," Milton answered.

"That's a pretty name. And her little girl?"

"Essie," Allan replied.

"And you're head-over-heels in love?"

"With both of them," Milton said.

"Wow, you got it bad, little brother," Judy laughed.

"I don't know why I call you," Milton replied.

"Get the ring first," Judy advised. "Then just ask her. Don't make a big production out of it, just take her out on a walk and ask her. And when she says yes, which I'm sure she will, take her out to celebrate. That's how I wish we had done it."

"Thanks," Milton said. "That helps a lot."

"I want to meet this girl," Judy said.

Chapter 24

Thursday

Allan left the farm after talking to Gordon, drove straight to his house, parked the Silverado and went to his office. He had to think, but his mind was going crazy. He sat down at his computer, found the lonelyfarmers.com site and brought it up, but he could not bring himself to concentrate on it.

Allan picked up his office phone and dialed Peggy's office number. The receptionist answered.

"This is Allan Proctor. I would like to speak to Mrs. Bentley, please," he told her.

"Just a minute." She put him on hold.

Allan wasn't on hold long. "Allan, where are you?" Peggy demanded.

"I'm at home, in my office catching up on some paperwork," Allan answered.

"Did you listen to your messages?" she asked. Allan could hear the frustration in her voice.

"No," Allan said in a calm voice, "but I saw that you tried to call me several times, and I called you back several times to see what you need."

Peggy didn't say anything for a moment. It was just like Allan to shift the blame on her for him not getting back to her. She gathered herself together and took a deep breath. "There isn't any documentation in that pile you gave me for any trips to Princeton after the middle of July," she said, and waited for a response.

"That's strange," Allan answered. "I told Gordon to get all of them to me; he must have missed a few."

"Well, I need them now," Peggy replied. "And there better be more than a few."

"Okay," Allan said thoughtfully. "I'll bet they're still in the tanker truck. He keeps them in a folder behind the seat."

"I need them now." Peggy was getting exasperated.

"I know you do," Allan responded. "Gordon is actually hauling a load down to Princeton right now. I'll call him up and have him check. If they aren't there, I don't know where they would be."

"God damn it," Peggy responded. "You need to run a tighter ship."

"I thought I was," Allan replied. "But evidently I was putting too much trust in Gordon. That's my fault. But I've never had any problems with him before. He's always been all over it. But right now, all I can do is call him on his cell and see what he says. Maybe they are at the house down on the farm. If they are, I can run down and get them right away. Let's hope that's the case. If not, we'll get them as soon as he gets back."

Allan's voice had a calming effect on Peggy. She was starting to breathe easier, and her heart was no longer pounding. "Allan, I can't just manufacture them. You need to find them and get them to me."

"I know that," Allan said. "I'll call you right back."

"I'll be waiting," Peggy said as she ended the call. She actually felt better after talking to Allan. It was just a mix-up, she was sure. Allan would get them to her, and she really didn't need to get them sent over to the state until tomorrow. They had time. Peggy just liked to be on top of things, and this investigation was making her nervous.

Peggy told herself that everything was fine, they just had to get the documents in order.

Allan sat back in his chair. He had to think. He took out his cell phone and listened to each of Peggy's messages, and deleted each one when he was done. She was coming unglued. If there was a loose cannon in this whole thing, it was Peggy. If he could keep her from going bonkers, they might get through this without drawing attention to Allan, but he had to get control of her.

Gordon was another story. It would be good for Gordon to disappear. Allan thought about going down to the farm, handing Gordon a wad of cash and telling him to leave the state. Maybe tell him to leave the country. He could go down to Mexico and stay with his relatives down there until this investigation blew over. Then Allan could pitch all the blame on Gordon. But Allan didn't want to just pitch the blame: he wanted to stay completely out of it. The blame had to go straight to Gordon, and not through Allan. Besides, Allan didn't even know if Gordon had relatives in Mexico.

Allan tried to think of the alternatives. He needed more options. He knew from experience that he could not count on one plan to work; he had to have two or three plans. When something that he couldn't control started coming apart like this, he had to be able to switch directions quickly. Gordon disappearing was a plan, but not the best plan. He had to come up with better ones. Ones that would keep Allan out of the spotlight. Allan was wracking his brain. He was wondering if there was any way that he could implicate Peggy to take the suspicion away from himself. Peggy and Gordon had to take the fall. Allan needed deniability.

Allan was tossing the idea around in his head. "Peggy and Gordon," Allan thought. "This has potential. How do I do this?" Allan was working it. Peggy and Gordon were having an affair, and Gordon was in cahoots with Peggy. Allan was just a pawn in their scheme. Gordon was illegally dumping the wastewater, and Peggy was getting kickbacks from Gordon. She knew all about it. Allan, in the meantime, was paying Gordon to take the wastewater to Princeton, totally unaware of the illegal arrangements between the other two.

It was a good plan, but of course they would refute his story. It would be their word against his, two against one. Allan had to figure out how to counter, and the best plan would be one that he didn't have to figure out how to counter. Because if he had to counter, that would mean he was suspect as well. Allan thought about that.

Then he had an idea. Allan would pay Gordon to admit that he was having an affair with Peggy, and that the two of them had hatched up the scheme. And then Gordon would disappear. That would leave Peggy holding the bag. The authorities would probably want Allan to testify against them, but he could say that he didn't know anything was going on, that he was the victim in their deception. That would be the end of it for Allan: he would simply say that he didn't know anything, then walk away from it like it never happened

Allan heard the bus stop out in front of the farm, and he could hear his kids yelling at their friends as it pulled away. A few minutes later he heard them come into the house and head for the refrigerator. He had a plan. Admittedly, there were a few holes to fill, but it was a plan. He just had to pull the right strings at the right time to make it work.

Allan got up from his chair to go out and say hi to his kids, ask them how their day had gone. Almost as an afterthought, Allan turned to the gun safe in the corner of his office and turned the dial back and forth, opening it up. He removed a Glock 9mm, checked to make sure that it was loaded and slid it under his waistband, pulling his shirt over it. Then he walked out of the office to talk to the kids.

He found the two at the counter in the kitchen. One had a bowl of cereal, the other was eating a cherry Popsicle that was dripping on the floor.

"Don't make a mess," Allan told the two.

"We're hungry," his son said, as if that explained everything.

"I can see that you're hungry," Allan lectured. "Don't make a mess."

The two were not listening.

"Hey," Allan barked, to get their attention. The two youngsters looked up. "I got some things that I need to get done, so I'm taking off. When your mom gets home, tell her that I'll be home for supper. Maybe a little late, but not too late."

His daughter nodded her head.

"Okay," Allan said. "Behave yourselves, and don't make a mess." Allan accentuated the "don't make a mess."

He left the house and got into the Silverado. He drove north on the blacktop and then west on New 30, toward the ethanol plant. He pulled into the implement dealership across the highway and parked in the parking lot. He got out his cell and found Peggy's office number in his contacts, then pushed the call button. The receptionist answered.

"Proctor, for Mrs. Bentley again."

"Just a minute," the receptionist replied. She sounded like she was being put out by Allan's calls. He thought that she probably had her nose stuck in a magazine, too busy to do her job.

"Find 'em?" Peggy asked first thing.

"He's got them," Allan replied. "But there's a problem, and I think that you need to take a look at something before you do anything."

Peggy didn't respond.

"We got a big problem," Allan went on. "Gordon has been fudging a bit along the way here, and I think that you need to see what he's been doing. Because I think we are going to have to explain what is happening and I want you to tell me what you think."

"I'm confused," Peggy replied. Her head was starting to hurt. "I don't understand what you just said. What do you mean, 'Gordon has been fudging'? What does fudging mean? Fudging what, documents?"

"Not just documents," Allan replied.

"Well, bring them in and let me take a look, then," Peggy said.

"It isn't just the documents that we have a problem with. There's something else, too," Allan said in a resigned voice. "Seriously, you need to take a look at this. I can't explain it over the phone. I need for you to meet me someplace, and not your office."

"Why can't you just tell me?" Peggy asked, exasperated. "Are we going to be implicated in this DNR investigation? Is that what you're saying?"

"Peggy, listen, you need to see it," Allan repeated. "I'll meet you at the lake. We probably don't want anyone to see you getting into my truck there at the plant. I'll meet you at the lake, at our usual spot. I'll take you down and show you what Gordon has been doing, and then we'll talk about it."

Peggy felt a bit uneasy about going off with Allan, but her curiosity and fear of what the state regulators would find were getting the better of her. She was sure that he wanted her to see this problem—whatever it was—so that she could come up with a plan to bail him out. Her better judgment was telling her that it was probably something of his own making and that the less she knew, the better off she would be.

"Okay, I'll meet you at the lake," she said resignedly.

"I wouldn't tell anyone, either," Allan said. "At least until you get a look at it first."

Peggy did not respond. "Just saying," Allan continued. "We might want to keep this on the down low for now."

"I'll see you at the lake," Peggy reiterated.

"In an hour," Allan said.

Peggy hung up her phone. Her heart was beating, she could hardly breathe and her head hurt. She felt like she was going to throw up. She went to the restroom and closed the door. Ten minutes later, her receptionist called through the door, "Mrs. Bentley, are you alright?"

"I'm fine," Peggy called out. "I have an unexpected meeting, and I'm just getting myself ready."

"Okay," Peggy could hear Sandra walking away.

Peggy left the restroom and went back to her office, changed out of her heels and into the walking shoes that she kept in her office for when she had to spend time out in the plant. She gathered up her phone and her purse and left her office.

"I don't know whether I'll be back today or not," Peggy instructed the receptionist. "Remember to lock up when you leave."

Sandra nodded. Peggy walked down the hall and made her way through the parking lot to her car. She got in, started it up and went out onto the highway, toward the lake. When she got there, Allan was in his pickup truck, already in the lot. Peggy parked and got out of her car. Allan reached over and opened the door for her.

"Hop in," he said from the driver's seat.

Peggy climbed into the truck, which was difficult in a skirt. She was glad that she had worn her walking shoes.

"So what's this all about?" she asked, a little nervous.

Allan had started the truck and was backing out.

"Whoa, where are we going?" she asked.

"I have to show you something," Allan replied.

"Where?" Peggy repeated.

"Down at the farm," Allan said. "You'll see when we get there."

Peggy was panicking a little. She started to open the door.

"What are you doing?" Allan asked her.

"I'm getting out," Peggy said.

"Calm down," Allan said, as he reached across and pulled the door closed. "Why are you being like this?"

"Why are *you* being like this?" Peggy countered.

"Calm down. I'll bring you back as soon as you see what's going on. We'll come back here and talk about it," Allan reassured her in a calm voice.

Peggy sat back, resigned. She could see that Allan was not going to tell her anything, and that there was not going to be any conversation until she saw whatever it was that he wanted to show her. She was certain that it was going to have to do with the disposal of the wastewater, and that made her very nervous.

When they got out to New 30, Allan spoke up. "So just how much do you and Gordon talk?"

"Gordon?" Peggy was confused. "I hardly ever talk to Gordon."

"You don't talk to Gordon about the business? About me?" Allan pressed.

"No, I don't," Peggy replied.

"He doesn't come up to the office there and visit with you?" Allan asked.

"I don't think he has ever been to my office," Peggy replied defensively. "Why are you asking all these questions about Gordon? I hardly know him."

"Because I don't think that Gordon is in this by himself," Allan continued. "I don't know how he would get it past me if he didn't have some help."

"You think that I have something to do with this? Whatever this is?" Peggy demanded.

"I don't know, do you?" Allan asked.

"I don't even know what it is you're talking about!" Peggy was becoming exasperated with the conversation.

"I'm just saying that I don't know who to trust anymore," Allan said, making sure to put an edge of anger in his voice. "I thought that I could trust you and Gordon, but now I don't know who I can trust."

Peggy was silent. She was trying to figure out what Allan was implying, and something about the way he was acting was making it hard to breathe. Had Allan discovered that Gordon was doing something illegal? And did he think she was involved, too? She wished that she had gotten out of the truck at the lake. She wished that she had not gotten into the truck in the first place.

"I'm just going to have to ask you right out, I guess: have you and Gordon been having an affair?" Allan asked.

"Are you fucking crazy?" Peggy blurted. "I've been having an affair with you, Allan. Do you remember last night? And I'm more than ready to end it right now, right here. You can just let me out on the side of the road. I don't need to go any farther."

"You haven't answered my question: are you having an affair with Gordon?" Allan calmly asked again.

Peggy was becoming afraid. Allan slowed down to turn the corner onto a gravel road and Peggy thought about jumping out, but then decided against it when she realized that she would have to unbuckle the seatbelt, open the door and jump out of a moving vehicle in a pencil skirt. Sure, you saw it all the time on TV, but Peggy knew that she was not up to the task. She resigned herself to the ride.

Allan drove by Elizabeth's place and looked out over the pasture. He wondered if Gordon had spread a load from the holding pond over it yet. He couldn't tell. As he pulled into the drive at the farm, he saw Gordon's truck parked next to the house and the honey wagon parked down the hill next to the pond. The hose from the pump was in the blueish-brown water that filled the pond. The gasoline-powered pump was running.

"We're here," Allan announced.

Peggy unbuckled her seatbelt and got out of the truck as quickly as she could.

"Come here and take a look," Allan said, leading her down toward the honey wagon. "Over there we have the hog confinements," Allan was explaining as they walked. "You've been down here before, haven't you?"

"I've never been down here," Peggy said.

"Gordon's never brought you down here?" Allan asked.

"No!" Peggy almost screeched. "Gordon has never brought me down here. Gordon has never brought me anywhere!"

"So one of the confinement buildings is full of hogs, the other one is empty," Allan continued. "Both buildings have manure pits under them." Allan looked over at Peggy to make sure she was following what he was saying as they were nearing the ponds. "So we have these ponds, and sometimes we pump the manure from the pits into these holding ponds." Allan stopped above the ponds and looked over at Peggy. She was looking out over the ponds as well. "Do you see all that hay spread out down there? That's covering up dead grass, which is dead because Gordon has been dumping the wastewater from BioForce into the pit under the empty confinement building, and when the pit gets full, he pumps it down into the ponds."

Gordon walked down the hill, stopping beside Allan and Peggy. He didn't say anything.

"So the wastewater is working its way through the ground and into the creek down there beyond those trees," Allan continued.

"That's about it," Gordon said. He was relieved that Allan was showing Peggy what was going on, getting it out in the open. It would be better all the way around.

Peggy looked over at Gordon. "Why?" she asked.

"Why what?" Gordon asked back.

"Why not haul it down to Missouri, like you are supposed to? Like I pay you to do?"

Gordon looked over at Allan, expecting him to answer.

"That's what I've been wondering, myself," Allan replied.

Both Peggy and Gordon gave Allan a confused look. Allan took a couple of steps back, pulled the Glock out of his waistband and pointed it toward the other two.

"I think that we've seen enough here," Allan said. "Let's walk back up." He stepped aside and waved the gun up toward the way that they had come. Peggy and Gordon started walking. Allan fell in behind them.

"Allan, this is getting out of hand," Peggy pleaded. "This is getting way out of hand. This isn't helping anything. We need to tell the authorities what happened, and then deal with the consequences. This, right here, is not how we handle things."

"Just keep moving," Allan replied calmly. "I know how to take care of this."

Most old farms like Allan's had a well pit, which was usually covered with a concrete pad with a heavy hatch on top of it. The pits went down eight feet to the well itself, where a pump and a pressure tank reside below the frost line. Allan directed Peggy and Gordon to his well.

"Gordon, if you would be so kind as to pull open the hatch there," Allan pointed to it with the barrel of the Glock. Gordon did as he was told. The pit was dark and cold. One light bulb inside connected to a switch that was installed on a pole beside the pit. In the winter, the 100-watt bulb generated enough heat to keep the well pit from freezing. A metal ladder attached to the wall led down to the floor of the pit.

"Down we go," Allan instructed Gordon and Peggy. They didn't move. "I really don't want to shoot either one of you," Allan said, "but you're going down there one way or another. Gordon, you first."

Gordon climbed through the hatch and down the ladder into the pit. Allan waved his gun at Peggy to follow. When both of them were in the pit, Allan pulled the hatch closed. He fastened the hasp that locked the hatch down, then slid an old rusty screwdriver through it. A two-inch pipe in the lid provided ventilation. "Just sit tight there," Allan yelled through the pipe. "I'll get you out when I have everything ready."

"Turn on the light," Gordon screamed. "Give us a little light down here."

"If you promise to keep quiet," Allan called back. The two were silent. Allan went to the pole and flipped the switch. Then he walked down to the honey wagon and turned off the engine on the pump. The pipe gauge on the side of the tank showed that it was almost full.

Allan walked back to his truck and drove home.

Chapter 25

Friday

Gordon had been awake all night, trying to figure out what was going on and how he and Peggy could get out of the well pit. They had heard Allan drive away, leaving them trapped. Gordon had pulled out his cell phone, but he got no reception. Cell reception was spotty everywhere at the farm as it was, but it was nonexistent in the well pit. Knowing that had not stopped Gordon from trying every few minutes all night, anyway. He had tried to call and he had sent a dozen text messages. He had tried to get some bars of service by holding his phone as close to the vent as he could. He had tried to send emails. But nothing had gone out. When he turned on his phone now, it would just spin, all the emails and texts in a queue, trying unsuccessfully to send.

It took a half hour or so for Peggy to realize what a predicament she was in. Then she started crying. Gordon had tried to reassure her that they were going to get out of there eventually, but he wasn't sure he believed it himself. Later she fell asleep, emotionally exhausted. She had awoken at five-thirty. The two talked for a while, piecing together what each knew to try and figure out what was up Allan's sleeve, but now she sat silent in the corner of the pit while Gordon stood as high on the ladder as he could get, head bent, his phone held up to the vent, trying one more time to call out. His battery was almost dead.

"So it was all a lie from the start?" Peggy asked. "Allan just wanted the cleaning contract?"

"Yes," Gordon answered.

"And you knew this?"

"Yes," Gordon admitted. "At first it was just Allan taking advantage of a business opportunity," Gordon explained. "He hired me to supervise the illegals that we were bringing in to do the work and to drive the tanker truck. But then the tanker truck got so bad off that it couldn't make the trip to Missouri, and I came up with the idea of dumping the wastewater in the pit until we could get something more reliable, which just never happened. I guess I hoped we would, but I think that I always knew that Allan wasn't going to ever buy a new truck. So we just kept dumping in the pit 'til it was full."

Peggy was only half listening to Gordon. She was frightened. More frightened than she had ever felt in her life, and more helpless. "What's going to happen now?" she asked.

"Honestly?" Gordon said.

"That would be a nice change," Peggy said, showing a little pluck.

"I don't know," Gordon continued. "I'm not sure if Allan knows."

"I have to pee," Peggy said.

"Try to do it over in that corner behind the pump," Gordon told her. "Away from the well. We will have to drink out of there if we are in here much longer. I won't look."

Gordon averted his eyes while Peggy squatted in the corner. She watched the urine make its way toward the well itself. She placed her foot on the floor to block the flow. It was all she could do to focus on the stream of urine on the floor of the well pit at the moment.

"To be honest," Gordon started again, "I don't see a good way out of this for Allan. He's crossed over the line. If he comes back we might try to convince him that we won't tell anyone what happened, but I don't think he will fall for that. But we need to try."

Peggy did not reply. Gordon looked at her, still squatted in the corner, hiding there from the reality. Gordon had hoped that if Allan came back, Peggy would be able to sweet talk their way out of the pit, but Gordon could see that she was not going to be able to do that. He had no illusions that he could talk any sense into Allan. Somehow they would need to escape. Gordon tried the phone again. It beeped and shut itself off.

"Fucking shit," Gordon screamed. Peggy began to sob. "I'm sorry, I didn't mean to yell like that," Gordon tried to calm her down. "Please quit crying. Crying isn't going to help us. We need to keep it together. If we get an opportunity, we are going to have to move fast and take advantage of it."

"What kind of opportunity?" Peggy asked timidly.

"I don't know, but if we get one I'm going to move, and you need to be ready to move with me," Gordon told her.

Max had just arrived at the agency. As always, Skip was already there and watching out the window, his jacket over his arm. Just as he got ready to go out the door, the phone rang. Skip thought about not answering it, but turned around and answered it, anyway. It was not his usual practice. Skip seldom answered his own phone, let alone the office phone, but something told him that he needed to. Perhaps it was Higgins returning his calls.

"Yep," Skip said into the phone receiver. He was watching Max, out in his car, watching him talk on the phone.

"Is this the G&B Detective Agency?" the familiar but shaky voice asked.

"Yep, it is," Skip replied. "And who's this?"

"This is Travis Bentley. Is Skip or Max around?"

"Oh, Travis," Skip replied. "This is Skip, here. I recognized the voice, but I couldn't place it. What's up?"

"Peggy didn't come home last night," Travis said.

"Okay," Skip said. He was waving to Max to come in. "Tell me about it. Start at the beginning."

"I came home around ten," Travis started. "And she wasn't home. No messages, no nothing. So I texted her and asked her when she was coming home and if she wanted me to wait up for her."

"She ever do this before?" Skip asked. "Be gone late like that. Is it unusual?"

"Hardly ever," Travis replied. "Maybe once or twice, but she always sends me a text to let me know. But last night, nothing."

Max was walking in the door. "Just a second," Skip said to Travis. He pulled the receiver away from his face. "It's Travis on the phone. Peggy didn't come home last night. I'm getting all the info." Skip returned the phone to his face. "Go on."

"Well, I waited until midnight, then I tried to call her, but she didn't answer. I left her a message that I was worried about her and that I wanted her to call me, then I sent her another text, then I went to bed and tried to go to sleep. But I couldn't, so I just waited. I don't know how long I waited, but then I must have dozed off. When I woke up ten minutes ago, she still wasn't home. So I called you."

"Okay," Skip said. "Let's not panic right yet. There are a lot of reasons that she might not have come home."

"Do you think that she ran off with someone?" Travis asked. "That was my first thought, but she didn't pack anything. All her stuff is still here. I mean, if she ran off with somebody, wouldn't she at least pack a bag?"

"I don't know," Skip said. "I've got to think about this."

"Do you think I should call the police department and report her missing?" Travis asked.

"No," Skip replied. "I mean yes, call the PD, but don't report her missing. Adults go missing all the time, and they have the right to go missing. The cops aren't going to put out a missing person's report unless there is some reason, like you can show them that she is a danger to herself or others. Tell them that you are worried about her, that she didn't come home last night and you want them to put out a welfare check on her. Tell them that you're afraid that her car broke down somewhere or something. It's all semantics, but that's the way the system works. Don't say you want them to find her, say you want them to look for her or her car to make sure she is okay. They'll do that. They'll put that out to all cars."

"I guess that I knew that," said Travis. "I have clients not show up all the time, so I kind of understand how that works. That's why I wanted to talk to you first."

"Good," Skip said. "So call it in, and Max and I will go looking for her, too."

"What's going on with your investigation?" Travis asked. "Have you found out anything?

"There has been some stuff going on," Skip replied. "But right now is not the time to discuss it. We probably need to locate her right now, not talk about what has been going on. Let's just concentrate on finding her and go from there."

Travis didn't reply right away.

"We're heading out right now to see what we can find out," Skip said. "You stay home, just in case she shows up there. If you hear from her, or if you get any ideas where she might be, call me right away. Call my cell. If we locate her, I'll call you and let you know."

"Okay," Travis finally said. "I hope she is okay, that's all."

"We'll call you with anything we come up with," Skip said, and ended the call. He laid the receiver back in the cradle and looked up at Max. "What now?"

"Let's make a fast run past the plant, run over to the lake and check there, then check both of Proctor's places on the way to give Higgins the heads-up. We can figure out where to go from there." Max said.

"Sounds like a plan," Skip replied. "Let's take the 'Stang."

"I kind of figured that you would want me to drive," Max snorted.

The two were getting ready to leave when Skip stopped. "I gotta go get my Sig."

Max was surprised; Skip didn't usually carry his gun. He also usually didn't rely on his gut feelings. Skip was very calculated, but this case had been different. Skip was winging it, and that was more Max's role. It actually made Max a little nervous. Skip was the one that kept Max on an even keel, not the other way around.

Skip came up to the front, threading his belt through the holster that held his Sig Sauer .40 cal pistol, and tucking it under his shirt. "You packing?" Skip casually asked.

".38 special, carrying Cambridge," Max replied, referring to the small town of Cambridge, where the locals were thought to either not have enough money to buy a holster for their gun, or they were not sophisticated enough to carry their guns in holsters, preferring to shove them into one of their pants pockets. Either way, Max was prone to carrying Cambridge.

When they got into the car and sat down, Skip wiggled around, pulling two fully loaded magazines for the Sig out of his back pocket and placing them in the cup holder.

"You're loaded for bear," Max commented. "You didn't tear my seat with those, did you?"

"No, I didn't tear your seat," Skip replied. "Let's just get going."

Max pulled out of the parking lot and made his way to New 30. There he held it at ten over, eastbound. As they drove past the ethanol plant, they both scanned the parking lot. Skip was on his phone, sliding his finger up and down the screen.

"What are you doing?" Max asked.

"Looking for Peggy's office number."

Skip dialed, then put the phone to his ear.

"Hello," he said into the phone. "Is Mrs. Bentley in? This is Ben Ralston, and she is expecting a call from me this morning."

Max could not hear the other side of the conversation. He slowed to the speed limit as he hit the outskirts of Nevada.

"Yes, well she asked me to call this morning," Skip was saying into the phone. "Do you have any idea when she will be in?"

Max strained his ears.

"You don't happen to know where she is right now, do you? She was expecting a call from me and it is urgent that I talk to her."

Max was wishing that Skip would hurry up with his call. He hated listening to his one-sided conversation.

"Okay, I'll call back later."

"Didn't show up for work," Max guessed as soon as Skip ended the call.

"Didn't show up, didn't call in," Skip replied. "And her receptionist does not know where she is."

"Process of elimination," Max observed. "We know where she isn't: at home or at work."

As soon as they left the city limits, Max brought the speed back up. He flew past the Maxwell turnoff, went over the river, then turned at the sign that pointed to the lake, three miles to the south. Max made short work of those three miles, drove around the east side of the lake, past the boat ramp and into the Snow Bunting Lodge parking lot. The first thing that both detectives saw as they pulled in was Peggy's Lexus, parked in the same spot it had been on Wednesday night. Max parked right next to it.

The two detectives got out and looked through the windows, being careful not to touch the car. If there was foul play, which neither believed there was at the moment, they did not want to contaminate the scene. It was habit. Skip took out his handkerchief, put it over one finger and carefully slipped it through the door handle and tried to open the driver's side door. It was locked. He came around the front of the car and held his hand over the hood. The engine was cold.

Max went to the shelter house, opened the door and looked in.

"Nothing," he called back to Skip. He went inside and looked around. There was nothing to indicate that anyone had recently been there. Max walked back to the car. "No sign of anyone staying in there last night. Someone must have picked her up here. Maybe she did run off with Allan. I mean, what else is there?"

Skip shrugged his shoulders.

"Peggy," Max shouted toward the trees that lay between the parking lot and the lake. "Peggy!" he shouted again.

The two looked around, waiting and looking for any sign of movement.

"Let's walk down by the lake." Skip suggested. The two detectives took the well worn path from the shelter house down to the lake, scanning the woods. There was little underbrush, and the two detectives could see into the woods on both sides. It was just a short walk. The two stood looking across the lake at the opposite shore.

"I don't think she's here," Max said. "I just don't."

"I don't, either," Skip replied.

"Peggy!" Max shouted again. The two detectives stood in silence for a minute.

"Let's go," Skip said.

The two backtracked to the parking lot, took one more look through the windows of the Lexus, then got back into Max's car. Max started the engine, backed out of the parking space and drove out the way they had come in. When he got to New 30, he turned west, back toward Nevada. At the Maxwell turnoff, Max took the Mustang up to eighty, rocketing through the countryside.

As Max neared Allan's farm, he slowed down to the fifty-five mile per hour speed limit. Both men directed their eyes toward the Silverado parked in front of the house.

"He's there," Skip pointed. "He just came out of the machine shed."

They had already passed, and Max was turning to get a view of the farm that was now behind them.

"Might want to watch where you're going," Skip remarked.

"Should we go back and ask him if he's seen her?" Max asked.

"I don't know," Skip replied.

Max kept driving south. "Well, she probably isn't there with him," Max reasoned. "I mean, that's the home place, he isn't going to take his girlfriend home where his wife lives."

Skip did not reply.

"Should I go by the other place?" Max asked.

"Well, she isn't with Allan, at least at the moment. What would she be doing at the farm? Let's take care of Higgins first," Skip suggested. "We don't have any reason to think that she's in trouble. Who knows where she is off to? Like I said to Travis, she is a grown woman. At this point I think that we need to alert Higgins."

Max put the accelerator to the floor, and the Mustang rocketed down the two lane blacktop toward Maxwell.

Chapter 26

Friday

Allan came out of the machine shed at his new place carrying the old twenty-foot section of two-inch hose from the honey wagon that he had replaced several years ago. It still stunk, and even though he had flushed it with fresh water when he changed it out, pieces of dried pig manure clung to the fittings at each end. Allan looked out at the blacktop and saw the yellow Mustang go flying by. He had been seeing it around all week, and thought that it might belong to that goofy insurance agent he had met at the West Café earlier in the week. It was a nice car, but it was looking dirty. Those guys must be hitting it pretty hard. He wondered who would use a nice Mustang convertible like that as a company car. Allan had thought about selling crop insurance himself at one time, but the timing wasn't right. There probably was money in it, but it sure seemed like there were a lot of insurance agents around. One thing Allan knew, and that was that he was sure as hell smarter than the idiot who was driving that Mustang. Allan had that guy figured out the minute he introduced himself.

Allan threw the hose into the back of his Silverado and went into the house. He sat down and read his email for a while, then went back outside and got into his truck. He pulled out of the drive and turned south, toward the farm. He had a plan, and it was a good one. He was going to have to take things a little farther than he ever had taken anything before, but he was ready to do what he had to do. He could see the light at the end of the tunnel.

Allan drove past Elizabeth's house. He couldn't see any movement. He would have to be careful with her. On still fall mornings like this one, sound carried a long ways. Even though their farms were a quarter of a mile away from each other, in the mornings, and sometimes in the evenings, Allan could hear Elizabeth talking to her friends from his place. He could always tell when she was having one of her parties out there. He would hear the laughing and voices. Most of the time he couldn't quite make out what they were saying, but he could hear them talking nonetheless.

Allan drove into his barnyard, backed his truck up to the well pit and turned off the engine. He opened the door and got out.

"Allan," he heard the muffled voice of Gordon coming from beneath the concrete slab. "Allan, what's going on? Let us out of here. We can help you. You need us to help you."

Allan walked up on the slab and put his ear to the vent. He didn't say anything.

"Allan," Gordon called out again, trying to control his voice. "I can hear you walking around up there. Let us out of here. We're all in this together. We need to work together. You're not solving anything by holding us down here."

"I got a plan," Allan shouted into the vent. "It's a good plan."

"Great," Gordon yelled with encouragement up into the vent to Allan. "Let us out of here, and we'll help. We can figure this out."

"No," Allan yelled back. "You two are fine where you are for now."

"Listen to me," Gordon was starting to sound frantic. "Let us out of here."

Allan wasn't listening. He walked to the truck, lowered the tailgate and dragged the hose out of the bed.

He took one end and stuffed it over the exhaust pipe of the truck as far as he could get it to go. He took the other end up on the slab to the vent and knelt so that he could shove it into the vent pipe. He kept pushing until he got it halfway past the bend, but it would not go any farther. He pulled it out and tried again, but it got stuck in the same place. It would have to do.

Allan stood up and walked to the truck. He reached through the open window and took Peggy's purse from the seat, then went to the house. He entered through the front door and took a look around. Gordon was actually a good housekeeper. It was much more tidy than Allan would have imagined. He walked up the stairs to the master bedroom. The old double bed that he and Brenda slept in when they lived out there was being used by Gordon now. It was all made up, but it looked like it had been done so hastily. The covers were wrinkled and laying a little crooked. At least Gordon wasn't completely domesticated. Allan dropped the purse next to the bed.

Allan looked through the closet. He found a laundry basket full of dirty clothes on the floor. He took it out and scattered the contents around the bed. He threw the basket back through the open closet door where it clattered around as it fell to the floor. He turned toward the bed and pulled down the covers. Allan pulled a pack of Camel cigarettes from his pocket and lit one, putting the pack on the nightstand next to the bed. Allan had not smoked in twenty years, and he coughed the first couple of times he inhaled. He sucked on the cigarette hard, burning it down as fast as he could, letting the ashes fall as they might. When he was finished with it he snubbed it out on the nightstand and lit another two.

Allan walked downstairs to the laundry room smoking both cigarettes at the same time. He opened the dryer and cleaned the lint screen. Then he dug past the empty laundry detergent bottles in the garbage can looking for more dryer lint. When he had accumulated as much as he could find, he went back to the bedroom. On the way he made a tour of the first floor, picking up all the newspapers, magazines and junk mail that he could find lying around. In the bedroom he snubbed out the cigarettes on the night stand, as he had done with the first. He left the butts on the stand, then went to the bathroom and got the wastebasket that he found there. He pulled a handful of toilet paper off the roll, wadded it up and put it in the can, along with the papers that he had gathered, and positioned it next to the night stand. He put the dryer lint on the very top. Allan surveyed his work. It looked good.

Allan walked back outside, got in his truck and started the motor, then got out and shut the door. He went to the rear of the truck and surveyed the hose leading from the truck exhaust to the vent. Phase one of his plan was in place. He figured that a half hour should do it. Probably five minutes, but he had never done anything like this before. A half hour would be plenty of time.

He would have to get the tractor and front-end loader to lift the bodies out of the pit and carry them to the house after they died. Allan spotted the tractor hitched to the honey wagon off by the pond. He walked toward it.

When Allan got to the tractor, he realized that the honey wagon was still full. He looked up the road at Elizabeth's place and smiled. He climbed on the tractor, started it and drove up the hill, past the truck and out the drive.

As soon as Allan started the engine of the truck, the stench of exhaust fumes spewed through the vent.

"Jesus Christ, he's gassing us," Gordon said. "Allan! Allan," he shouted through the vent, but his words were forced back into his face by the exhaust. Gordon pulled his handkerchief from his pocket and shoved it into the vent as far as he could, using his phone to push it farther. He took off his shirt and jammed it against the opening. He thought that he could hear Peggy screaming, but his concentration was focused on the vent and the exhaust that was seeping through his shirt. He pulled it away and ripped it into strips so that he could get them shoved up higher into the pipe.

"Give me something to stick up here," he was shouting to Peggy. She started to unbutton her blouse. "Not that!" he shouted. "Give me something that I can get up in this hole; give me your underwear!"

Peggy did as she was told, stripping her underwear down past her feet and handing them to Gordon, who was standing on the ladder. He shoved them into the vent and tried to push them and the strips of shirt farther with his phone.

"Give me something else!" he yelled. He heard tearing and looked down. Peggy had already taken off her blouse and was ripping the seams at the sleeve with her teeth. Gordon reached into his pocket, fished out his pocket knife and threw it down to Peggy, hitting her in the face before it fell to the floor. She grabbed it up, opened the blade and started to cut her blouse into strips, handing them to Gordon as fast as she could cut them. He shoved each one into the vent with his phone. Gordon was working furiously, but he was starting to feel lightheaded. It was all he could do to hang on to the rung of the ladder with one hand and shove the strips of cloth into the vent with the other. When he felt like he could not summon the strength to go on, he heard the metal fitting at the end of the hose fall against the concrete slab, and he realized that he had forced the hose back out of the vent, hopefully winning them a reprieve. He crawled down the ladder and sat on the wet floor. Peggy sat down beside him, dressed in her bra, what was left of her blouse in one hand, the pocket knife in the other.

"Are we okay?" she asked shakily.

"Maybe," Gordon answered. "I hope so, for now."

Elizabeth heard the roar of the tractor and came out of her indoor arena to see Allan come into her drive at road gear speed, the honey wagon careening to one side and looking like it would tip over as he turned in. Elizabeth sprinted out into the tractor's path, yelling and waving her arms. For a moment she thought that Allan was going to run her over, and she was about to reverse directions to get out of the way when he slammed on the brakes and slid to a stop.

"I'm going to spread this in your pasture," Allan called down from the tractor seat.

"I don't want it spread in my pasture!" Elizabeth yelled back.

"Yes," Allan corrected her. "It's good for the grass. It is fertilizer. You're going to be happy about it."

"No!" Elizabeth said. "You're not going to spread it in my pasture. That's the final word." She stood her ground, hands on her hips.

Allan was losing patience. "Fucking bitch!" he shouted. "Get out of my way."

"Get off my fucking property!" Elizabeth shouted back.

The two stood looking at each other. Suddenly the tractor lurched forward and Elizabeth jumped out of its path, expecting Allan to continue to the pasture. But instead, he wheeled it around toward the road. Just before he came to the gate, he opened the valve and spread the hog manure on her driveway. He continued to dump the brown noxious liquid on the gravel road as he drove back to his place, turning the surface into a mess of liquid manure, wastewater, dirt and gravel. Elizabeth reached into her back pocket and pulled out her phone. She pulled up her contacts and scrolled through them to Max's number. She was glad that she had put him in her contacts list when she did. She pushed call, and the phone started to ring.

Max had just pulled into Higgins's drive. The place still looked deserted, just as it had the evening before. Pete and Repeat met them as they pulled in, barking and snapping at the tires of the Mustang. Max stopped the car. Skip was looking around to see if he could locate anyone.

"Pull up to the pasture and see if anyone is out there," Skip suggested.

Max pulled ahead, escorted by the two snarling dogs. When he got to the gate going into the pasture he stopped. The two could see the grow in the distance, untouched, just as it was the last time they had been there.

"No Higgins," Skip commented quietly. "No cousin, no nothin'."

Max backed the Mustang around and turned toward the driveway. Skip tried Higgins's number on his cell phone again, and got the message that his voicemail box was full. Max stopped in front of the double wide and hit the horn. The two scanned the barnyard for any signs of movement.

Max drove out the drive and turned left. The two dogs stopped at the gate, watching the car leave, making sure that it wasn't coming back.

"Where you going?" Skip asked.

"Casey's," Max answered. "See if Bonnie is there."

"Might as well," Skip agreed.

Max proceeded towards the convenience store. As they turned onto Main Street, Max's phone rang. He squirmed around, trying to fish it out of his pocket.

"Hello," Max put the phone up to his face and answered.

"Max, this is Elizabeth Beckman. You told me to call you if anything weird was going on over at Proctor's place, and there is a lot of weirdness going on right now." She stopped to take a breath.

"What kind of weirdness?" Max asked.

"Well," Elizabeth started again. "He came over here just a few minutes ago. He was yelling at someone over at his farm earlier, but I don't think anyone else is there. I haven't seen or heard anyone else over there since yesterday. It's been real quiet until this morning. But this morning he's yelling, and he's ramming around in his truck and just raising a ruckus. Then he came over here and wanted to dump his honey wagon in my pasture. He almost ran me down with his tractor, and when I ordered him off my property, he called me a fucking bitch! Then he turned around and dumped the whole honey wagon out on my drive and all over the road between my place and his. It is a fucking mess." Elizabeth stopped to take another breath.

"Holy shit, it sounds like he's out of control," Max remarked, as he turned the Mustang around in the middle of the street and headed north. "Call the sheriff's department and tell them to get a car out there. Nine-one-one! Call nine-one-one, and tell them that Proctor is out of control over there. Do it now, and stay far away from him." Max ended the call before Elizabeth could respond. Max turned to tell Skip what Elizabeth had said as he accelerated out of town.

"I heard," Skip said before Max could talk. "This is getting crazy all of a sudden."

Allan emptied the honey wagon on the road. He pulled it into the drive of his farm and parked it next to the hog confinement building. He got off the tractor and pulled the clevis pin to unhitch it from the drawbar. Allan was thinking clearly now. Phase two of the plan: pull the bodies up out of the pit with the front end loader and take them to the house. Then drag them upstairs to the bedroom, strip them naked and put them in the bed. Just like the lovers they were. Then he would burn the place down. Make it look like the two were in bed, and that Gordon was smoking a cigarette, fell asleep and dropped it in the trash can that he so carelessly left setting where a cigarette could fall into it. The fire would spread to the mess of clothes lying on the floor, and then burn the house to the ground before the volunteer fire department could get there. That kind of stuff happened all the time. Gordon and Peggy, the two lovers, the co-conspirators, taking advantage of a situation, and Allan knew nothing about it. It was so sad. Allan was starting to feel bad for them. Allan would be devastated by the whole thing, so devastated that he would not even be able to talk about it. He smiled. It was a great plan.

Allan drove the tractor to the well pit. As he approached, he saw that the hose had fallen out of the vent onto the concrete slab. He climbed down from the tractor and went to the truck, reaching through the window and turning the ignition switch, killing the engine. He walked on to the well pit and got down on his knees to look inside the vent pipe where he had inserted the hose.

"Allan," he heard Gordon call out. "Allan, think about this. You can't do this."

Gordon's voice was muted. Allan was trying to put the hose fitting back in the vent, but it was blocked. He reached in with three fingers and pulled out a dirty handkerchief. He tried to stick the hose back up again, but it was still blocked. He reached back in again and pulled out a pair of women's underwear.

"What the heck are you two doing down there?" Allan laughed. "I knew that you two were up to something."

"Allan," Peggy yelled. "Let us out."

It was the first time that he had heard Peggy call out. She sounded so pitiful, so defeated. "I think that you lost your undies, Peggy. What's Travis going to say?" Allan laughed again. "Hang on, we're going to get this done here pretty soon and everything will be back on track. Don't you worry."

Allan tried the hose again, but it was still not going in. Then he looked up as he heard a car coming up the road. It was coming fast, throwing up a spray of pig manure mixed with wastewater as it went. Allan got up and climbed onto the tractor. He knew that the car was coming for him, and he was going to block it at the road. As he put the tractor into gear, he saw that the car was coming too fast. It was going to beat him to the gate. He pulled the tractor to the side of the drive and waited.

Chapter 27

Friday

Max hit the city limits of Maxwell going out of town at eighty and climbing, trying to remember exactly where the turnoff for 340th was. He was pretty sure it was the next one. The other times that they had gone past Proctor's place, they had come in from the south, but as Max had rocketed out of Maxwell, he decided to take the straight shot up the Maxwell blacktop, then come back from the north. It might be a little farther, but not much, and a lot less gravel to navigate. It was six of one, half-dozen of the other.

Max wasn't sure he had made the right turn until he was running west on the gravel, fishtailing as he accelerated. He could see the bridge over the creek just ahead, and the next intersection beyond that. As he roared over the bridge and made the turn, the Mustang was fighting for traction, sliding through the turn. Skip sat calmly, bracing his arm against the door as Max fought for control of the car. It was nothing new to him, and he had complete confidence in Max's ability to get them through in one piece. Max let up on the accelerator and the car straightened out. As soon as it did, Max was back on the gas. They flew past Elizabeth's drive. Skip could see her standing by the fence, watching them go by.

"Fuck me," Max shouted, as dirt, dust and liquid manure from the road coated his windshield. He flipped on his windshield wipers. They only smeared the goop around. He pushed the button for the wash and was able to see just in time to slam on the brakes and turn into Proctor's drive. The side windows were not much better than the windshield. Skip tried to peer through the brown coating streaming down the window. All of a sudden the car lurched sideways and began to lift. The passenger side door airbag went off, and Skip turned his head as the glass in the window shattered. When he turned back to look, all he could see was a wall of metal, and all he could hear was the roar of a motor wound tight.

"What the fuck?" Max was yelling as the right side of the car was lifted toward the sky. The car rolled onto the driver's side and sat balanced there for a moment. Skip put a foot on the console between the seats and was able to take enough pressure off of his seat belt to unbuckle it. He pushed down the half-deflated airbag and cautiously stuck his head out the window, standing on Max in the process. He saw Proctor driving a tractor, backing away from the Mustang and lowering the front end loader to take another run at them. Skip pulled the Sig Sauer out of his holster and fired two rounds at Proctor's head, the only part of him that Skip could see over the loader. The tractor began to come forward again, and Skip ducked down, slipping on Max's squirming body and falling on him.

"He's attacking us with a tractor," Skip shouted as Max got out from under him.

The car started to tip again and the front airbags exploded, knocking Skip back between the seats and trapping Max in the driver's seat. The car rolled over onto its top, crushing the canvas convertible roof. The windshield buckled and shattered, but the frame held the weight of the car. Skip saw his chance and dove through the front window of the car, rolling and crawling on the ground. As he did, he saw Proctor getting off the tractor, a gun in his hand, taking aim.

Skip's training took over. The natural tendency is to get tunnel vision, but Skip forced his focus to take in everything around him. He stayed low and below Proctor's line of sight, knowing that it was harder to aim under a gun than over. As he rolled, he turned his body so that it was angled toward the target. Proctor fired. The bullet went over Skip's head and ricocheted off the ground behind him. Proctor fired again, the shot flying high and hitting almost exactly in the same place as his first one. Skip brought his gun up, made a calculated and conscious effort to aim for a specific point on Proctor's body and avoid firing away in the general direction of his target. He got a good grip on his Sig. Skip concentrated on the front sight, centering it in the rear sight, lining it up with his target, which lay slightly blurred before him. He kept his gun positioned straight up and not tilted to one side or the other. Then he pulled the trigger slowly, firing off a single round. It only took a moment for Skip to do it all. He had done it thousands, maybe tens of thousands of times on the practice range. Proctor fell like the proverbial sack of potatoes. Skip held his sights on the prone body writhing on the ground, ready to follow up with another shot if needed. Proctor's gun had fallen from his hand. He was making no attempt to retrieve it.

"Coming behind you," Skip heard Max call out, letting Skip know where he was at.

"Cover him," Skip instructed. He got to his feet, circled to his left, out of Max's line of fire, and approached Proctor, who was laying on the ground. He kicked the Glock farther from Proctor's reach as he came closer. Skip stood over Proctor, who was lying in a fetal position, groaning, his hands clutched over his lower abdomen.

"What, did you shoot him in the balls?" Max was right beside Skip looking down at Proctor with his revolver pointed toward the ground and away from Skip.

"No, I busted his pelvis," Skip replied.

Max didn't say anything.

"While you SWAT guys were always preaching to 'shoot center mass to stop the threat,' I always wondered what would happen if you just blew out their foundation, you know? I mean, didn't you guys ever play football?"

"Well, there you go," Max exclaimed. "And now we don't have to wonder anymore."

The two detectives heard the sound of cars with sirens coming down the road. Skip didn't take his eyes off of Proctor. Max turned and looked.

"Cavalry is here," Max remarked as the cars came into the drive.

Carlisle had just pulled into the parking lot at the dead end road where he and the DNR officer had arranged to meet. The DNR officer's truck was already there, the officer at the wheel and another man, who Carlisle assumed was the biologist, sitting on the passenger side. As he pulled in, the two got out of the truck. Carlisle parked his patrol car and reached for his radio to call out with dispatch.

"Eighty-five-twelve," the dispatcher's voice came over the radio before Carlisle could call out.

"Go ahead," Carlisle said into the handset. "I'm out here in Maxwell with the DNR on special assignment."

"Eighty-five-twelve, respond to three-zero-six-hundred-fifty-four, six-hundred-forty-fifth. Report of a WMA threatening neighbor and dumping hog manure on the road there," the dispatcher replied.

"I'm on special assignment here in Maxwell," Carlisle repeated over the radio.

"Ten-four," the dispatcher replied. "You are the closest car. Shift commander says for you to respond. Sounds like the party involved is out of control. He almost ran the caller down with his tractor."

Carlisle sighed and looked at the DNR officer and the biologist, who had been listening to the call.

"I gotta go," Carlisle looked up apologetically.

"We'll come along and back you up," the DNR officer said to Carlisle. "Then we can come back."

"Sounds good," Carlisle replied. He got back into his patrol car. As he drove out of the parking lot. His radio squawked again.

"Eighty-five-twelve, shots fired," the dispatcher reported. "Repeat, shots fired."

"Ten-four," Carlisle clicked the mic.

Carlisle heard the siren come on behind him. The DNR officer must have been monitoring county radio. Carlisle turned on his own red lights and siren as he slammed the accelerator to the floor. He cut through town, passed Higgins's place and took the road that went past the ball diamonds out of town. When he hit the gravel he let up a little on the accelerator to make the turn north. In his rearview mirror he saw the DNR truck right behind him, red lights flashing in the dust. It was surreal. As soon as he made the turn, he nailed it to the floor again. The DNR truck fell back a little, but then caught up. "That guy can drive," Carlisle thought as he barreled down the gravel road toward Proctor's place.

It took Carlisle and the DNR officer less than three minutes to negotiate the three miles of loose gravel between Maxwell and Proctor's farm. Carlisle began scanning the scene before he even got to the drive. As he pulled through the gate, he saw Skip Murray standing over a body with his gun drawn, Max Mosbey standing next to him, also gun in hand. Carlisle picked up the radio mic and keyed it.

"Eighty-five-twelve, I'm out at the scene. I got DNR with me. One man on the ground, two armed individuals appear to be covering him. We're probably going to need an ambulance here. I'll let you know what we have in a minute." Carlisle paused, then almost as an afterthought he picked up the mic again.

"I know the two armed subjects," Carlisle said over the radio, for the benefit of the DNR officer pulling in behind him. "They're private detectives."

Carlisle pulled to a halt, with the DNR truck pulling up behind him. Carlisle bailed out, pistol in hand. Both Skip and Max bent down and placed their weapons on the ground, then held their hands up where the officers could see them.

"You're good," Carlisle called out as he came toward them. "What you got?"

"This is it so far," Skip replied, still holding his hands up. "One down, belly wound. I don't know if there is anyone else."

"Go ahead and pick up your weapons," he instructed them.

Both Max and Skip bent down and retrieved their pistols. Skip put his back in his holster; Max stuck his in his waistband. Carlisle was on his knees next to Proctor.

"I need a first aid kit," he instructed the DNR officer.

"It's behind the seat," the DNR officer relayed to the biologist, who turned and ran back toward the truck.

"We need to clear this place," Carlisle said to the men standing around him. "Skip, you, Max and the DNR officer here, check those hog confinement buildings and the house. Me and the biologist will see what we can do for Proctor."

Skip and Max started to move out.

"Can you turn off that tractor?" Carlisle called out as the men turned to start their search. Max jumped up onto the drawbar of the tractor, reached over the seat and switched the key to off. The tractor went silent.

"Help! Let us out, help us!" The four men suddenly stood motionless when they heard the faint voices. It took a moment for them to locate where they were coming from. Max and Skip were the first to reach the well pit. Max reached down and tried to pull the hatch up, but it was still held closed by the hasp. Skip quickly pulled the screwdriver from the hasp and flipped it down, then Max hauled the hatch open, letting it clang on the concrete slab as it fell. The two detectives, the DNR officer and Carlisle were all on the slab looking down into the well pit. They saw two faces looking up at them, smeared with dirt and sweat, Gordon standing shirtless with strips of Peggy's blouse in his hand, still ready to stuff them into the vent. Peggy stood in her skirt and bra, her face dirty and tear-streaked, her hair matted and wet.

Gordon took Peggy's arm and propelled her to the ladder, helping her get started on the first rung. It was clear that she was in shock. Gordon averted his eyes as she made her way up through the hatch and stepped out into the sunlight. Gordon followed.

"Anyone else around here?" Carlisle asked as he gave Gordon his hand and helped pull him up through the hatch.

"I don't think so," Gordon replied, looking over at the prone body of Allan curled up on the ground, the biologist bent over him. "Proctor was trying to kill us." Gordon looked up at Carlisle. "He was trying to gas us with exhaust from the truck."

It was the first that anyone had noticed the hose extending from the exhaust pipe of the truck to the well pit.

"He tried to gas us," Gordon repeated.

"Why was he trying to kill you?" Carlisle asked.

"Because he was afraid that we would spill the beans on him," Gordon replied.

Carlisle looked around. He was about to ask Gordon what they were going to spill the beans over, but then he decided the questioning could wait. Carlisle led Peggy by the arm to his patrol car, opened his trunk and pulled out a blanket, laying it over her shoulders. He sat her in the back seat of the car, leaving the door open. He went back, led Gordon to the light pole by the well pit and had him sit down.

"Stay put right here," he ordered. "Don't get up and don't go wandering around. If you do, I'll put you in cuffs. Understand?"

"Yes, sir," Gordon said quietly as he sat.

"I don't want you talking to the lady," Carlisle added.

Carlisle went over to where Skip and Max were standing over the biologist and Proctor.

"What the hell?" Carlisle exclaimed. "Did you shoot him in the balls?"

"No," Max replied. "Skip shot him in the pelvis. Broke his pelvis."

Carlisle stood looking at Max and Skip. He didn't reply.

"Dropped him like a ton of bricks," Max added.

"On purpose?" Carlisle asked.

"Yep," Max nodded. "On purpose."

Carlisle shook his head. A Maxwell/Collins volunteer first responder was coming through the gate, another deputy right behind him.

"Okay," said Carlisle. "Me and the DNR guy are going to check around. I want you two to go sit down somewhere and keep yourselves available. I'll be back. And don't be talking to each other, or I'll have to separate you."

"You got it," Max replied. "We know the drill."

Carlisle met the other deputy getting out of his car. Another first responder pulled into the driveway. Carlisle surveyed the scene. There was a lady on a horse standing ten feet away. He had not even seen her come up. Carlisle realized that he needed to secure the scene quickly, before it completely got away from him. The biologist was getting pushed out of the way by the volunteer first responders. He stood for a moment watching, then turned toward the hog confinement and walked in that direction. Carlisle considered telling him not to go wandering around, but decided to let him go. He had a hunch that Proctor trying to gas two people in a well pit had something to do with the pollution of the creek that ran behind his farm. It was one hell of a coincidence if it didn't.

Max and Skip stood looking at Max's car. "I think it's totaled," Skip remarked.

"I think so, too," Max agreed.

"What you going to do?" Skip asked.

"I guess I'll have to report it to Ben Ralston and get him to file a claim," Max replied.

"I guess so," Skip said. "I suppose we might want to see if someone can come down here and pick us up, because we aren't driving that." Skip said. "Or maybe the deputies can take us home."

"I'm not going to ride in the back of a patrol car," Max said. "I'll call Monica and see if she can pick us up. If she can't, I'll get Gloria to come down."

Skip didn't say anything. Max got his phone out of his pocket and dialed Monica's number. Skip went over to the Mustang and bent down, looking at the interior where he and Max had been trapped. Max walked off to the side. Monica responded after three rings.

"Hey, Max," he heard her answer.

"What are you up to right now?" Max asked.

"Just got out of class," she answered. "Heading over to the office. Was going to sit over there in case anyone called. Maybe get some homework done. Why?"

"Because we're out at Proctor's place, and my car got totaled. We need someone to come and get us."

"How did your car get totaled?" Monica asked, concerned. "Are you both okay?"

"We're fine," Max said. "It is a long story, but we're okay. We found Peggy, and she's okay, and we just need you to come down and get us. You know where Proctor's farm is, the one with the hog confinement buildings and the ponds? You Googled it, right?"

"I can find it," Monica replied. "I'll punch the address into the GPS on my phone."

"Listen," said Max, "there is a mess on the road down here that you're going to have to drive through. Skip wants you to drive the Mercedes down here instead of your car. No use you getting your car all messed up and dirty. His keys are in the upper right-hand drawer of his desk. Just drive it down here to pick us up."

"Okay," replied Monica slowly. "I'll do that if that is what he wants. Then I don't have to take the carseat out of mine."

"Right," Max said. "Best all around if you just drive Skip's car down here."

Max ended the call. Skip was walking toward him, Elizabeth on her horse walking along beside.

"This is crazy!" Elizabeth exclaimed. "Wow, I can't believe it."

"Be something to tell your friends about next time you have a party out here," Max agreed.

"No kidding," Elizabeth said. "He tried to run me down with that tractor."

"He rolled my car over," Max replied.

"I know," Elizabeth said. "I saw it. I came over on my horse as soon as you guys went by. I saw Skip shoot Proctor. I've never seen anyone get shot before." Elizabeth was beside herself.

Max turned his attention to Skip. "You think we should call Travis and tell him that Peggy is alright?"

Skip raised his eyebrows. "I thought about it. But I don't want to step on Carlisle's case. I'll leave it up to him. Travis will just have to wait until he's done here."

Max shrugged his shoulders. "I think you're right."

"Did you get someone to come down here and pick us up?" Skip asked.

"I can take you guys home," Elizabeth said.

"That's okay, Monica's on the way," Max replied.

Carlisle was walking toward them with a hand full of papers and pens.

"I need statements, guys," he said as he approached.

He looked up at Elizabeth sitting on her horse. "Ma'am, what are you doing here?"

"I'm the neighbor," she replied. "I called 911 when this all started. I saw everything. I even saw Skip shoot Proctor."

"Okay," said Carlisle. "You need to climb down off your horse and start writing, too. I need you to write it all down, from start to finish, and no coaching from these two, either."

Elizabeth swung her leg over the horse and dismounted, a wide smile on her face. She was excited to be a part of the investigation. "I attended the Ames Police Citizen Academy," she informed Carlisle.

"Great," he replied. "That's great."

Chapter 28

Friday

Monica was sitting in Skip's Mercedes watching the show through the windshield. When she had arrived at Proctor's farm, she was met at the gate by a deputy who instructed her to park it and not get out. She could see Max, Skip and a woman with a horse, papers of some sort in their hands, chatting it up. Skip had given her a wave when she got there, and a couple of times he or Max had acknowledged that they knew she was still there by giving her a questioning shrug, but so far it had been a waiting game. Monica had tried calling her mother to ask her to pick up Essie at preschool, but she hadn't answered. So she had called Milton, and he was going to pick her up after he got off work. He seemed happy to do so. Monica was starting to feel close to Milton. She had put him on the list at preschool to allow him to pick up Essie, who loved it when he did. She could count on him. It was almost as if she had a partner in life all of a sudden. That was something that she had not experienced before: someone who put her and Essie first. It was nice.

A flatbed truck, followed by a wrecker, pulled into the drive and stopped. The driver of the truck was discussing something with the deputy at the gate. The deputy spoke into his portable radio, then finally waved the truck through. The wrecker backed up to Max's Mustang, and the two men got out of their trucks. One attached a cable over the undercarriage of the car and hooked it on the other side. The wrecker driver then wound the cable, pulling the car over, crashing first onto its side then onto its wheels. The driver then backed the flatbed up to the Mustang, attached a cable to the back axle and pulled the car up onto the bed. Monica watched them strap it down.

The Mustang was a mess. When Max had told her that the road was covered with hog manure, Monica had plotted a course that would take her south into Maxwell, then up to Proctor's place from the other direction, hoping that she could avoid it. She had driven Skip's Mercedes slowly up the gravel road, trying to keep it from getting any more dust on it than she had to. Looking along the side of the car through the side mirror, it looked to her like she had done a good job of it.

Carlisle had waved at her when she had first parked the car. Now she saw him walk over to the two detectives and the woman with the horse to collect the papers that they had in their hands. He talked to them for a moment, then shook hands all around. The three stood watching the flatbed leave with the Mustang, then walked to Skip's car, the horse trailing along behind them.

"Monica, Elizabeth," Max introduced the women through the open window. Elizabeth reached in and shook her hand, smiling.

"I'm going home," Elizabeth said to Max. "We need to get together; I'll let you know the next time I have a barbeque. Bring Gloria and your friends here, too."

"Sounds like a happening," Max responded.

Elizabeth placed her foot into the stirrup and deftly swung herself up into the saddle while the horse sidestepped away from her. She waved as she guided the horse toward the gate. Skip told Monica to stay where she was and climbed into the passenger seat. Max got in the back.

"What've you got going?" Skip asked. "You have some time?"

"I do," Monica answered. "Milton is picking Essie up from preschool, and he can bring her over to my place when I get back. He said that if I'm late, though, he's going to take her to some fast-food restaurant and stuff her full of unhealthy deep-fat-fried food, so I need to save her from that."

The two detectives laughed. "Turn left," Skip instructed her. "Let's run down to Higgins's place and see if he's there. Carlisle and his crew are a little distracted right now, but he's like a bulldog; he hasn't forgotten about Higgins."

Monica turned left as Skip had told her to, and drove slowly on the gravel road toward Maxwell.

"So what's the deal?" Max asked from the back seat. "How did you keep Skip's car from getting dirty?"

"Took the long way around," Monica replied. "You told me about the mess, and I thought that I would come in from the other side and see if it was better, and it was."

Skip turned around and grinned at Max. "Pays to hire smart people."

"I guess so," Max sulked.

Skip directed Monica to Higgins's place. As they came down the street in front of the acreage, they saw his truck parked in front of the double-wide. Monica drove through the gate. Pete and Repeat met them and trotted along beside the car until Monica parked it and turned off the ignition.

"I'm staying in here," Monica said, eyeing the dogs looking up through the car window at her.

"Looks like Higgins is here," Max said, slowly opening his door. "The dogs are friendlier when he's around."

The two dogs ran around to Max's door and wagged their stubby tails, nudging each other aside, trying to get close enough for Max to give them a pet.

"These are two crazy dogs," Max remarked.

Skip opened his door and got out. The two dogs ran over to him. Higgins was coming out of the barn.

"What's up?" Higgins asked as he approached the car. "You find out anything yet?"

"Yep," reported Skip. "Case solved. It was that guy Proctor, up the road north of town. He was dumping poisonous cleaning water from one of the ethanol plants that he contracts with into his hog confinement pits, and it was making its way into the creek. The DNR is up there right now taking a look."

"No shit," Higgins exclaimed. "I knew that guy was an asshole."

"Yep," Max replied. "That's why Skip shot him."

Higgins's eyes widened.

Skip ignored Max. "So where've you been?" Skip asked. "We've been trying to call you since yesterday afternoon. We've been down here three times looking for you."

Higgins pulled his phone out of his pocket and looked at it. "Says I have seven missed calls," he remarked.

"They're just from us, asking you where you are," Skip interrupted. "You might want to clean out your voicemail box sometime."

Higgins closed his phone and put it back in his pocket. "Bonnie took me home with her," Higgins explained. "She said that whenever I'm around my cousin I get in trouble. So she made me go to her place until he got done doing what he had to do."

"So did he?" Max asked.

"I guess so," Higgins answered. "It's gone."

"Is it in the barn?" Max turned his gaze to the barn door.

"Nope," Higgins answered, "Bonnie took the phone while I was talking to him and told him to get that shit off my property, every leaf and stalk of it."

"Good for her," Skip remarked.

"So what've you guys been trying so hard to call me about?" Higgins asked. "Just that you found out who was killing the fish?"

"No," said Skip, "we wanted to tell you that the DNR and a deputy are going to be coming up the river here soon, and they're going to be looking around. You need to make sure that there isn't any evidence of that grow out there in the pasture, and don't take potshots at them when they come up and look over the fence."

"I don't do that anymore," Higgins said indignantly.

"And don't sic the dogs on them, either," Max said.

"They aren't like that anymore," Higgins said.

"Not when you're here," Max informed him. "But when you're not, they are the same old dogs, maybe worse."

The three men looked over at Monica, still in the car, window rolled down, petting the two dogs who had jumped up on the door of Skip's Mercedes and were soaking up the love.

"Really?" Higgins said.

"Really," Max responded.

"Maybe it is just you guys," Monica added to the conversation. "They seem like really nice dogs."

"Maybe," Higgins nodded, appreciating Monica for defending his friends.

"I don't think so," Max said defensively, dropping the subject.

"Okay," said Skip, "I think that we got everything covered. You got any questions?" he asked Higgins.

"Did you really shoot that guy, Proctor?" he asked Skip. "I always figured if one of you was gonna shoot someone, it would be Max."

"It is a long story and I'm not in a mood to relive it right now," Skip said decisively.

Higgins accepted that. "When them guys coming through?"

"Don't know," Skip answered. "They're finishing up their investigation at Proctor's place. I don't know how long they'll be up there. I don't even know if they will come up the creek now, with the case solved, but they probably will eventually, just to see how extensive the fish kill is. I just wanted you to know."

Higgins thought for a moment. "So are you guys done?" he asked.

"I think we are," Skip replied.

"How much I owe you?" Higgins asked.

"What did we agree on?" Skip replied. "Two hundred, I think. Cash."

Higgins turned and walked toward the double-wide.

"You going to take his money?" Max asked.

"I sure am," Skip answered.

Higgins returned after a few minutes with a wad of twenties in his hand. He offered it to Skip and Skip took it. He shook Higgins's hand. "Pleasure doing business with you," Skip said.

Higgins reached out to Max and shook hands, then he stepped over to the car and shook hands with Monica. "Thank you for your help, too, Miss," he said to her.

Skip and Max got back into the car with Monica, and she backed around. Higgins watched them leave. The two dogs escorted them to the gate. Skip handed the bills to

Monica, who steered with one hand and took them from Skip with the other.

"What do you want me to do with these?" she asked.

"Keep 'em," Skip replied. "Bonus for coming down and getting us."

Monica handed the bills back to Skip. "Okay, that's great, but could you just hang on to them until I'm done driving us back?"

Skip took the bills back and sat with his hands in his lap, while Monica drove the speed limit back to the agency.

After work, Milton went home to change clothes, then drove by the agency to get the carseat out of Monica's car. Then he went to the preschool to pick up Essie. As always, she was all smiles when he showed up. The ladies who ran the preschool were all smiles as well. They sensed that something good was going on between Monica and Milton, and they were always glad to see him, hoping for some revelation about the two of them. They were a little disappointed when Milton simply thanked them for taking care of Essie and took her by the hand out to the jeep. They were sure that if anything happened, they would be the first to know. Didn't everyone tell the preschool teachers first?

"Wanna go to the mall?" Milton asked Essie after he made sure she was securely fastened into her seat.

"Yeah," she laughed, ready for an adventure. "I wanna go to the mall."

"Good," said Milton. "We'll get a pretzel."

Milton drove through town and made his way to the mall parking lot. He parked and shut off the engine, lifted Essie out of her seat and took her hand again as they went into the front doors. When they were inside, Essie tried to pull her hand away and free herself. Milton let her go. She ran full speed through the mall toward the pretzel stand. Milton followed along behind, keeping an eye on her.

"Two pretzels," Milton ordered when he caught up to Essie waiting at the stand. "Nice, salty, buttery ones," he added.

The girl working the stand took a pair of tongs and started to put the pretzels in a bag.

"We're going to eat them," Milton stopped her. "Just give us some napkins." He looked down at Essie who stood smiling up at him. "Give us lots of napkins."

Milton paid for the pretzels and gave one to Essie. The two walked slowly back toward the mall entrance and the jewelry store that sat just inside the front doors. Milton felt like he was not in control of his feet. The ring was drawing him through time and space; Milton was just along for the ride. When he walked into the store, the same woman he had talked to before looked up and smiled.

"Came back," she observed, looking at Milton, then at Essie. "Who do you have here?"

"This is Essie, my girlfriend's daughter," Milton answered.

"Did you bring her along to see if she thought that the ring was okay for her mom?" the woman joked. Essie wasn't listening, she was busy chewing on her pretzel and watching the crumbs fall on the carpet.

"Nah," Milton laughed. "I just brought her along for company. Her mom's at work and I picked her up at daycare."

"Are you still looking, or have you decided?" the woman asked.

"I think I want the one you showed me," Milton said, a little surprised that the words had come out of his mouth.

The lady walked over to the display case. Milton followed, herding Essie along with him.

Milton looked at the rings in the case, trying to spot the one that had caught his attention. He kept one eye on Essie. He knew that she could disappear in a second if he didn't keep close watch on her. She sat down on the carpet and put her pretzel on the floor.

"Don't put your pretzel on the floor," Milton laughed. He leaned down, picked up the pretzel, inspected it and then gave it back. Why had he picked this moment to buy a ring? He could have waited until he didn't have Essie, but for some reason he felt like he needed her along.

Milton stood up. His own pretzel was on the counter. "That one right there," Milton pointed at the ring.

The woman reached into the display case and brought it out. She laid a felt mat on the counter and placed the ring on it. Milton picked it up and inspected it. He had no idea what he was looking for. He just knew that this ring had caught his eye.

"I'll take it," Milton said, a bit of panic coming over him.

"Do you know what size?" the woman asked.

Milton felt another wave of panic.

"Do you know what size your fiancé's finger is?"

Milton wanted to tell her to put it back, that he would come back when he had the size.

"You can buy it now," the woman smiled. Milton was not her first nervous boyfriend. "Then, when you give it to her, she can bring it in and we will size it for her."

Milton tried to think. "Okay, that's what I'll do," he told her.

"This is a beautiful ring," the woman remarked. "She is going to love it, I'm sure."

Milton tried to get Essie to her feet. He grabbed her under her arms and lifted her, but she kept her legs bent up and would not put them down to stand up. Milton carried her that way to where the woman was at the cash register and put her back on the floor. When he looked up again, the woman placed a receipt on the counter. Milton looked at it, and a third wave of panic came over him.

"Do you take Visa?" he asked.

"Yes, we do," the woman said with a smile.

Milton handed over his card and looked down at Essie, while the sales woman processed the purchase. She placed the receipt on the counter.

"Just sign here," she said, offering him her pen.

When Milton and Essie walked out of the mall, Milton took her little hand in his, the bag with the ring in his other hand.

"What's that?" Essie asked.

"Nothing," said Milton.

Essie seemed satisfied with his answer. He was relieved when she didn't ask him more questions, and he was glad that she was with him. He didn't think that he could have done it without her.

Chapter 29

Saturday

Milton drove his patrol car into the parking lot of the G&B Detective Agency. Monica's car was parked in her reserved space in front of the door. Next to her car was Deputy Carlisle's patrol car, and next to that was Skip's Mercedes. Monica had told Milton all about the events at Proctor's farm when he had brought Essie home. He was a little envious that he had missed out on all of the action. Especially because it had involved Skip shooting Proctor.

Milton parked and went into the agency. Monica was at her desk and Carlisle was sitting in one of the easy chairs, smiling and joking around. Skip was back in the bar. Milton took the other chair. Monica gave him a wink and a smile as he sat down.

"Waiting for Max," she said. "He has to ride his bicycle in, now that he doesn't have a car."

"He has another car," Milton corrected her, "but he would rather ride his bicycle and tell everyone that he doesn't have a car, and *why* he doesn't have a car."

Monica laughed. "You're right, and here comes Mr. Got No Car right now."

The two officers looked out the window to see Max ride his Cannondale Road Warrior up on the sidewalk in front of the building and to the front door. Monica got up and held the door open for him while he rolled his bike into the waiting area and leaned it against the wall.

"We should get a bike rack," Max observed.

Skip came out of the bar with a bloody mary in one hand and a screwdriver in the other. He handed Max the screwdriver.

"Breakfast," he said as Max took the drink.

"You talk to Travis yet?" Max asked.

"Talked to him a little while ago. Sounds like Peggy told him about Proctor, about her affair and everything else that happened, after she got cut loose from the sheriff's department yesterday. He went over there to pick her up."

"So, how's he taking it?" Max asked.

"Hard to tell," Skip replied. "They were on shaky ground before this happened. I don't know if they can put it behind them or not."

Monica had gone back to the conference room to get some more chairs. She came up the hall pushing two office chairs.

"Sometimes I wonder what you two would do without someone to take care of you," she said as she placed the two chairs in the waiting room.

"Let's just hope we never have to find out," Max replied.

"What are you going to do when I graduate?" she asked.

"Max can't think that far ahead," Skip joked.

Max gave Skip a dirty look. The two detectives took their seats.

"Okay, we ready now?" Carlisle asked. No one responded, but the four turned their attention to the deputy.

"About a year ago, Proctor was looking around on the internet and he came across a dating site, lonelyfarmers.com," Carlisle began. "I think that you know some of this from your investigation, but I'm going to take it from start to finish." He paused a moment. "Proctor is sort of an opportunist and a scammer, and he finds Peggy Bentley on the site. She's just lonely and looking for a little company, and Proctor senses some vulnerability in her. So he internet stalks her and finds out that she is responsible for most of the subcontracting at BioForce. Proctor sees an opportunity, works it so that he can get close to Mrs. Bentley, they start having an affair, then he lands the cleaning contract for the equipment at BioForce."

Carlisle stopped to see if anyone wanted to comment. No one said a word, so he continued. "Okay, so Proctor gets this contract and he hires Gordon to work for him because Gordon has some experience with cleaning the equipment, but more importantly because Gordon has a direct line to undocumented laborers who are willing to do the dirty work at minimum wage, a cut of which Gordon is taking. And everything is going fine until the old tanker truck that he's using to haul the waste cleaning water breaks down. Now, instead of hauling the wastewater all the way to the disposal plant in Missouri where they are supposed to take it, they start dumping the water at Proctor's farm.

"They fill the pit under the hog confinement, so then they start pumping it into the holding ponds. Then wastewater starts leaking into the ground, finds its way into the creek, polluting it and killing the fish. Then the DNR gets to snooping around and they go over to BioForce to talk to Bentley about it." Carlisle stopped for effect. "So then Bentley goes to Proctor because she doesn't have all the paperwork, and Proctor comes unglued. I mean really unglued. He comes up with this big idea to put Gordon and Peggy in the well pit, gas them with exhaust from the truck, haul them out of the pit with the tractor, take them up to Gordon's bedroom in the house and put them both in the bed together. He was planning to burn the place down and try to make everyone believe that Bentley and Gordon were the ones having the affair and doing all this illegal dumping, and that he had no idea what was going on." Carlisle took a breath. "Then you guys came along, and you know the rest."

The four others looked at each other.

"Wow," Max said. "That's just craziness, but it has a bit of sense to it. I'm not saying that it was a good plan, but I can see how he got to it."

"That scares me," Skip said. "That you can understand his reasoning."

Max shrugged his shoulders. "I said it wasn't a good plan."

Skip cleared his throat. "So, Carlisle, you got involved in this because you just happened to be in Maxwell helping the DNR investigate the dead fish in the creek when you got the call to respond to shots fired at Proctor's place?" he asked, guiding the conversation. "That was pretty good luck, that you were right there."

"Yep," Carlisle said. "We were going to walk up the creek and see what we could see, but we never got the chance."

"You going to try to go up there again?" Skip asked.

"Probably not, now," Carlisle replied.

Skip could see that Milton was getting nervous with the direction that he was going. He felt a little bad that he had put Milton in that position.

"What's the story now, with Skip?" Max inquired. "I mean, shooting Proctor and all that?"

"Right now, the county attorney is saying self defense, and unless something comes up to change that, I guess there isn't anything more to it," Carlisle replied. "Proctor's still in the hospital, and he's going to be there a while. I guess it takes some time for a broken pelvis to heal. I don't think he's going to be running any races for a while."

"Was he a big runner?" Max asked.

Carlisle looked at Max to see if he was serious, but he couldn't tell from the questioning look that Max was giving him. "No, not that I know of," Carlisle answered. "Why?"

"Just wondering," Max responded. "I run 5Ks, and I've never seen him running one."

Carlisle still couldn't tell if Max was screwing with him or not, so he continued. "The judge put a million dollar bond on him this morning. I don't know if he can make that or not, but if not, he goes to jail as soon as he's released from the hospital. He's still maintaining that it was all Gordon and Mrs. Bentley, and that he didn't have any idea what was going on."

"How does he explain those two in the well pit and him attacking us?" Skip asked.

"He doesn't," Carlisle replied. "He just says it is all Gordon and Bentley's fault."

The others said nothing. Carlisle stood up. "Well, if you don't have any more questions, I'm going back out on the road. There will probably be some follow-up from some of the agencies involved. There's our investigation, but the DNR might have something as well, and maybe even the feds. But at the moment, I've got nothing else."

"Thanks, Carlisle," Skip stood up and shook his hand. Max followed suit. "I appreciate you coming in."

"No problem," Carlisle responded as he shook their hands. He nodded toward Milton. "Catch you later at the truck stop?"

"Probably," Milton answered. "Unless I get a call."

The four watched the deputy walk out to his patrol car, get in and pull away.

"Wow, that was something," Max said. "I'm going over for a cup of coffee. Wanna get out of here and come along?" he asked Skip, winking and nodding toward the other two.

"Sure," he answered. The two detectives went out the door headed for Filo's across the street, leaving Milton and Monica in the office.

"What do you have going on today?" Monica asked.

"Nothing," Milton replied. "Gotta work, then I don't have anything. I thought maybe we might do something."

"I should maybe spend some time with Essie," Monica said.

"That's fine, let's do something with Essie," Milton responded.

"We could go to the mall," Monica suggested.

"What do you want at the mall?" Milton asked.

"Nothing," Monica replied. "It's just that Essie said you two went to the mall and she had fun. She wants to go again."

"What else did she say about the mall?" Milton asked, feeling a little bit of anxiety, wondering if Essie had told Monica about the ring. He was pretty sure that she had been focused on her pretzel, but you could never tell about Essie. It was hard to get anything past her. He should have known better than to bring her along with him.

"She didn't say anything else about the mall," Monica replied, wondering why Milton was so worried about it.

"Let's go to Des Moines to the mall," Milton suggested. "It's bigger. She'll like it better."

"Okay," replied Monica. "We can go down to Des Moines if you want."

"Settled," Milton said.

Monica made a mental note to ask Essie exactly what she and Milton had done at the mall. Maybe he had bought her Christmas present, although Christmas was a long ways off. For a cop, he wasn't very good at keeping things secret.

"Okay, gotta go," Milton said abruptly. "I'll see you later, then."

Monica grabbed his arm as he turned to leave, pulled him down and gave him a kiss. Milton looked around to see if anyone was looking through the windows at them, then leaned down and gave her another one.

Monica followed Milton out the door, locking it behind her. She waved in the direction of Filo's, knowing that her two bosses were watching, even if she could not see them through the reflection on the windows across the street.

"What do you think?" Max asked Skip, as they waved back at Monica.

"I think those two are in love," Skip replied.

"So are we going to throw them a big wedding when they get hitched?" Max asked.

"They aren't even engaged," Skip replied.

"I think we should," Max remarked.

Chapter 30

Monday

Max sat down at the table with his cup of coffee and looked across the street at Skip's car parked in front of the agency.

"I'm over here," Max texted. It was a long shot. Skip didn't pay much attention to his phone.

Max's phone chirped. "Over in a minute," Skip texted him back.

Max got the attention of the barista, held up one finger, and mouthed the word "cappuccino." He nodded back and went to work on the drink. Max turned to the window and watched Skip make his way across the street.

"What's up with you?" Skip asked as he sat down across the table. "You order me anything?"

"Yep, cappuccino," Max told him.

"I don't think that I want to do that again," Skip remarked.

"You mean another case, or shoot someone one again or another cappuccino?" Max asked.

"Both," Skip chuckled.

"You know, the plan was to not take any cases," Max exclaimed. "You just wanted an office to go to. How are we getting into these things?"

"I think that you started it," Skip said.

"I think that Gloria started it." Max corrected him.

"And this last one was Marjorie's fault. I didn't want to take it," Skip assured Max. "We need to stop letting people manipulate us."

"I thought that's what we had Monica on the payroll for," Max responded. "Isn't she supposed to make sure we don't have cases to work? Next time one of the girls comes up with a case, we tell them that they have to go through Monica. We tell them that we don't make those kind of decisions."

Skip nodded.

"So," Max changed the subject. "Did you talk to Travis any more?"

"Talked to him twice yesterday afternoon," Skip sighed. "I don't know. I don't think either one wants to give up on what they thought they had. But I don't know if there is anything left in that marriage to hold them together. Frankly, I think I'm becoming his therapist."

"You make a good therapist," Max replied.

"Thanks," Skip said in a sarcastic tone.

"No, seriously," Max went on. "You're a good listener."

Skip's cappuccino arrived. The two detectives looked out the window.

"Monica coming in today?" Max asked.

"I have no idea," Skip replied. "You going car shopping?"

"I think I better," Max said. "I called Ben. He had me call an insurance adjustor and they are getting the police reports. But I can't go without a car, and I don't want to drive that little overpowered go-cart that Gloria calls a car."

"I'll go with," Skip suggested.

"Okay," Max replied with enthusiasm.

The two detectives sat back in their chairs, sipping their coffee, watching the world go by on the streets outside Filo's and making plans to find Max a new car.